PRAISE FOR

MORE THAN JUST A PRETTY FACE

A YALSA Top Ten Best Fiction for Young Adults Book

"The kind of book I've been searching for my entire life....
This is a must-read for everyone." —Adiba Jaigirdar,
author of *The Henna Wars*

"Exactly what we need more of on our shelves right now and
always.... As deeply hilarious as it is unendingly tender."
—Leah Johnson, author of *You Should See Me in a Crown*

"A wildly entertaining, stereotype-shattering rom-com debut.
Total Netflix movie material." —Sarah Henning, author of
Throw Like a Girl and the Sea Witch duology

"Hilarious and teeming with heart.... Danyal has secured his
place as a heroic protagonist for the ages.... I am a forever fan."
—Erin Hahn, author of *You'd Be Mine* and *More Than Maybe*

"Funny, openhearted, and utterly charming.... This is a
spectacular debut." —Katie Henry,
author of *Heretics Anonymous*

"I couldn't have been more charmed by Danyal.... One of the
most unique and likable characters I've come across. This book
has such a kind, expansive heart." —Rahul Kanakia,
author of *We Are Totally Normal*

MORE
Than JUST
a PRETTY
FACE

Syed M.
Masood

(L)(B)

LITTLE, BROWN AND COMPANY
New York Boston

Copyright © 2020 by Syed M. Masood
Excerpt from *Sway with Me* copyright © 2021 by Syed M. Masood

Cover art copyright © 2020 by Sammy Moore
Brick wall texture © Sayan Puangkham/Shutterstock.com
Cover design by Marcie Lawrence
Cover copyright © 2020 by Hachette Book Group, Inc.

Little, Brown and Company
Hachette Book Group
1290 Avenue of the Americas, New York, NY 10104
Visit us at LBYR.com

Originally published in hardcover and ebook by Little, Brown and
Company in August 2020
First Trade Paperback Edition: August 2021

Little, Brown and Company is a division of Hachette Book Group, Inc.
The Little, Brown name and logo are trademarks of
Hachette Book Group, Inc.

The publisher is not responsible for websites
(or their content) that are not owned by the publisher.

The Library of Congress has cataloged the hardcover edition as follows:
Names: Masood, Syed, author.
Title: More than just a pretty face / Syed Masood.
Description: First edition. | New York : Little, Brown and Company, 2020. |
Summary: "When self-proclaimed 'not very bright' nineteen-year-old
Danyal Jilani is chosen for a prestigious academic contest, he hopes to
impress a potential arranged marriage match, only to begin falling for the
girl helping him study instead"—Provided by publisher.
Identifiers: LCCN 2019023874 | ISBN 9780316492355 (hardcover) |
ISBN 9780316492386 (ebook) | ISBN 9780316492393
Subjects: LCSH: Pakistani Americans—Fiction. | Muslims—United
States—Fiction. | CYAC: Pakistani Americans—Fiction. | Muslims—
United States—Fiction. | Interpersonal relations—Fiction. | Arranged
marriage—Fiction. | Preparatory schools—Fiction. | Schools—Fiction.
Classification: LCC PZ7.1.M37642 Mo 2020 | DDC [Fic] —dc23
LC record available at https://lccn.loc.gov/2019023874

ISBNs: 978-0-316-49236-2 (pbk.), 978-0-316-49238-6 (ebook)

Printed in the United States of America

LSC-C

Printing 1, 2021

For my wife,
Saira Amena Siddiqui,
the most beautiful heart I know

CHAPTER ONE

"*I'm more than* just a pretty face."

"Oh really?" Kaval Sabsvari asked, her warm brown eyes sparkling with suppressed laughter. "Tell me, Danyal Jilani, how exactly are you more than just a pretty face?"

I gave her an adorable, irresistible grin. "I'm an absolutely gorgeous face."

She rolled her eyes.

"I'm just saying, I may not be at the top of the graduating class—"

"Aren't you actually at the bottom of the class?"

I shook my head. "They don't keep track of things like that at my school."

"They do. We go to the same school. We're, like, literally here now."

Kaval was right. We were both seniors at Aligheri Prep

and were standing outside Mr. Tippett's history class, waiting for the door to open. She was so popular that I rarely had the chance to be alone with her. Now that I had the opportunity, I was going to use it to flirt shamelessly.

You couldn't blame me. Hotter than my grandmother's homemade, weapons-grade, unripe mango *achar*, Kaval was the star of my spiciest dreams. Unfortunately, she was also Sohrab's twin sister, and Sohrab was one of my best friends, so I usually had to pretend I didn't have feelings for her.

"You know," I said, "I've heard that women shouldn't insist on being told the truth. It isn't attractive."

"Wow. Well...fuck you very much."

I gasped dramatically. "Ms. Sabsvari, how are your parents going to find a good desi boy for you to marry if you use your mouth to say such scandalous things?"

Kaval crossed her arms at her waist. She was wearing a deep purple floral dress that came down to her ankles. It was supposed to be modest, I guess, but this girl's body had not gotten that memo. She could've made a burka look sexy.

Okay, so she couldn't really, because that's impossible. Still, it would've been nice to be brave enough to say that kind of thing to her.

"Then what should I use my mouth for?" Kaval asked, tilting her head to one side. Was she flirting back? As a stupid grin spread across my face, she held up a finger in warning. "Don't. I know it's difficult for you, but please don't say something gross."

"Fine...but only because you're cute."

Her smile returned. "Really?"

"Not as cute as me, though."

"Of course. Still, you think so?"

Yes. Definitely.

Honestly, I was completely gaga over Kaval. In fact, I liked to tell myself that I'd gotten held back in the seventh grade on purpose so I could be around her more. It wasn't what had happened, but that wasn't important.

What *was* important was that I now had a chance to say something sweet to Kaval. I tried to come up with a good compliment, but that's hard to do when you've just been called out for fudging the truth about your grades a tiny bit. I decided to say something perfectly accurate.

"Sure. I mean, you aren't the most beautiful woman in the world or anything, but—"

As her jaw dropped open, and I realized I should probably stop talking, the bell signaling the end of the lunch period went off. I sighed, glancing down the dull green hallway that would start filling up with other students soon. My alone time with Kaval was about to end, and I hadn't come close to saying what I wanted to say.

I'd wanted to talk to her about...well, not a date, exactly, because neither one of us was allowed to date. I guess I'd wanted us to have a conversation about having a conversation.

You know, the Muslim version of first base.

Instead, she'd asked me if I'd done the assignment that

was due today—I hadn't—and that had somehow led to a discussion of how poorly I was doing in Mr. Tippett's class. This was not how I'd imagined things would go when I'd seen Kaval leaving the cafeteria and had abandoned my *shami kabab* and ketchup sandwich to hurry after her.

"Nice," she said, her tone cold and sour with irritation.

"Sorry. I didn't mean for it to sound like that. You know that I'm an idiot, right?"

Thankfully, Kaval chuckled a bit at that. "Everyone knows, Danyal."

That was a little harsh, but also undisputable. Anyway, it didn't matter. All that mattered was finding a way to move this conversation from being about *me* to being about *us*.

As I opened my mouth to do just that, Kaval spotted a couple of her friends and waved them over.

My moment was gone.

〰

It wasn't long before the hallway was crowded with thirty or so other students, all of them buzzing about who Tippett would choose to enter into this year's Renaissance Man. It was the kind of thing that was typical of a bougie private school like Aligheri Prep—a contest where teachers picked their best students to present a paper to an auditorium full of proud parents and bored friends.

Tippett always got a pick because history was a core class that was taught all year, not just for one semester.

4

English, math, physics, bio, chem, geography, and econ were the others. The heads of those departments always rushed to nominate a senior to represent their subject, each trying to scoop up the crème de la crème before someone else did. Tippett, for some reason, usually waited until the last minute.

All around me, I heard the same tired grumbling as every year. Why did the different kinds of sciences each get their own entry, but calculus, trigonometry, and algebra had to share one? Why did they even bother with geography, when it never won? Stuff like that.

I'd never understood why everyone got so worked up over Renaissance Man. Sure, it looked great on college applications, and you got a tiny gold-painted statue that looked a lot like the Academy Award dude was clutching a book to his chest, but I didn't care about any of that.

Of course, there was also a $5,000 cash prize and a free pass on the final exam of the subject you presented your paper on. Both of those things I could use.

Students like me, however, didn't get picked for Renaissance Man. It was only for the best and the brightest.

Ignoring talk of the contest, I spent a little time with my phone, occasionally sneaking glimpses of Kaval with her pack of friends, until Intezar found me, a frown on his face.

"You totally ditched me, *yaar.*"

This was true. When I'd rushed out of the cafeteria to follow Kaval, I'd not only abandoned my sandwich, but also my other best friend. "Yeah. Sorry about that."

"You're such a *dupatta* chaser," Intezar grumbled. "I ate the rest of your lunch, by the way."

"Fair," I said.

He gave a pointed nod toward where Kaval was standing. "How'd it go?"

"So great. We talked about my grades."

Intezar snorted. "Smooth. Hey, who does she think Tippett is going to enter into Renaissance Man? There's a rumor that it might be her."

Kaval hadn't mentioned that. Maybe she just didn't want to get her own hopes up. Renaissance Man would definitely appeal to her. She didn't need the money or the help with college admissions, but she was super smart and she'd want to win.

"It didn't come up. She probably forgot all about the contest because of how distracting she finds me."

"Right," Zar said, making no effort to hide how unlikely he thought that was.

Then, to change the subject more than anything else, I demanded to know when he'd get up the nerve to ask Natari Smith out.

Zar was between girlfriends, and he was always a little depressed when that happened. It didn't help that his latest crush was someone he thought was out of his league. It also didn't help—though he'd never admit it—that his parents had recently separated, and he was living with his father, who was always out of town on one business trip or another. Zar wasn't very good at being alone.

Anyway, I let Zar go on about how wonderful Natari was. I'd heard it all before, more than once, but he needed to repeat himself. I got it. I was the same way when it came to Kaval, and Intezar was the only one I could talk to about her. He never interrupted me when I got started either. Good friends, after all, care enough to pretend to listen.

܀

Algie Tippett had a small plaster bust of Winston Churchill on the podium from which he delivered his lectures. It was his habit to place a hand on the bust's bald head before he started teaching. His voice was thin and reedy, and he spoke slowly, like a stoned turtle.

He'd been working at Aligheri Preparatory Academy for an eternity—like forty years or something—and his lectures felt like they'd gotten old with him. There were people who thought he was a great teacher, but as far as I could tell, all he did was deliver long speeches from memory in a really bored voice.

It wasn't long before I found myself thinking about Kaval, not as she looked today, but as she had looked two days ago, when I'd dropped by to visit Sohrab, and she'd opened the door a little out of breath. She'd been wearing a tank top and leggings and had obviously been working out, because her ponytail had been messy, the hair around her ears damp, and her skin flushed. Her brown eyes had seemed even brighter than usual.

I let out a sigh. She was so beautiful. Like a perfect molten chocolate lava cake.

Then I realized that everything had gone quiet. Tippett had stopped reciting his speech. I glanced up at the clock. Class wasn't over yet.

"Mr. Jilani?"

Had Tippett asked me a question?

He must have. Shit. What had he even been talking about?

"You seem awfully preoccupied. What has so completely captured your attention?"

I should've made something up. Instead, for some reason, I told him the truth.

"A girl."

Laughter from the class. Not from Mr. Tippett, though.

"Danyal," he said, "on your feet, please."

I managed not to roll my eyes as I stood up.

"Can you tell me," Tippett asked, "what we were discussing?"

I couldn't. He knew that. Why did he have to be a jerk about it? I heard snickering from some of the other students.

I folded my arms across my chest. Fine. I could be a dick too.

"History," I said.

The class laughed again.

Tippett's lips narrowed into a thin line. "Indeed." He ran a hand that trembled a little over his heavily wrinkled face. "Your history, in fact."

8

I glanced around. A couple of people mouthed the answer, but I couldn't figure out what they were trying to tell me. "What do you mean?"

"The history of your country, Mr. Jilani. You were born in India, correct?"

"San Diego, actually."

Tippett sighed. "Yes, but your parents were born in India, were they not?"

I shook my head. "Pakistan."

"Those are very nearly the same thing," Tippett said, "historically speaking, of course. Regardless, our subject was the great Sir Winston Churchill. As you are aware, Churchill was posted in India when he grew into the kind of man he was going to be."

I was aware of no such thing, but I nodded anyway. I just wanted to sit down.

"What else can you tell me about Churchill, Mr. Jilani?"

What. Was. His. Problem?

Churchill. Churchill. What did I know about Churchill? British dude from a while back. Face like a bulldog. Body of a manatee. That probably wasn't the kind of information Tippett was looking for.

"Uh . . . he was . . . well, you know, he was—"

A familiar and welcome trilling bell sounded. Freedom. I glanced up at the heavens—well, the ceiling anyway—and thanked God for the assist.

"We'll pick this up next time," Tippett promised, before finally looking away from me.

9

Principal Weinberg's office was surrounded by something like a hundred and fifty kids. It was as if half the school was standing around, waiting to see if the list of Renaissance Man contestants would be updated today. This was something of a January tradition at Aligheri Prep, this feeding of the sheeple at the end of every school day, just as you were trying to get home. It would go on until the last participant was announced.

I wondered sometimes if the principal hated Tippett a little for dragging this nonsense out every year by refusing to announce his pick till the last minute.

I shouldered my way through the crowd. Zar was waiting by the heavy, bright mustard double doors that led out to the parking lot. "History was brutal," he said. "You okay?"

"Fine." I marched out into the cool afternoon, heading straight for my rickety tan 1997 Honda Odyssey. That's right. I drove an ancient minivan. It didn't look like much, but it was functional. I told myself that every day.

I'd bought it for two reasons. First, Intezar and I had been planning to start a band, because I can play the guitar and he'd said he could play the drums. I'd figured it'd be a good way to haul instruments and equipment to gigs. Second, a van would be a convenient place to sleep with all the hot girls who loved my band's music.

A year later, I had to assume that my lack of a band

was the reason I was still a virgin, and *that* was entirely Zar's fault. He'd grossly overstated his musical abilities.

Well, there was the whole Muslim thing too. We're the last Keepers of Virtue in this world, the sworn Guardians of the Hymen. I'd discussed this with Intezar in some detail—a previous girlfriend had relieved him of his virginity a while ago—and he'd argued that clinging to old-world views about sexuality was not a wise long-term plan. He said that Muslims were setting themselves up for disaster, because after the zombie apocalypse, when we reverted back to a savage society and human sacrifices resumed, how would people identify virgins? That's right. They'd look for the hijabis.

"You're sure?" Zar asked as I let myself into the van and leaned over to unlock the passenger-side door. "You don't seem fine. You seem pissed."

"Well...I really am fine." I smiled at him, as if being humiliated in front of Kaval and everyone else hadn't bothered me at all. "But this probably hurts my chance of being Tippett's pick for Renaissance Man."

Intezar laughed, a little harder than necessary, and buckled in. "I heard some people talking, and they're just going to ask him who he's nominating."

"Whatever. I don't want to talk about Algie."

Zar held up his hands in surrender. "Sure, dude. Let's go fry some Sectoids."

"Or, you know, we could play a game that isn't old."

"*XCOM 2* is a classic, all right? Being old is how

something gets to be a classic. Besides, it's all about the brown experience."

The game was actually about aliens who invade Earth, take over all governments, and have to be fought off by a small resistance force of elite soldiers the player recruits from various countries. Intezar thought the whole thing was a metaphor for colonization. I, on the other hand, seriously doubted the developer had been thinking about the plight of our ancestors when the game was made.

Anyway, I was a little bored of it. "Let's see what Sohrab wants to do," I said, because I knew he felt the same way about Zar's *XCOM* obsession. "Maybe we can just play some *2K*."

"Fine," Zar grumbled, folding his arms across his chest. "If you feel like being lectured about praying on time or something for the rest of the day, I guess."

Sohrab was the last member of our trio. We'd all been close once, but recently he and Zar had seriously cut back on the time they spent together. This was mostly because Sohrab couldn't help but talk about religion, and Zar didn't want to hear anything about it.

Arguing about whether to call Sohrab ended up being a waste of time. He couldn't hang out with us because he'd apparently decided to join some after-school Quran study group. I told Zar that he sounded sorry to be missing out, which was true, but Zar just rolled his eyes and made me play *XCOM 2* after all.

The forces of humanity weren't doing all that well when my phone rang half an hour later. It was my mom.

Not a lot of Pakistani guys could say this, but my mom was cool. She was the one who taught me to play the guitar, who secretly told me it was okay to go to a culinary school if that's what I wanted, and who had passionately argued against my getting a minivan, suggesting a 1977 Pontiac Firebird instead. I think the name of that car spoke to her soul. She'd loved it since she'd seen it in a movie with Burt Reynolds. She'd said that Reynolds was the only man she'd leave my father for. Knowing my father, I'd have thought the list would be longer.

"Come home," she said.

"I'm kind of in the middle of something, Mom."

"The Akrams are here."

"Okay. And?"

"They have a daughter. She's your age."

I groaned. "Mom."

"Just come home. I know you're probably with those nerd friends of yours, playing games on the computer, *haan*?"

"No."

"Hold on." I could hear Dad's voice in the background. When she got back on the line, she said, "Your father says not to be a nonsense fellow and to come home right now."

"How long do I have to listen to him call me names?"

"Probably as long as he's alive."

I grumbled under my breath. For someone who was usually awesome, Aisha Jilani was being a real mom right now. "How long is this thing with your friends going to take?"

"Not long. I promise."

"Fine," I sighed. "I'll see you soon."

"Excellent. And Danyal? Keep an open mind about this girl. She's not, you know, hot, exactly, but she's got...sex appeal."

I made a gagging sound. Not a phrase that was okay for mothers to use.

"I'm serious," she insisted.

"Those are the same thing," I told her.

"No," she said, in the manner of someone imparting an ancient wisdom. "They really aren't."

"Have to head out?" Intezar asked as I hung up the phone.

I told him where I was going, and he made a face. This wasn't my first *rishta* meeting, where I'd be introduced to a girl because our parents hoped that we'd hit it off and ultimately decide we liked each other enough to get married. I was "on the market," as Zar put it.

He thought arranged marriages were really old-fashioned, but they were pretty much the only option in my opinion. Muslim men and women aren't supposed to hang out alone with each other or go on dates, which makes finding someone to marry on your own pretty hard.

And getting married is super important because, Islamically, if you're going to have sex with a girl, you need permission from your parents. And her parents. An imam has to sanction it. And the state has to be informed, of course, and the proper paperwork has to be filled out. And you need witnesses who can swear that all the necessary parties were advised. You also need to throw a party, so everyone you know can dress up in their best clothes and come to congratulate you about the fact that you're going to finally get fucked.

It's the way things are done in polite, proper society.

Once you have your official papers in order, what was once forbidden becomes legal. It's like getting your driver's license, except going to the DMV is a lot less frustrating than going through the arranged marriage process.

"We're way too young, dude. Your parents are crazy. No disrespect."

I really was pretty young for the market, but my parents were looking because, as they told me, they feared my personal charms and extraordinarily poor judgment would lead me into sin.

Anyway, getting an arranged marriage didn't bother me. What *did* bother me was that even though I'd dropped a ton of hints about Kaval, my mother had completely ignored them. I was going to have to just spell it out for her soon, so we could stop with these pointless *rishta* meetings.

Because no matter how great the girl I was meeting now ended up being, she'd still be a distant star next to the shining moon that was Kaval Sabsvari.

CHAPTER TWO

The Akrams—was I supposed to know these people?—were seated in the formal living room of my parents' deceptively nice house when I snuck in. Mom and Dad had bought it with the only serious money they'd ever had, my father's inheritance, and were lucky that they'd made the purchase just before houses in the Bay Area got crazy expensive.

So now my parents were house rich. Their home was all they really had in the world, which was fine. It wasn't like we were living in the earthquake capital of the world or anything.

The house was their fortune and their misfortune. It made people expect that they would live lavish lives, hosting and attending parties, driving cars that cost more than they could make in a year. I don't know why my parents cared about what "society" thought of them, but they did, at least enough that it made their finances really tight.

It would have given them hope, I think, to imagine that there was help coming from their son, that he could grow up to be a doctor or lawyer or engineer, capable of making the facade of their lives real.

I think they'd gotten to know me well enough, however, to realize they shouldn't dream such dreams.

The slightly sweet smell of saffron-infused chicken *biryani* that lingered in the air distracted me from the guests and lured me into the kitchen. Given the pile of plates stacked in the sink, it was obvious that everyone else had already eaten.

Grabbing a spoon, I took a bite straight from the pot and let out a happy sigh. The basmati rice was perfect, each grain separate from the others. It was somewhere between spicy and mild, and the baked chicken wasn't dry. Mom had the proportions of her *dum biryani* down to a science.

I was only going to have one bite, but there is nothing like the first spoonful of *biryani* to make you realize how hungry you are. Hoisting the entire steel pot onto the dining table, I began shoveling food into my mouth as fast as I could.

That was how Bisma Akram saw me for the first time.

"Hi," she said.

I cleared my throat and wiped at my mouth with the back of my hand. "Hello."

"Bisma."

"Danyal Biryani. I mean, Jilani. Danyal Jilani."

She smiled.

Bisma was one of those people who, but for one defining feature, would've been unremarkable to look at. In her case, it was her swift smile. It caused her nose to wrinkle a bit, and her cheeks dimpled. She didn't have anything remotely like Kaval's scorched earth beauty, and she didn't have the figure to make everything she wore look a little tight. Bisma was willowy—no, that makes people think of movie stars and models. Wrong plant. Bisma was ... palmy.

Was it weird that I was so focused on her looks? A little, I guess, but that's the reality of the arranged marriage process. Normally, our parents would have exchanged photos and biographical information before any of this happened—it was the old brown people version of trading baseball cards—and the picture alone would've determined whether or not we even met each other.

So don't judge me for being shallow. Judge all desis.

Anyway, my mom was right. Bisma wasn't hot.

There was, however, something undeniably attractive about her. Her vibe was very geek-California. She had on a pair of retro square eyeglasses that were slightly big for her face. Her long, light brown hair hung in loose waves. In white jeans and a baby-blue T-shirt with Spider-Man's face in the shape of a heart, she obviously didn't care enough about being set up with me to dress up. I liked that.

"Do you want me to twirl around or are you good?"

Crap. I'd stared too long. I could feel my face get hot. That was probably the first time in my life a girl had made *me* blush.

"Sure," I joked. "Go ahead."

She blinked, obviously a little taken aback, then shrugged her narrow shoulders and spun around.

I hadn't expected her to actually do that.

"Well?" Bisma asked, hands on her hips.

I knew I should say something nice.

"Nice," I said.

She let out an exaggerated sigh of relief. "Thank God. I feel super validated."

Bisma laughed then, and I couldn't help but join in.

"Hear that?" I heard my mother say from the other room. It was practically a squeal. "They're getting along. I think now is a good time to send them out for coffee, don't you?"

Going out for coffee was actually kind of a rare event in my limited arranged-marriage-process experience. Most parents don't let their girls go out with a "prospect," even for half an hour, without a chaperone. The Akrams were being rather liberal, and I suppose I should've been grateful. I was, however, too busy being mortified by the way Bisma raised her eyebrows when she saw my minivan.

"Sexy," she said as she got in.

I felt myself blush again. What was it about this girl

that made my face do that? "Makes it easier to move guitars and speakers and stuff."

"You play?"

I nodded.

"Are you good?"

"I'm very good."

Bisma chuckled. "Well, you don't have any self-esteem issues."

"Groundless confidence is one of my special skills." I turned the ignition, and the old engine coughed itself to life. "Where to?"

"Anywhere."

We drove in silence for a few minutes. Finally, she said, "You're nineteen, right?"

"Yeah. You?"

"Yup. So how come you're still in high school?"

I bit back a sigh. Desi uncles and aunties had been asking me that question for years. I hated it. I was pretty sure that by now my family's entire acquaintance knew I'd been held back a grade in middle school, and they only pretended to be ignorant to feel superior about their own spawn. Jerks.

I guess it was a fair question, though, coming from a girl your parents were setting you up to potentially marry. I projected my best devil-may-care attitude. "I'm not very bright."

Bisma laughed, but not unkindly. "I doubt that's true."

"What about you?"

"I'm actually very bright."

I smiled. "I mean, where do you go to school?"

"Berkeley," she said. "For microbiology."

I glanced over at her. Berkeley? Wow. She *was* bright. What the hell was her family doing trying to set her up with someone like me?

"What?" Bisma asked when I didn't say anything.

"That's a good school."

"It's got something of a reputation, sure."

"I mean, that's something that desi parents would approve of."

She nodded.

"So . . . what's wrong with you?"

Bisma frowned. "What?"

"You're smart. And you're okay to look at." I winced as soon as I said it. "Sorry. I don't know what is going on today. I'm usually much better at giving compliments. Anyway, what I'm saying is, given everything that you've got going on, why are your parents shopping for a husband in the bargain bin?"

"Wow. I was wrong about you not having self-esteem issues, wasn't I?"

"This isn't about what I think of myself." I sounded defensive, but . . . well, Bisma knew what I was trying to say. Why was she making me explain? "It's about how uncles and aunties value people. I mean, I don't care, really, but I know what my worth is on the market."

"If I were an English major, our parents putting us together would make more sense to you?"

"Yeah. I'm not saying that's the way it should be. I'm just saying no desi parent wants their daughter to marry a guy planning to attend a culinary institute."

She didn't say anything for a while. Just looked out her window at the quintessential suburbia that was my hometown. Finally she said, "This is a waste of time. I'm sorry. I can't get my mother to stop setting these meetings up."

I sighed. I'd been too rude. Too direct. Or maybe she hadn't known about the wanting-to-be-a-chef thing. Whatever. It wasn't like I was trying to impress her anyway.

We drove in silence for another moment or two. Then Bisma said, "Let's just go back."

Except she didn't say it like it was something she wanted to do. She said it like it was something she was agreeing to, like I was the one who wanted to bail. It bothered me. What was her deal?

"Did you kill someone?"

Bisma chuckled. "I think my family would prefer it if I had."

"Are you a cyberterrorist or something?"

"Worse."

We pulled up to a stoplight, and I had the chance to look at her. She was staring at her hands and had slunk further into her seat, as if she was trying to disappear into it. Then it hit me.

What was worse than being a terrorist when it came to an arranged marriage?

"You're not . . . I mean, you've had . . . you've done—"

"I'm not a virgin."

"That's what I meant." When she didn't say anything further, I said, "That's like...whatever, you know. I don't really understand why desis make such an issue out of it. They treat it like it's the end of the world or something, but it isn't a big—"

"There's video," Bisma told me, very quietly. "Is that apocalyptic enough for you?"

"You haven't said anything in a really long time," Bisma pointed out softly.

I pulled into a parking spot in front of a small coffee shop I liked. They made the best mocha, which was the only drink I ever ordered, because it was the brownest of all coffees.

"Danyal?"

"I'm not sure what to say."

"That's okay." Her gaze was still fixed on her lap.

More silence.

"So...in this video, you're—"

"Fucking."

I knew she'd used that word to shock me. I could respect that.

"What are you waiting for?" Bisma asked. "Take me back."

I shook my head, not at her suggestion, but at the situation she was describing. How was there video? That was insane. It was the kind of thing the reputation of a Pakistani girl would never, ever recover from.

Did anyone know? Did her parents? I had so many questions. I chose to ask one.

"So . . . you're a porn star, then?"

Now Bisma did look up at me, eyes flashing with indignation. "What? No! How can you—holy shit, I'm not—"

I held up my hands. "It was a joke."

"Was it?"

"Yeah. Of course."

"It didn't sound like a joke."

"I'm super dry."

She scowled at me. "It was stupid. There was some stuff going on at home and I was really angry. I went to a party because my parents wouldn't want me to and drank because they wouldn't want me to and . . . Anyway, I decided to sleep with this guy and I didn't realize he had a camera in his room. I guess he thought it'd be funny to record it or something. Then he posted it online. He called it 'Muslim Girls Like Dick Too.' "

"*What?* Seriously? That's . . . wow, that's *messed up.*"

Bisma ran a hand through her hair. "Yeah. Well, then his friends showed their friends. By the time he agreed to take the video down, because I told him I'd go to the cops, it was too late. It was all over school, and then the mosque. Then my parents heard about it, and my father almost kicked me out. Anyway, we couldn't live there anymore. We moved to California to make a fresh start."

"And that's why you're in the bargain bin."

"Yeah." She sighed. "So now that you know, can we please go back? After we leave, you can tell your family all about how I'm a slut who slept with a white boy, and the whole world saw it. They'll never mention me again."

"You're probably right."

"I know I am," she said, sounding very tired, and something she'd said came back to me.

I can't get my mother to stop setting these meetings up.

"This has happened before," I guessed. "You've had to tell this story before."

"Every single time my parents introduce me to someone. I get my mom to ask the guy's mom to send us out for coffee, and then I have this conversation with them. There's no point in talking to someone who can't handle what happened."

"And you've had a lot of coffee?"

Bisma laughed and wiped roughly at her eyes. "It never gets that far. They hear my story, and they're nice—I mean, you know, most of them—but they drive me back. I don't blame them. This isn't going to stay a secret. Someday, someone is going to find out, and his family will be the one with a tramp for a daughter-in-law. I'm over it. I've made peace with it."

"Peace is good," I said, just to have something to say.

"Sure. Yeah. It's great."

I didn't really think much about what I would do next, which wasn't all that unusual for me. I'd agreed to have coffee with her before she'd told me about her past. All I had to do was ask myself if learning her story had changed my opinion of her at all. If it hadn't, there was no reason to change our plans.

"Can I ask you something?"

Bisma shrugged.

"Do you like nuts in your brownies?"

"What?"

"Some people like their brownies plain, you know, just pure chocolate batter. And that's cool, but I think having nuts in there makes for a better experience."

"Are the brownies a metaphor?" Bisma asked. "Because if so, that's pretty racist."

"Two things," I said. "First, membership has its privileges, okay? Second, no, it isn't a metaphor. This place has good brownies, but they make them with nuts. They put a little sea salt on top, which I think really...anyway." I turned off the ignition. "Come on. Let's go inside."

She stared at the keys as I withdrew them from the car, then she stared at me, and then the entrance to the cafe. "This is a nice gesture, Danyal, but I don't need your pity."

"It isn't pity. My mother told me to have coffee, so that's what I'm going to do. You in?"

))

"So," Mom demanded as soon as the Akrams left, "what did you think?"

"Who cares what he thinks?" my father asked. To a

stranger, he would've seemed inordinately annoyed by my mother's question. I knew, of course, that this was his default setting. I'm pretty sure Ahmed Jilani came into this world with a frown, and the odds are good he'll be frowning when he leaves it. His autobiography would probably be called something like *A Series of Continuous Disappointments*. I'd have a feature role.

"Should I request your opinion, then?" Mom glared at him. "Are you going to marry her, or will he?"

Ahmed Jilani gave a grunt. He grunted like happy people smiled—that is to say, often. There were different types of grunts, and if you spent enough time with him you learned to tell them apart. This one, drawn out at the beginning, then abruptly cut short, was dismissive.

"He should be grateful anyone even considers giving him their daughter. He's just a bloody part-time cook. Hasn't even graduated high school yet. He might never manage it. Why would the Akram girl even consider marrying your son?"

"*Acha*, he's my son only now?"

This argument happened every time my future came up. My father had strong opinions about what I was doing—or not doing—with my life, and he wasn't shy about voicing them.

"Of course," he said. "Wasn't it the great-uncle on your mother's side who had a restaurant? Danyal doesn't get that nonsense from my side of the family, I'll tell you that."

My mother huffed and came back with her stock reply.

"On your side also there is art, okay? Wasn't it your mom's mom's brother who was a poet?"

"Poetry is different. Food isn't art, woman. Besides, there are lots of respectable poets."

"Like who?"

Before Dad could launch into a long history of the Urdu poets of Lucknow, the city in India where my paternal ancestors lived before 1947, I said, "She was fine."

My father glowered in my direction. "What?"

"He's answering my question. About the girl," Mom explained. "So, Danyal, did she seem interested in you?"

"If she is interested in him," my father interrupted, "we shouldn't be interested in her. No woman with good judgment would..." He leaned forward in his chair, then said, "Wait. Aisha, how did you say you came to meet these people?"

Aisha Jilani, who somehow knew everybody, outlined for her husband a complicated chain of friends and acquaintances, none of whom I recognized.

"And how well do all of these people really know the Akrams?"

"What are you trying to say, Ahmed?"

"I'm saying that there is something strange in this *daal*. Why would they be interested in this one?" He pointed to me. "We should look into it."

"Or," I suggested, "we could just not eat the *daal*. We could get something else entirely."

I thought that was a perfectly reasonable comment, but

it still drew another grunt from my father. It was an "are you sure this idiot is my child, woman, because I'd rather have been cuckolded than believe my blood flows in this fool's veins" grunt. I'd heard it a lot.

Mom just ignored me. "You never give our son—"

"Your son."

"*Uff.* Fine. You never give my son enough credit. Look how handsome he is."

"Yes. He's lucky he got my looks."

"*My* son," my mother said, "*my* looks. The point is that he may not be all that well qualified, or that intelligent, and he probably doesn't have a very good future—"

"Hey!"

She waved off my objection without even looking at me. "But he'll make lovely babies. Think of it like an old-school arrangement. When our elders got married, they looked at the boy's education and the girl's looks only. Just think of Danyal like that. Like an eighteenth-century girl from a remote Indian village. Then it all makes sense."

Ahmed Jilani gave his "you make a decent point but I'm not convinced" grunt, which was the closest he'd probably ever come to admitting anyone else might be right. "Those women had skills. They managed their homes, raised families. Will this one do that? He's just a pretty face."

"I'm more than just—"

"Anyway," my father went on, "I still think their interest in Danyal is strange."

"Okay, fine, *baba,* I'll ask around some more." My

mother masterfully switched over to a placating tone all of a sudden. It was what she did when she realized that reasoning with her husband would get her nowhere. It was something she'd gotten a lot of practice at over the years. "I'm sure people know them. We'll get plenty of references."

I grimaced. The last thing Bisma Akram needed was a bunch of desi aunties prying into her life. Someone, somewhere, would have a relative who knew the Akrams before they moved here, and that someone would know a friend, who would know a brother-in-law who'd once mentioned an Akram Sahib's daughter who made erotic videos and posted them online. By the time Bisma's story reached my mother, it would be exaggerated all to hell, and it'd spread like wildfire, burning her reputation down in California too.

"No," I said. "Don't do that."

Now it was my mother who frowned at me. "And why not?"

"Bisma seems like a nice girl and everything, but I don't think it's going to work."

"*Allahu Akbar.*" My father threw his hands up in the air. "Of course it won't work. Because you have an allergy to work, don't you? This won't work. That won't work. She won't work. The only thing you're good for is wasting my money and eating my food, isn't it? Bloody idiot. Get married to a qualified girl now, so you can live off your woman's earnings like a shameless—"

"Ahmed!"

"No, Aisha, let me give him a dose of truth, okay? How long are we going to live, *haan*? When we're gone, he'll be cooking in a crappy diner somewhere. Or maybe he'll be homeless, playing music at the side of the road, guitar case open, begging for scraps. He'll see then if the Akrams even deign to look at him."

So...pretty harsh. Not the worst I'd gotten from my father, though. Since I'd first told him I wanted to one day open my own restaurant, this kind of blowup had been happening a lot. When he finally stopped speaking, his face red from the exertion of his words, I gave him a small smile, the most I could manage, and said, "Are you done?"

My father snarled and slapped his hands against his thighs before getting up and stalking out of the room. I sat there with my mother in silence for some time.

Finally, she said, "Danyal?"

"It's fine, Mom."

"He loves you, *jaan*, and he worries about you—"

"I said it's fine."

Aisha Jilani sighed and came to sit next to me on the sofa. Her autobiography would probably be titled *I'm Here to Make Sure You're Okay*. She ran a hand over my hair. "You're sure I shouldn't ask around about this Bisma girl? You didn't like her?"

"I liked her fine, Mom. It's just..."

"It's okay. You don't have to tell me why. Just tell me

you're not saying no to Bisma because of Sohrab's sister, that Kaval. Just tell me this isn't about her."

I smiled at the gentle way my mother spoke, like I was a fragile thing right now. "Her I really like."

"I know." My mother chuckled. "I think everyone knows."

"So why don't you talk to her parents?"

"Because I also know what they're going to say."

That stung a little. Maybe even more than a little. "You agree with Dad, then? That I'm worthless?"

"No, *beta*, but..." She let out a weary sigh. "For you to have any chance, Kaval would have to fight for you. I've seen that girl grow up. And I can tell you that she won't do it."

"You've never really been that crazy about her."

"You've always been crazy enough about her for the both of us," she joked. When I didn't respond, she said, "Have you asked her if she loves you?"

I gave her a cheeky grin. "Everybody loves me."

"This is true. I'll tell you what... if Kaval says that she is interested in you, that she'll stand against her parents' objections, then I'll go over to their house myself and beg for her hand."

"Really?"

She nodded. "Yes. Trust me."

Something about the way my mom said this gave me pause. I'd heard that tone of voice before. On TV. On the news. My mother was making me a politician's promise. One she didn't expect to have to keep.

"You really don't think Kaval will do it. Why?"

My mother paused, as if she didn't know exactly how to explain this to me. "She wears a lot of makeup."

I rolled my eyes. "That's the reason?"

"Kaval wears a lot of makeup, Danyal, and it's Chanel."

"So?"

"It's expensive. And the purses she carries? Her newest one, it's Gucci. More than twenty-seven hundred dollars. Before tax. And don't get me started on her shoes."

"Mom, she can care about fashion without having expensive things. I do it. And it's not like they're her whole life. She's fun and smart and really serious about school."

"People can be more than one thing," my mother replied carefully. "They always are, in fact. Still, my sense is that she cares about having expensive things. That's what you're not getting. Anyway, look, let's not argue. You ask her if she wants you as you are, and if she says yes, I'll be happy for you."

I nodded. "Okay, I'll ask her. You better get your sales pitch ready for her parents, though." I started to get up, but Mom grabbed my forearm and held me in place.

"Listen. I can't believe I never explained this to you before. I should have but I guess I never got around to it."

"What is it, Mom?"

"You need to know that there are two kinds of beauty in this world. There is beauty that men appreciate, and there is beauty that women appreciate."

"And Kaval has the kind of beauty that men appreciate."

"Oodles of it," Mom said. "It's a little unfair how much."

When she didn't say more, I asked, "What's your point?"

"Oh. Just that you should always remember that men, almost entirely without exception, are complete idiots."

"Not me, though," I said. "Right?"

"Sure, *jaan*. Whatever you need to tell yourself."

CHAPTER THREE

Mrs. Sabsvari had one of the most amazing home kitchens I'd ever seen, but according to Sohrab and Kaval, she never used it. They said their mother wanted to be known as a terrific cook but had no desire to actually make food.

This was great for me. Whenever it was Mrs. Sabsvari's turn to host the almost weekly get-togethers that society uncles and aunties held at their homes—get-togethers that their children were forced to attend—Mrs. Sabsvari paid me to cook for her and not tell anyone about it.

Honestly, the kitchen, with its massive gas range and loaded pantry, was so awesome that I would've worked there for free, but I liked getting paid just fine.

The fact that Kaval dropped by every once in a while was a bonus. Sohrab came to hang out with me too, but that was a lot less exciting. In fact, it was a little annoying. Any edible ingredients close to him were always in danger of disappearing. The amount of cardamom he'd swallowed over the years had to be toxic.

The menu Mrs. Sabsvari had downloaded from an #auntylife blog for this particular event was pretty standard for a desi party, or *dawat*. There was a ton of food— because otherwise what would people say—but the level of difficulty was low. I was grinding masalas with a pestle for Bombay *biryani*, the cheering fragrance of cinnamon and the dark bite of black pepper blossoming in the air, when Kaval bounded in.

She was wearing a pink T-shirt with a Louis Vuitton symbol on it and sweatpants. Her hair and makeup were, as always, perfect.

"Sorry I'm still in my pj's. I know it's noon already." She arched her back and stretched. "I'm having such a lazy day."

I missed the mortar and stoneware clinked against the countertop. "It's cool," I said, perfectly casually, I'm sure.

"Sohrab isn't down either?"

I shook my head.

"I hope he got some sleep. He's obsessed."

"With what?"

"With being Muslim."

"He's definitely been getting serious about it. I haven't seen him much lately."

"He's always been serious," she said. "Now he's getting . . . I don't know . . . it's becoming the only thing he does. If he doesn't stop making comments soon about what I wear or how I don't pray enough, I'm going to slap him."

"He's been irritating Zar too."

"Yeah, well, Intezar doesn't have to live with him."

Kaval stepped toward me, moving a little closer than was necessary to get a look at what was going on with the food. When she saw the chunks of lamb I'd just finished cleaning the fat off of to reduce their gamey smell, she made a face. "I don't know why you keep letting Mom take credit for your cooking. I'd have told everyone it was my food ages ago. People rave about it, you know?"

"I don't really mind. Besides, I need the money."

"Your parents won't give you some?"

No. I mean, I could ask, but I wouldn't. I knew things weren't easy for them—I'd overheard them stressing about bills and stuff—though they'd never admit it. They were probably regretting ever sending me to Aligheri Prep. I think my father had hoped that going to a fancy private school would somehow make me smarter.

"Also"—I decided to step around Kaval's question—"I love being here."

"I know. It's super cute, actually. I like the way you smile when you're cooking."

I tried to smile like I was cooking, but she didn't comment. Maybe I didn't do it right.

"I'd help but I just got a manicure the other day and I really don't want to ruin it. Oh, I meant to show you!" She suddenly reached down into the front of her shirt, and my mind exploded with question and exclamation marks until she pulled out a pendant and held it up.

It was a key shaped like a fleur-de-lis, sparkling with what looked like a lot of really intense diamonds and one deep red ruby. "I thought you'd like it because you're all Frenchy."

I wouldn't have called myself "Frenchy," though the restaurant I worked at, Remarquable, certainly was. It didn't matter enough for me to bother correcting her.

"It's beautiful," I said, because it was true, and also because she was beautiful, and it struck me that that was what I should say right then.

"I'd better go start getting ready."

What? Oh, the party. I frowned. "People won't be here for another six hours."

"What's your point?" Kaval asked. She gestured up at her face and then down to the rest of her body. "This doesn't just happen, Danyal Jilani."

"Yeah?" I pointed to myself. "This does, though."

She laughed, extended a certain rude finger toward me, and walked away. It had been a chance to talk to her about "us," I guess, but the moment hadn't felt right. Hopefully soon an opportunity to speak to Kaval in private would present itself in a setting where dead animals featured less prominently. When that moment came, I promised myself, I would seize it.

$$\text{\scriptsize ∿}$$

I've always loved making simple food. I guess that's weird for someone who wants to be a chef and works at a fancy restaurant, but...I don't know, there's like...truth in a beautifully made omelet, and easily recognizable perfection in mousse that sets and feels just right. Sure, complex dishes are fun, and everyone goes nutty bananas for them, but only the basics ever really feel like home. I guess that's why le pâté en croûte isn't anyone's idea of comfort food.

So I was actually enjoying boiling basmati rice in milk to prepare kheer for dessert when Sohrab ambled in and made a beeline for a canister of cardamom, shoving three pods into his face before I could stop him.

"Dude," I said by way of reprimand.

"What?"

"It's super weird how much you like that stuff."

"Everybody loves cardamom."

That had not been my experience, but there's no accounting for taste, I guess.

"How's it going in here?" His hand slithered toward a plate of samosa filling with the speed of a venomous snake, but I pulled the potato mixture away in time.

"Back off," I warned him.

Sohrab held up his hands in surrender. That was when I noticed that his eyes were a little red and he looked tired.

"You okay?"

"Yes. I didn't get a lot of sleep. I was reading and lost track of time."

"Reading? Sometimes, dude, I just don't understand you."

"I could say the same thing," Sohrab said, looking pointedly at the stove. "How do you keep from eating while you're cooking?"

I smiled and went back to stirring the milk.

"Anyway," he went on, "I wanted to apologize for not hanging out with you and Zar the other day. I'm committed to that Quran class."

"It's cool. We understand. You were doing something important."

Sohrab gave a serious nod. Can a nod be serious? It can when Sohrab does it, because everything is serious with him. He's a serious nerd, a serious student, and a serious member of the Muslim Students' Association, a social club organized around religion that has a presence in pretty much every major school, college, and university in the States.

I was technically a member. I'd gone to a couple of their pizza parties, but because Intezar thought the club was full of tools, we didn't really hang out with them that much.

"What did you guys end up doing?" Sohrab asked.

"Not much. My mom called me home for a *rishta* meeting."

"How'd that go?"

"The usual," I told him.

"Not interesting?"

"Too interesting, actually."

Sohrab grinned. "Well...I am glad you're taking the meetings. We should look to find what is good for us in this world, don't you think?"

"What do you mean?"

My friend opened his mouth to speak. Then seemed to think better of it. When he eventually spoke, he said, "I was reading *Al-Baqarah* last night—"

"Wait. You were up late reading the Quran?"

"Of course. What did you imagine?"

"I don't know. A novel or something."

"What is the point of a novel?"

"To...have fun, I guess?"

Sohrab harrumphed—it sounded awfully like one of my dad's grunts—and said, "Anyway, there is a part of that chapter where God says that sometimes you think you love something, but it isn't good for you. And sometimes you don't want something, but that thing ends up being best for you."

"I still don't get it."

"I am just saying that you should keep taking the *rishta* meetings. You haven't found what is best for you yet, even if you think you have."

Was he talking about Kaval? No way. I was so careful to never let on that I liked his twin sister. We'd been friends forever. I didn't want to make things weird between us.

I was caught so off guard by Sohrab's advice that I almost missed his hand sneaking toward a plate of *kababs*. "Step away from the food, *yaar*. You know what? Get out of my kitchen."

"It is actually my kitchen," he reminded me.

That was a fair point, but I still scowled at him hard.

"Fine. I'll see you at the party," Sohrab said. "You'll have fun. Your fan club is going to be there."

Mrs. Sabsvari was known throughout the Bay Area for her amazing *kofta korma*. She told everyone the recipe for it was ancient, passed down to her from her great-grandmother in exchange for a promise that it would never be shared with anyone who did not also share her blood.

I'd actually come up with this particular recipe during an econ test. I'd been pretty sure my variation of the classic dish would turn into something special, but I hadn't been able to try it out until Mrs. Kapadia had graded our papers and returned them a whole week later. I'd failed. Apparently, Mrs. Kapadia didn't have much of a culinary imagination.

Still, I loved making the dish, especially because I got to use the Sabsvaris' massive, exquisitely crafted Moroccan clay tagines. Humming and bopping along to the latest Spotify playlist Zar had sent me, I rolled out beef meatballs seasoned with cilantro, mint, green chilies, ground Kashmiri and red peppers, pureed roasted onions and all.

The soul of this *salan* was ground almonds and cashews, which added a beautiful texture and richness to the curry. Whistling, I whipped them together with yogurt, poppy seeds, coconut, and dry spices. Once I'd sautéed the yogurt mixture, I'd add cream and water, and then wrap up the prep by trusting the oven with a tagine full of everything I'd prepared, along with the beating hearts of pretty much all desi food: ginger and garlic.

I could tell it was going to be good before it was done. I loved that feeling, that certainty in the excellence of my own work, which I'd only ever found in a kitchen. Sure, I got a lot of attention for looking good, but the ability to *create* something beautiful was so much better because it was something I'd earned, not something that I'd just been given.

As awesome as the food can be, *dawats* still suck. Men sit in one part of the house and women sit in another. So while there are all these pretty, dressed-up girls near you, you don't actually get to talk to them much. Instead, you get heavy uncles having heavy uncle conversations about religion and politics—international, federal, state, and mosque—and other stuff that no one cares about. The amount of information I've ignored about the Indian and Pakistani cricket teams from the seventies and eighties could fill the Internet.

Thankfully, if you're young enough, you're usually

allowed to sneak off after a while to hang out with people your own age, so Zar, Sohrab, and I can chill. But it also means that we have to be around other guys, some of whom are totally uncles in training. Zar thinks that Sohrab is becoming one of them. It is the curse of brown boys everywhere. We either die young or we live long enough to see ourselves become uncles.

At least some of Sohrab's cute cousins—my "fan club"— were invited to this *dawat*. They found all kinds of excuses to walk past where I was sitting to say hi, and then, as soon as they'd gone a few feet, they'd burst into whispers and giggles. Both Sohrab and Kaval thought they were ridiculous, and Zar was always irritated they didn't want to talk to him.

"I like your shirt," one of them said shyly when she stopped by. "Looks good on you."

"Everything looks good on me," I said with a grin.

She laughed and laughed.

As she drifted away, Sohrab rolled his eyes so hard that I was worried he'd hurt himself.

"What?" I asked. "I'm hilarious."

"No. You really aren't."

"I'm funny and charming. Ask anyone. Right, Zar?"

Zar didn't answer, studying the peas in the samosa he was holding like they were works of art.

Sohrab added, "You know that girls only laugh at your jokes because they find you attractive, right?"

"Whatever. No one thinks that. Right, guys?"

When the uncles in training all just sat there in silence, I jumped up and walked off in a huff.

The problem with walking off in a huff is that it isn't really effective if you don't have anywhere to go.

I didn't want to sit with the uncles because they were talking about boring stuff like the fate of the world or whatever. I couldn't go hang out with the aunties because I was a dude, even though all aunties loved me. And I couldn't go hang out with the girls because... well, I don't know what would happen, actually, because no one I know had tried, but it probably wouldn't be good.

I also couldn't go to the kitchen. Mrs. Sabsvari was very clear that I was to steer clear of it in order to avoid suspicion.

So I made my way outside. The Sabsvaris had a sprawling backyard with a massive pool and a concrete half basketball court. As I walked toward the hoop, laughter and talk from the *dawat* got quieter and quieter until, for a second, it felt like I was all alone, under a dark night sky.

That was when I heard the dull *thwap* of a basketball hitting the ground. I looked behind me and Kaval was there, her shimmery *shalwar kameez*, trailing *dupatta*, and high heels all at odds with the casual confidence with which she was dribbling.

"You look lost," she said.

"Usually am, I guess."

She didn't smile. Not even a little. Maybe Sohrab had been right. Maybe I *was* having an off night bringing the funny. Instead, she asked, "What were you thinking about?"

"Nothing. Just... I don't know.... There aren't any stars out. It seems like there are fewer stars in the sky than there were when we were kids, don't you think?"

"They're still there. Our lights are just so bright now that we can't see them."

I'd never thought of it that way. I was trying to figure out how to respond, when Kaval whipped the ball toward me and it smacked into my chest, startling me. "Want to play?"

I frowned. "Now? With you?"

"Sure," Kaval said, stepping out of her heels and pulling her *dupatta* from around her neck. As she tied the long piece of delicate fabric around her waist, she added, "Unless you're scared."

"Terrified."

"Don't worry. I'll go easy on you."

I nodded toward the house and the "party" going on inside. "What if someone sees us? All the aunties will freak out."

"If you're not scandalizing aunties, Danyal Jilani, what is even the point of your life?"

That was impossible to argue with, so I tossed her the ball. "First to get to twenty-one?"

"Sure."

That was when Kaval Sabsvari, sugar and spice and

all things nice, stepped behind the three-point line and drained a jumper that would've stunned Steph Curry.

"What was that?" I exclaimed.

"What was what?"

I grinned and shook my head, jogging up the court to get the ball. Typical Kaval. Always a badass. As I passed it to her, she went for another jumper that, even though it clanged around the rim a bit, ultimately dropped through the hoop.

"I can do that all night, Jilani. You're going to have to get closer and actually guard me."

"Oh." It came out squeakier than I would have liked. "How . . . um, how close can I get?"

Kaval crossed her arms behind her back and walked up to me, slowing down as she got closer, until her chest was almost touching mine. I wasn't sure if my heart had ever beat as fast as it was beating now.

"How close do you want to get?" Her eyes were shining with the intense promise of being up to no good.

How was I supposed to respond to that?

"There you are."

I jumped so high at the sound of Sohrab's voice that, had an NBA scout been around, I would've gotten signed right there. Kaval, however, stayed exactly where she'd been standing, somehow not startled by her brother's interruption.

Sohrab had a vaguely disapproving frown on his face,

but that was kind of how he always looked. Zar, who was following him, flashed a wicked smirk that I desperately hoped he would put away as soon as possible.

"Mom is looking for you," Sohrab told his sister.

"Really?" Kaval said in "I Don't Believe You Times a Hundred" font.

"Yes."

Kaval narrowed her eyes at Sohrab, then glanced at Zar, who gave her a "what're you looking at me for" shrug. "Fine," she said, turning to me. "But we're not done talking."

"What? Oh. Right. Sure," I said. "Talking at school, then. We'll talk, I mean at..." Kaval didn't wait for me to finish. She picked up her heels and marched across the grass barefoot. I turned to my friends. "We were just... talking."

"About what?" Zar asked, not at all helpfully.

"Nothing. Just, you know, stars."

"Stars?" Sohrab asked.

"Yeah. I was telling her that it seems like there are a lot fewer of them now. Remember when we were kids? The sky was beautiful then."

"Maybe you're just standing in the wrong spot and looking in the wrong place," Sohrab suggested.

That made zero sense, just like his "advice" in the kitchen earlier. At least, I thought so. Zar, however, nodded along like he understood. So maybe it was just me.

"Come on," Intezar said. "We came to find you because they're serving dinner. Let's eat. You know the food is always amazing here."

"Yeah," I said. "I'm sure it's all right."

〜

Work the next day was super stressful but being around Chef Brodeur could be like that sometimes. I'd started working at Remarquable part-time three years ago, when I was sixteen. My mother knew the saucier somehow—often it seemed like she knew the whole world—and she'd told him how much I wanted to work in a restaurant.

He'd said they were looking for a dishwasher, and I'd jumped at the chance. Since then I'd been bumped up to a line cook, and last year to something like an apprentice. As such, I was required to learn every position in the kitchen. At least, that's what I was told. So far as I could tell, I was the only apprentice the relatively small restaurant had ever had, so they were probably making the rules up as they went along.

Anyway, Chef Brodeur, a lean, hawk-eyed Frenchwoman, was sharp with her criticism, so days when you weren't perfect could be rough. My coworkers said she wasn't as tough on me as she was on them, but I think that only seemed true because I wasn't considered worthy of the night shift.

Instead, I worked during lunch on the weekends, and sometimes helped prepare for the dinner rush, though I always had to be out by six. I kept waiting for Brodeur to tell me I was good enough to work at night, but that hadn't happened yet.

Whatever. My toque was off, and I didn't have to think about work for a while. Instead I tried to figure out what I'd make when I got home. It'd have to be something basic. My father wasn't an adventurous eater. According to Ahmed Jilani, if you had to use your imagination to make it, it wasn't really food.

I'd just resigned myself to making a *korma* or something and serving it with defrosted naan like a barbarian when my phone rang. I was driving and I didn't recognize the number, so I shouldn't have answered it. Not sure why I did. Maybe that'll be the title of my autobiography: *I Don't Know Why I Did That.*

"Hello?"

A deep voice replied, *"As-salamu alaykum."*

And just like that, the chances of it being a wrong number went down to nearly zero.

"Wa'alaykum," I said as I pulled out of the BART station and onto the street. "This is Danyal."

"Yes, Danyal, this is Jaleel Akram."

I raised my eyebrows. Bisma Akram's father. Why was *he* calling me? "Uh . . . yes, sir."

"We came over to your parents' place a couple of weeks ago. About my daughter's hand in marriage."

"Of course."

Silence.

"Mr. Akram? Are you still there?"

"I'm here," he said. "Bisma made you aware of her ... situation?"

"Umm ... yes, sir."

"I got your number from your mother. I ... just wanted to thank you. After you met with her was the only time we've come back from one of these *rishta* meetings and I haven't had to watch my daughter weep."

I wasn't sure what to say to that.

"You're a very decent young man. I wanted to let you know that I appreciate it."

"Thank you."

There was another pause. Then he said, "I was wondering if you could come over to our place to talk."

I let out a deep breath. "Mr. Akram, Bisma seems wonderful, but I'm not ... This is really something you should discuss with my mother and—"

"I have a business proposition for you," he interrupted. "I think you'll find it interesting."

"What kind of business?"

"You're into cookery. Let's say it is about the cookery business."

"Okay." I tried to keep the skepticism out of my voice but ... well, I was skeptical.

"We'll expect you after school on Friday, if that works. I'll text you the address."

He hung up.

I stared at the stylized *H* on the van's wheel and shook my head.

"Okay," I told the aging machine, since there was no one else around to talk to, "that's going to super suck."

CHAPTER FOUR

Kaval walked up to me in chem. She somehow managed to look glamorous in the protective goggles we had to wear that day. "Hey, partner," she said.

"Part...where's Aaron?"

Our chemistry teacher had assigned lab partners at the beginning of the year, and I was supposed to work with Aaron Mendes. We got along fine, mostly because he actually knew what he was doing, and I tried my best not to touch anything that looked like it might explode.

"We switched for today." A little smirk played on Kaval's lips. "You're not complaining, are you?"

Me? Complain about working with her? Impossible. "Of course not. I thought we weren't allowed to switch, though."

"I asked nicely. Mr. Jang said it was fine. He was very sweet about it."

I frowned. Our chemistry teacher had never been sweet to me. I looked around the classroom, and sure enough, Aaron was clear on the other side of the room, and Mr. Jang didn't seem like he had a problem with it. In fact, he didn't seem to care about anything but his plans for Renaissance Man, which he was discussing intently with Trinity Selassie, whom he'd picked to represent chemistry.

I let Kaval take the lead as we set up the experiment. She was a better partner than Aaron, in that she didn't hesitate to order me to do things. Aaron usually did everything, even though I was happy to help. I wasn't lazy. It was just that I usually only had a vague idea of what I was supposed to do. Today I lit the Bunsen burner when Kaval told me and fetched the test tubes we needed.

"So," Kaval said, her voice totally casual, "we didn't get to finish our conversation last night."

"When I was showing you up on the basketball court, you mean."

She raised her eyebrows at me.

"What?" I asked. "That's how I remember it."

Kaval shook her head. "Whatever. I never got to say what I wanted to say to you."

"Say it now."

"I'm getting to it."

I raised my hands by way of apology and almost spilled

the purple liquid in the test tube I was holding. What was this stuff, anyway? Boron? No. Potassium? Sodium, maybe? It looked like it might taste like lavender, but taking a sip was probably inadvisable.

"I heard you had a visitor recently."

I carefully placed the tube on a rack before I could mess up. "Visitor?"

"I heard some aunties gossiping. Apparently, some girl came over to your place. You know, a marriage prospect."

She'd heard about Bisma Akram, obviously. "Yeah, you know, parents . . ."

"I heard your family liked her. Did you?" Kaval's eyes were locked on mine, and her gaze was very intense.

"Um . . . I mean, you know, she seemed nice, but—"

"Not for you."

"Right," I said. "Exactly. It's not happening."

"I'm glad," Kaval said, and then she giggled at my surprised expression. "I'm just saying, you know, it would be a shame if you made a decision like that without talking to me first." She brushed her hand up against mine as she reached for the test tube full of purple.

I tried and failed to keep my expression neutral as my heart danced with the knowledge that Kaval Sabsvari was flirting. With me. We had chemistry together. I stood up straighter and a huge grin spread over my face. This. Was. Awesome.

"Are you saying—" I started with hope.

"I'm not saying anything, except that it's a big decision. . . .

Just don't jump into anything without talking to your friends. I mean"—her smile got playful—"you're not the best prospect in the world or anything, but..."

"Very funny. I guess I deserved that."

"Yes. You definitely did."

What Kaval had said made me so weightless that it was impossible to concentrate during history. She hadn't said that she liked me, of course, but she'd totally hinted at it. Right? Yes. Definitely. I wasn't wrong about this.

Why hadn't she just come out and said it, though? Saying "don't jump into anything" seemed a long way off from what I wanted to hear.

I was reaching into my pocket as stealthily as possible to text Zar to ask his opinion, when I realized Mr. Tippett had stopped talking in the middle of his lecture. I looked up, wondering if he'd seen what I was doing.

He hadn't. Kaval had raised her hand. This wasn't really done in Tippett's class. He didn't like questions.

"What is it, Ms. Sabsvari?"

"We're all wondering if you've picked someone for the Renaissance Man."

"Be precise, Ms. Sabsvari. Who is 'we'?"

"Like...everyone."

There was a murmur of agreement from the rest of the class.

I rolled my eyes.

"Indeed? Am I to understand that all of you are conspirators in this delightful disruption to my day? Surely there is someone here who does not care about this ridiculous award."

I should've just kept my mouth shut, but I've never really been good at doing that. I raised my hand. "I don't care. Like at all. If that, you know, helps."

There was some giggling and snickering. I sat back in my chair, content with the reaction.

"Yes, Mr. Jilani," Tippett drawled, his tone a little amused. "I'm familiar with your impressive talent for apathy. Anyone else share his lack of enthusiasm for puffed-up self-congratulatory pageantry? Anyone at all?"

No one else spoke up.

"Very well," Algie Tippett said. He fixed his gaze on me. "In that case, congratulations, Danyal. History will find you to have been, against all odds, a Renaissance Man."

A shocked silence followed Tippett's announcement.

When a pick for Renaissance Man was announced, there was usually a lot of cheering and backslapping for the chosen one. It was—as everyone polite who has ever been up for an award says—an honor to be nominated. It meant, at the very least, that one teacher thought highly of you.

That wasn't the case here. Tippett had just selected me

out of spite. I was nowhere near the best student in his class. I was, in fact, the absolute worst.

Our teacher smirked. I felt smaller than I ever had before.

Intezar, bless his big, dumb heart, actually started clapping, but when no one joined him, he gave up awkwardly.

"Very funny," Alan Rhodes called from the back of the class. "Who are you actually going to pick?"

I turned around to glare at Alan. What did he care? He was already in Renaissance Man. He'd been picked for mathematics.

"What was it about my statement that you failed to understand, Mr. Rhodes?" Tippett asked.

"You can't be serious. Jilani is an idiot."

There was some scattered laughter, before Kaval whirled around and said, "Don't be a dick, Alan."

I'm not going to lie. Seeing Kaval defend me almost made the humiliation of the moment worth it, especially because Tippett's ridiculous decision had to sting her the most. She wasn't going to get into the competition now.

There were a couple of *ooh*s around the room at Kaval's remark, as our teacher said, "Please don't be inappropriate, Ms. Sabsvari."

"But—"

"Enough," Tippett said. "Whatever intellectual limitations you all feel Mr. Jilani suffers from, he is going to represent this class in Renaissance Man. Anyone who has a problem with that can take it up with the principal. Right. Now."

This time no one said a word.

"Very good, then. Now, as I was saying, Winston Churchill...Oh, by the way, Mr. Jilani, you really ought to pay attention. You see, the subject of this lesson, Churchill, will be your topic for Renaissance Man. I trust you will be motivated to not make a public fool out of yourself. For once."

I glared at him, viciously pulled a cap off a pen, and prepared to take notes.

"Excellent. Let's get started, shall we? One must not keep history waiting...."

"You can't do this," I said, standing before Algie Tippett's desk, arms crossed.

With a shit ton of boredom in his eyes, my history teacher watched everyone else file out of the room. Kaval whispered "Good luck" as she hurried past, and Zar gave me an enthusiastic thumbs-up.

"Now," Tippett said, leaning back in the cheap, creaking plastic chair the school had provided him. "What, precisely, is the problem, Mr. Jilani?"

"You know what the problem is." I tried to stay calm. I was basically a superstar when it came to not raising my voice while frustrated. I'd lived with my father my entire life, after all. "The Renaissance Man."

"That hardly seems like a problem. In fact, I would go so far as to say that congratulations are in order, wouldn't you?"

"This isn't funny."

"As you mature, Mr. Jilani, I believe you will realize that most humor is simply a matter of perspective. There are many ways in which your current situation is objectively amusing."

I managed to resist the urge to pick up the apple on his desk—he got one for himself and displayed it prominently every day—and fling it against the wall. "I don't belong in that contest."

"Ah. Then you agree with Mr. Rhodes's assertion that you are, in fact, an idiot."

"No," I said. "Obviously."

"In that case, by all means, elaborate on the nature of your concern."

"I'm . . . not an, you know . . . I mean, I'm not an idiot—"

"A proposition that is becoming less certain by the second, I assure you."

"But I'm not good at school. I won't win. I've got no chance. So all that happens is that everyone who actually cares about being in Renaissance Man is going to be pissed at me for taking their spot—"

"I suspect that they're going to be rather more 'pissed' "—

he took the time to put up the world's slowest air quotes—"at me than they are at you."

"It isn't just them. My parents...my mother is going to get all excited, and then...I'm going to get laughed off the stage. I'm going to be a joke. Just, look, I'm sorry I was rude or whatever about Churchill the other day, but please, pick someone else. Anyone else. This should go to your top student."

"And if I were to assure you that it was not my intention to punish you, would that change your mind at all?"

That stopped me for a moment. I couldn't begin to figure out what he meant, though. "It wasn't?"

"Not entirely, no. Danyal, I've been at this institution for a little short of half a century. In that time, none of my students have won Renaissance Man." He harrumphed. "Now that I think about it, the name of the contest is getting rather dated. Perhaps I should talk to the principal about making it more inclusive."

"What about me?" I asked.

He clapped his age-spotted hands together. "Ah yes. The central question of youth. My point is that I do not expect you to win anything. That has never been a goal of mine."

That made no sense. What reason, outside of winning, could there be for entering a contest?

"Obviously, given how entrenched you are in your belief that you cannot succeed in any kind of academic pursuit, victory is impossible. However, I do expect you to *not* be a joke. That much, I am sure, is in your power. Do you understand?"

"But—"

"Excellent. Now, please excuse me. I'm old, my time is precious, and you've taken up more than enough of it for one day."

Shaking my head, I stormed out, trying to make sure I wasn't muttering unpleasant truths about Tippett loud enough for him to hear.

Almost the entire class was waiting for me when I stepped out. I gave them a little wave—no one waved back—and closed the door behind me. As soon as it clicked into place, Alan Rhodes demanded, "Did you ask him to pick someone else?"

I nodded.

"And?"

I shook my head.

Everyone groaned.

"This is completely ridiculous," Alan said, raising his voice to be heard over the noise. "We should put a petition together. Tippett can't demean Renaissance Man by picking someone like Jilani."

"Look, guys, I'm sorry, okay? I asked him to go with the top student in this class—"

"Will you sign the petition?"

I didn't see who asked, but some curious whispering followed. I was about to tell them I would when Kaval said,

"No. Why should he? This is bullshit. It isn't like only the top scorers in every subject get entered—"

"That's how it should be," Alan muttered.

"It isn't, though. And no one, ever, gets asked to drop out."

"Except Jilani will probably be a dropout entirely soon enough."

"Dick," Kaval snapped.

"Stop calling me that."

"Then stop being a dick." A couple of people laughed. When the bell for the next period rang, they began moving away. Alan left too, walking backward all the way down the hall so he could glare at me the entire time.

Kaval turned to me. "Look, Danyal, we all know that Tippett was being a jerk when he went with you. But this is a huge opportunity. You could show everyone what you're really made of. This could be your version of Tom Brady being picked in the sixth round of the draft."

Intezar stared at her. "You follow football?"

"I follow Gisele," Kaval said. "Anyway, I'm just saying, you know, this could be a turning point for you. Don't give it up."

"That's nice," I said. "Really. Except for one problem."

"What?"

"Tom Brady can actually play a little football," Intezar told her.

"Whatever. Look, I promise to help you. You can come over to my place. We'll work on it together."

How could I say no to that?

"Renaissance Man," Sohrab called out when he saw me. It was, I could tell, meant to be an exclamation, like someone shouting *Dude!* or *That's awesome!* Since it was Sohrab Sabsvari who said it, it came out calm and sober. He was incapable of getting fired up.

I made a face, like he'd said something gross. A couple of kids standing nearby rolled their eyes. I glared at them with all the venom I could manage, which wasn't much, but it had been, like, two hours, and I was already growing tired of all the whispers and snide comments I'd been getting since Tippett announced I was his pick.

"You don't seem very enthusiastic. How can you not think this is good?"

"It's not my thing. You know I'm not applying to college. I don't need the boost."

"But five thousand dollars would be nice."

I chuckled at the understatement. "Yeah. That would be huge. But I'd have to win to get it, and we both know that's not going to happen. Losing spectacularly, though, is very much in the cards."

"It's still an accomplishment," Sohrab insisted. "We should do something to celebrate."

"Like what?"

"Well...there's a fascinating scholar coming to the mosque next month after *Maghrib* to give a talk. We could go to that."

"How is that a celebration?"

Sohrab narrowed his eyes at me. "God is fun," he said, in a tone that suggested it'd be total blasphemy to disagree.

"Maybe. The people who like to get together and talk about Him, though . . ."

"I did tell you," he said, "that you're not as funny as you think, didn't I?"

"Don't start. Anyway, I just meant that a month seems a long time to wait before 'celebrating.' You're just trying to get me to come to mosque with you, aren't you?"

Sohrab rubbed the back of his neck sheepishly. "Maybe. But only because I always end up going to these things alone. I miss hanging with you guys."

Emotional blackmail. A total uncle move.

I had to admit it was effective, though. What was I supposed to say to that?

"Come on. Please? It'll be great. I'll text you the details. I should also invite Intezar."

"Um . . . no, you shouldn't."

"Fine. You know him better than I do."

I grimaced. The way he'd said that had been so . . . well, sad, I guess, but also lonely. To make him feel better about his fraying relationship with Zar, and because I really hadn't been spending a lot of time with him, I said, "Fine. I'm in."

"Fantastic," Sohrab said. I could tell he was excited because I knew him, but really there was no way to tell from his tone or his face. "You won't regret it. You talk so much about being handsome that you don't spend any time becoming handsome. I mean, of course, that you have to work on beautifying your soul—"

"Hey," I cut in. "Remember that time you said I wouldn't regret agreeing to go to the mosque with you?"

Sohrab frowned. "You mean a few seconds ago?"

"Yeah. Just so you know, I regret it already."

CHAPTER FIVE

"*My God! How* did you not immediately call me? This is so exciting, Danyal. We are so happy for you. All the aunties are talking about you and Renaissance Man. All of them are surprised. We aren't surprised, though, are we, Ahmed?"

My father, who was reading a newspaper—an actual printed newspaper because he thinks tablets change the way news feels, whatever that means—looked up from across the living room. He gave a short, sharp grunt. That was the "I completely disagree with what you just said but I'm going to be nice and ignore you now" grunt.

"Aren't you proud of our son? Don't you want to tell him that?"

My father gave a long, drawn-out sigh, folded his newspaper, and set it aside. "So, this is an academic contest?"

I nodded.

"And you were selected to enter, *haan*?"

I nodded again.

"Strange. What happens next?"

My mother let out an exasperated breath. "All the kids who get picked write an essay over the rest of the year. Like a proper thesis. Then there is a big event and they get up onstage and present their papers. One senior student for each subject."

"And what subject did you get?" Dad asked.

"History."

"Aren't you failing history?"

"I prefer to think that history is failing me."

My father frowned. "What does that mean?"

"I... don't know. It just sounded clever."

He shook his head. "So, you got in—"

"Picked by a teacher," Mom said.

"Yes, yes. Fine. Tell me, Danyal, are you going to win?"

I shook my head.

"That's what I thought," he said, reaching for his newspaper again. "I'll say this about your son, Aisha. He's never surprising."

Mom's hands were on her hips and her nostrils flared. "Danyal. Go to your room."

Great. I was going to be the cause of another shouting match. I could feel it in the air, like I was standing next to a burning oven. Not for the first time, I wondered whether my parents would've been happier together if I'd never been born.

I was barely to the top of the stairs when Mom started yelling and Dad replied calmly, because he always replied calmly at first, before he got angry and loud. It wouldn't even be about his reaction to Renaissance Man soon. I'd heard more than enough of these to know that the fight would become about old hurts that had never quite healed right, and it would go on and on, as sure as the moon rising in the sky, until finally there would be silence without peace.

When I turned seven, my father started throwing open my door at daybreak, turning on the lights, roughly shaking me awake, and yelling at me to get up. He was the world's most obnoxious, consistent alarm, and he didn't have a snooze button. I'd told him that I was responsible enough to get up to pray myself, but he refused to believe me, which was fair, but annoying.

"Get up, Danyal. It is time for *Fajr*."

I groaned.

"Prayer is better than sleep," he said, quoting the *adhan*.

"I know, I know," I mumbled, like I'd done a hundred thousand times, and dragged my unwilling body to the bathroom.

Honestly, I've never been able to square the dawn

prayer with the idea of a loving and merciful God. Why does a divine, all-powerful being require me to get up when it's still dark, when even early birds are sleeping, to pray to Him? I mean, I know that remembering Allah is important and all, but I could also do it during regular business hours.

Sighing and muttering under my breath, I made my way downstairs, where my father was waiting. As crazy as Intezar thought it was, getting married young would at least keep my dad out of my room at five in the morning. I'd decided a long time ago that I'd buy my wife scandalous stuff to sleep in—nightshirts and tank tops and shorts—just to be absolutely sure the old man was never able to shake me awake again.

He seemed tired this morning, and given the comforter and pillows piled on the couch, he'd slept in the living room. I've never figured out why he did that. There was a perfectly good bed in the guest room he could use when he and Mom fought.

Honestly, though, I'd stopped trying to figure Dad out years ago. What was the point?

"*Allahu Akbar*," he said, starting the prayer.

I raised my hands to my ears as well, hoping that my father would choose short verses to recite, so that I could crawl back to bed as quickly as possible.

He didn't choose short verses. He never did.

And I was the disappointment?

As soon as we were done, I was on my feet and heading back to my room, when my father called out, "Wait."

I groaned. "Yes, Dad?"

"Eat breakfast with me."

I glanced out a window. The sun had barely started to rise. I could squeeze in another two hours of sleep if I was lucky. "Now?"

"You shouldn't be wasting these early hours. The Prophet Muhammad said that there is great blessing in this time. Whatever you attempt, you will do well in."

"Yeah. It's the best sleep."

Ahmed Jilani gave a grunt. And we were off for the day. This was a "that was kind of funny, but I don't like you all that much, so I'm not going to smile" grunt.

"I'll cook," my father offered.

Oh...that was even worse. But there was obviously no way out of this. How had a holy undertaking made my morning so forsaken?

I played a quick game involving DC superheroes on my phone while my dad heated a pan on high and made sunny-side up eggs for us, the edges of the whites crisping. When the sizzle had died away, he sprinkled an excessive amount of red chili powder on them, before dripping hot oil over the pepper, and serving everything with toast. It was a very desi breakfast. Chef Brodeur would've had a stroke just looking at it.

"Thanks," I said.

He grunted in response and pointed to my phone. He was a big believer in doing only one thing at a time. With a sigh, I put it on the table, screen facing down. We ate in silence for a few minutes, the crunch of slightly over-done toast the only sound between us, until my father said something I'd never heard before.

"Your mother was right."

The piece of toast that had been on its way to my mouth dropped from my hand. "What?"

"About your contest. She had a point. I mean, she was also wrong. . . ."

And just like that, balance was restored to the universe.

"What I'm saying," he went on, "is that even if you getting into the contest is not worth celebrating, it is a good thing you are in it. At least this way you won't have to write a final in history. This is an opportunity."

I nodded. Here came the "it will look good on a col-lege application" speech, which would transition into the "I know you've got the brains of a stupid donkey, but you should go to college" speech, which would then become the "being a chef is not a viable career path" speech. It was a familiar mutation.

Instead of launching into a lecture, however, my father simply took a sip of chai out of a giant mug that my mother had gotten for him. It read WORLD'S OKAYEST DAD. Aisha Jilani could be savage when she wanted to be. Then he asked, "What are you writing about?"

"My teacher says I have to write about Winston Churchill."

"Why are they making you write about that fucker?"

I stared at Ahmed Jilani like I didn't know him.

I mean, there are things that you never expect to happen, but that your mind can still make sense of—alien invasions, zombie apocalypses, falling in love with a vampire—and then there is stuff so bizarre that stunned silence is the only possible response, such as the thought of my father using any variation of the f-bomb.

He looked embarrassed in the face of my shock. "Sorry," he said. "That is not a good word. Make sure you never use it. Even for Churchill."

"Um. Yeah. No. Totally. I mean, I don't even know what it means."

The super awkward silence continued, but finally Dad said, "What does your history teacher say about Churchill?"

"Tippett is a big fan. I thought everyone was."

He seemed to think about this for a long time, a pained expression on his face.

Why? Everything I'd ever heard about Churchill at school or seen in movies or documentaries had been positive...though, honestly, I hadn't really been paying close attention.

"Write what makes your teacher happy. That will get you the best grade."

I wasn't sure if that was a command or a question. "Are you sure?"

That was when Ahmed Jilani said something I'd never heard him say before for the *second time* in our conversation.

It was a sentence that I'd assumed all desi uncles and aunties lacked the capacity to utter.

"I don't know."

Even during the last class of the day—it was one of the maths, trig or maybe calc—I was still thinking about my dad's outburst at breakfast. What had that even been about? As was typical of him, my father hadn't answered any questions about his issues with Churchill. Instead, he'd just gone upstairs to make up with Mom.

I'd been wondering about it all day. In fact, I was so preoccupied with Ahmed Jilani's use of the f-word that Mrs. Wright's explanations about how angles can move or something because real life is not simple and two dimensional totally went over my head. Honestly, though, that would've happened even if breakfast had been boring and predictable.

I decided it was entirely possible that Mrs. Wright was making all this up. I mean, we'd have no way of knowing, would we? We put a lot of faith in our teachers, if you think about it. How do we even know a square root is a real thing?

It was then that the whole Renaissance Man thing got real. Principal Weinberg came by and pulled me out of class for orientation, along with Alan Rhodes. His petition to get me kicked out of the contest hadn't gone anywhere.

I thought it was kind of amazing that he'd put up a web

page dedicated to bashing my selection so quickly. Tippett, however, seemed less than impressed. The rumor was that he'd told Alan if the site stayed up, Alan's history grade might suffer. That was like threatening Alan's firstborn. He would do anything to protect his grades.

"You excited?" I asked as we walked out of class together.

Alan gave me the kind of look a desi aunty would give calamari if she ever found one in her kitchen—the "I don't know what you are or how you got here, and I can't believe I have to deal with you" stare. Then he picked up his pace and pulled away from me.

Still upset, I guess.

I followed him into a room where the six other Renaissance Man contestants were sitting behind desks, all of them with textbooks for various classes open. I resisted the temptation to roll my eyes. These guys were something else.

Alan stalked his way to the far side of the room without saying anything, but I waved to the group. "Hey, guys."

Only Natari Smith waved back. It was easy to see why Intezar had a crush on her. I made my way over and sat down next to her.

"Tough room," I whispered.

"Yeah. They absolutely hate you right now."

"Impossible."

She chuckled.

"What's their problem?"

"Danyal, you're the only one here that isn't a nerd."

"So I'm not cool enough to be here or something?"

"Something like that," Natari said. "A lot of people worked really hard for this. Many of them are our friends. They didn't get in. You stumbled in accidentally. Do you get it?"

I frowned. So much for Tippett's theory that everyone would be mad at him, not at me.

The idea of not being liked bothered me. I was used to being pretty much universally loved. "This whole thing will blow over soon, right?"

"Absolutely. Once we destroy you in the competition, things will go back to normal." Seeing the look on my face, Natari grinned. "You realize that everyone is going to go all out, right? No one wants to rank below you. They'd never live it down."

I winced.

"Sorry," she said.

"It's fine." I tried to put a matching grin on my face. "Do you want to beat me too?"

"Sure I do, Jilani. But I'm not shortsighted enough to be irritated you got in. Just makes for one entry I know I'm going to crush."

We stopped talking as Principal Weinberg walked in. She smiled at us all in her typically warm way. "Why don't we get right to it? Congratulations, of course, to all of you for getting selected for Renaissance Man. It is a remarkable achievement."

I felt a couple of people glance in my direction.

"There was a time when the principal of Aligheri Prep had to stand in this room and explain how the competition worked and tell the students why it was important. That time has passed. Everyone knows what the competition means now. It means that, in this school of high standards, you stand at the top of the mountain—"

There was a mountain? No one told me there was a mountain.

"—and so it is not surprising that every student who has ever won this contest has been accepted to an Ivy League school, many with impressive scholarships. And, of course, there is the cash prize. I understand that money means little to most of you." Weinberg's eyes seemed to find me as she said this, and I ducked my head. "But that sum is still a significant incentive, I would think."

I stared at my desk. Why'd she have to look at me? I mean, yeah, okay, I was probably one of the only kids at the school who didn't grow up wearing gold-plated diapers, but not everyone needed to know.

"When writing your thesis and preparing your presentation, I suggest that you remember the name of the contest. You are required to show mastery of one subject, but a pan-disciplinary approach typifies the spirit that the contest seeks to honor."

Whatever that was supposed to mean.

"Finally, as you know, you will no longer be required to write the final exam in the subject you've been chosen to represent. Your thesis will determine your grade.

Therefore"—this time Weinberg definitely paused to look at me in particular—"it would be a good idea to keep your teacher's interests and preferences, as well as what will play well to an audience, in mind when crafting your thesis. Any questions?"

I watched as seven hands shot up in the air.

Weinberg called on Natari. "Yes, Ms. Smith?"

"Can we write the final exam in our subject anyway?" she asked, in the tone of a kid asking for a pony. "Maybe for extra credit?"

Everyone in the room seemed to lean forward, as if very interested in the answer.

These people were not okay.

Weinberg, for her part, seemed unsurprised by the question. "No, I'm afraid not."

I pulled out my phone as the questions went on. I knew how the contest worked, more or less. And besides, they say that the devil is in the details, and I've always been taught to avoid tangling with the devil whenever possible. In a way, living carefree is the most Muslim thing you can do.

Sohrab thinks this philosophy of mine is "interesting and creative but plainly erroneous." I think that two out of three isn't bad.

Anyway, the only question I was interested in, the principal couldn't answer. What had been my father's deal at breakfast this morning?

I decided to google Winston Churchill to find out.

CHAPTER SIX

Research isn't easy when Google pops out a lot of results. I typed in "Winston Churchill" and got around ninety-one million hits. Just a little bit more reading than I was willing to do, thanks.

I ended up doing an image search instead. I mean, a picture is worth a thousand words, right? So if you look at ten pictures, you've already read like twenty books.

Math is my best subject for a reason.

Well...it's not, actually, but whatever.

Pretty much all the images that came up were useless, at least when it came to figuring out what my dad's issue with Churchill was. Assuming, of course, that Ahmed Jilani didn't just really hate bow ties, because it looked like Winston was crazy about them.

Anyway, it wasn't until I was on my way to the Akrams'

house that I realized that even though I didn't understand my father, there was someone who, against all odds, did. I could just ask my mom.

I also hadn't remembered to ask her why Bisma's father had called me. I glanced quickly at the van's rearview mirror, and then to my sides, just to make sure there were no cops around, and reached for my phone.

As soon as I touched it, it buzzed and started playing the theme song from Disney's *Ratatouille*. I nearly dropped the phone but recovered enough to see who it was.

"Hey, Zar."

"Listen, I got the number for a *pir* dude in Pakistan, in case you want it."

"You got whose phone number?"

"A *pir*. My momz knows some *pir* people in Pakistan. The holy guys who fight black magic and all that. They make amulets and stuff?"

I had heard of them. My parents had taught me most of these "holy guys" were charlatans and nothing more, but I guess Zar and his family believed otherwise. "Okay."

"And I just thought, you know, who could use a hookup like that? And then I thought you could, in case you want someone to pray for you to crush Renaissance Man. And to graduate this year. It never hurts to have a *pir* dude on your side."

"Is that his name? *Pir* Dude?"

"I don't think they have names, *yaar*," Zar said. "I mean, you know, obviously they do, but I don't think they share 'em. Ruins the mystic's mystique. He goes by Pirji, I think."

"Sounds legit."

"Gotta try it."

"I really don't."

Intezar let out an irritated sigh. "What could it hurt? These guys are like...miraculous, okay? One of my cousins was totally in love with this girl, and Pirji gave him a super secret prayer to recite like thirty thousand times a day or something."

"And your cousin got the girl he wanted?"

"What? No. He was so distracted trying to keep track of his thirty thousand recitations that he got into a car accident and died. It was horrible. Doesn't mean it wouldn't have worked, though."

I opened my mouth to argue, then decided against it. With Intezar, you just had to go with the flow. It was like trying to argue with a strong wind. All the logic in the world won't make it change its course, and it's possible you'll end up swallowing a bug. "Fine. Whatever. Let's talk about it later. I've got to meet the dad of that Akram girl I told you about."

"That's today? I'd forgotten. Damn, this uncle ain't wasting time. They're gonna lock you down."

I shook my head. I wanted to tell him that was not what was happening, but then Zar would demand an explanation, and I wasn't going to betray Bisma Akram's confidence.

"You don't seem interested. What's wrong? She an uggo or something?"

"No. Dude, uncool. We shouldn't talk about people like that."

"Whatever, man. Fuckability is a prime factor in arranged marriages."

I groaned. In addition to Intezar's theories about sex, he also had a number of opinions about arranged marriage. His primary thesis was that it was a low-tech eugenics program to create ideal brown people.

You take a smart man (smarts being measured primarily by the balance of his bank account or the potential balance of his bank account) and mate him with an attractive woman (attraction being measured by how light the color of her skin is within the brown spectrum) in the hopes of producing children that are both smart and attractive. It sounded ridiculous, of course, but that's why it also rang true. It seemed like something desi aunties would attempt.

"Yeah, yeah. I've heard it all before. Look, you know that I like Kaval, so the rest of this is a waste of time."

There was a pause. Then Zar let out a long breath. "You're shopping outside your price range."

"What?"

"It's like you're at the grocery store and you're trying to buy eggs. You, my brownther, you've got your eyes on some double A—or in Kaval's case, double—"

"Stop. And stop trying to make *brownther* happen."

I heard him huff. "You're a mean girl. And fine. I won't impinge the honor of your fair maiden, Mr. Jilani."

"What do you think *impinge* means?"

"I don't know. I heard that line on TV or something."

If he'd heard it on TV, it was probably a real word.

"Anyway," Intezar said, "Kaval is like free-range and organic and corn-fed and all that. She's prime eggs. Fresh. The problem is that you're broke. You're really only looking at like...Grade C eggs, all watery and flat and a little cracked. So, if your parents are able to get you Grade B eggs, I mean, they're a little thick, but you should go for it."

"You know a lot about eggs," I said.

"I looked up the USDA guidelines. I've been sitting on this for a while." Intezar chuckled. "Get it? Sitting on it—"

"Yeah. I get it."

"I'm right about this, Danyal," he said, his voice more serious than I'd heard it in a long time. "You should listen to me."

I sighed. "My mom said the same thing. You really think she's that far out of my league?"

"*Yaar*, Kaval is the NFL Pro Bowl, all right? You're like a game of *kabbadi* in a small village in fucking Gujranwala that no one showed up to."

"I appreciate the sensitivity with which you answered my question."

"What are friends for?"

"For helping. They're for helping."

"I got you the number for Pirji," he protested.

"Thanks for that. Hey, listen, I gotta let you go. I'm here."

〰

A girl of around fourteen or so answered the door. The family resemblance was so strong that, even if I'd met her somewhere else, I would've known immediately that she was Bisma Akram's sister. When I smiled and greeted her, she nodded but didn't smile back.

"They're in there." She gave a swift, jerky wave in the direction of the formal living room and then scurried away.

That was weird. Maybe she was just shy.

The three Akrams I had met before were waiting for me in a nicely—if traditionally—decorated room. There was a red rug with a paisley pattern, and thick, heavy wood furniture with flowers carved on it. There were a few coffee tables with an assortment of religious knickknacks on them, like a miniature replica of the Prophet's Mosque in Medina or a glass cube that said *Allah* on one side in Arabic, and *Muhammad* on the other.

On the far wall hung a painting with several verses from the Quran. The calligraphy was beautiful. It was from *Ad-Duhaa*, the chapter named "The Morning Hours." It read: *Did He not find you lost and guide you?*

The Akrams were each sitting in different corners of the room, almost as if they were trying to stay as far away from each other as possible. Jaleel Akram, Bisma's father, got up to greet me. He was one of those men I instantly resented a little because he had a gravity about him, something that makes you think that his broad shoulders and tall frame belong in a dignified black-and-white picture from the 1930s. I don't have that impressiveness. I don't think I ever will. He shook my hand.

"Thank you for coming, Danyal."

His wife, a pleasantly round woman, managed a smile, though I could tell from her eyes that she'd been crying. I glanced behind me at where Bisma was sitting, dressed in a plain white *shalwar kameez*, but she wouldn't look me in the eye.

"Sit here," Jaleel Akram said, pointing to a couch directly opposite Bisma, "so you can look at her when you make your decision."

I raised my eyebrows, but his back was to me already as he went and sat down next to his wife. I did what I was told.

Bisma's eyes remained fixed on the floor.

Her father cleared his throat. "As you are aware," he said, in a formal, emotionless manner, which made me think that he'd written out a script and memorized it, "my eldest daughter has, in her past, made a grave error, which has dishonored her and dishonored our family. She has left us unable to hold our heads high in society. She's cut the noses off our faces."

Bisma was picking viciously at her skin by her right thumbnail. I wanted to tell her to stop, that she would tear it open and make herself bleed, but I didn't. Her breathing was labored, and I was certain that if she looked up, there would be tears in her eyes.

"Despite this, my wife has a delusion that this wretched girl of ours can have a normal life. My wife wants to get her married, and wastes our time, and the time of other people, by parading this..." He trailed off and gestured toward Bisma. "...in front of prospects like yourself. It always ends badly. She tells the boys the truth and, if she wouldn't, I would. We won't perpetrate a fraud on anyone. All of them refuse, as they naturally must. Of all the young men she has met, my understanding is that you were the kindest to her, and for that may Allah bless you."

I didn't know what to say to that. I didn't even want to nod, because that would seem like I was agreeing with his cruel speech, but I felt like I should do or say something. Fortunately—unfortunately—Jaleel Akram was not done speaking.

"It is because of your kindness that I must now use you for a demonstration. My wife's ridiculous hopes for this girl must be killed. Her attempts at getting this girl married must stop. I just... I'm sorry but I have to put an end to this once and for all. I *must*. So, I am going to make you an offer to see if you—the kindest of her would-be prospects—will accept her." He reached into his pocket and pulled out a USB drive. "I have what is hopefully the only copy of her filthy video with that horrid white boy here. If you agree to marry Bisma, you can have it. That way you can be sure it never gets out. I will pay you also, to compensate for the deficiency in her character."

"Sir," I said, "with all due respect, this is—" I wanted to say this was fucking *insane*, but I was truly speechless. Nothing in my experience, or the experience of anyone I'd ever known, had prepared me for an encounter like this. Bisma's mother had tears running down her cheeks. She got to her feet to walk away, but in a cold tone, her husband commanded her to stay. Then, with a grimace, he turned his attention back to me.

"Ten thousand dollars?"

I shook my head, stunned. "What are you—"

"No? Twenty thousand, then."

"If you will just listen for a—"

"Fifty thousand?" he asked.

"Stop," Bisma pleaded quietly from across the room. "Please."

Mrs. Akram, for her part, bolted from the room, weeping.

Her husband watched her go in silence, then continued. "You know, they say that before the Prophet Muhammad stopped the practice, in the dark days of Arabia, they used to bury daughters alive when they were born. I never understood that until—"

"That is *enough*." I was on my feet, my voice raised, before I'd even fully considered what I was doing. In my life, I'd never spoken to an adult like this, and though I trembled with the daring of it, I couldn't stop myself. It was like a new part of my being had woken, a part of me burning with a righteous, unquenchable fire. "There are limits to the respect your age and your relationship to Bisma give you, and you, Mr. Akram, are... you're over that limit. This is mean, and it's... I'm sorry, but it's not how a man acts. It's disgusting."

I could feel the rage radiating from the older man. His eyes were wide with fury, and for a moment, I thought he might try to hit me. Somehow, I managed not to cringe at the thought of the blow. He didn't do it, though. Instead, he said, "Get out of my house."

Then, without waiting to see if I obeyed, he turned and stalked out of the room.

Bisma was sobbing now, slender arms wrapped around her waist, as if she was trying to comfort herself because there was no one else in the world who would.

I knelt down in front of her and took her hands in mine. "I'm sorry," I said.

"He's such an asshole," she managed to say. "I hate him so much."

I wanted to hold her then more than I'd wanted anything in my entire life.

That, however, wouldn't have been proper. It would've been a sin. I shouldn't have even been holding her hands, truth be told. I was surprised she hadn't pulled them away.

I wanted to do something for her. I wanted to console her, but I also wanted—needed—her to know that I didn't think the things her father had said were true. I wanted her to know... what? I couldn't even think of all the things that I wanted to say, much less figure out how to say them.

An image from my childhood came to my mind. I'd dropped a Quran on the floor once, when I was a kid. It just slipped from my hand. I remember watching as my mother knelt down and picked it up. Then she pressed the Quran to her lips, kissing it once, and then raised it to one eye and then the next. It was an apology and a show of reverence for something holy that, even if it fell, would forever be exalted.

I leaned forward and kissed Bisma's hands.

I raised them to one eye, and then the next.

Then I got to my feet.

Bisma's younger sister was standing at the threshold to the room, staring at us. As soon as I stepped away, she rushed past me and threw her arms around Bisma.

I let myself out.

$$\text{\textit{⸞⸞}}$$

I just drove. Something about my anger longed for the growl of a powerful mechanical beast, converting fuel and fury into motion on the open road.

Of course, those are the dreams of muscle cars; I was driving a minivan with 150,000-odd miles on it. Even if I could've floored the accelerator, the aged Odyssey would've only managed a weak mewl.

I was near the heart of Silicon Valley, and there were no open roads. All the arteries feeding souls to San Francisco were blocked. The red brake lights of an endless supply of cars stood before me, stopped in the middle of a freeway, like a glowing river of blood. It was a picture of a cardiac arrest, painted in traffic.

I slapped a hand hard on the steering wheel, which did nothing but hurt.

I swore, swerving onto the shoulder and accelerating past the other trapped cars, prompting indignant honking from them. I took the next exit and headed to the BART station.

I parked in a nearly deserted lot, climbed out, and slammed the door shut. I ran a hand through my hair, pacing up and down aimlessly, wondering when the beat of my heart would return to normal, when the crushed weeping of Bisma would fade from my ears.

What Jaleel Akram had done was so messed up. It was practically inhuman. I'd never thought I'd see someone treat their own child that way. My dad railed against me all the time, but he'd never shame me in front of a stranger, and he'd never make me break like I'd seen Bisma break today.

Even worse, I knew that I could save her from that little hell she was trapped in. All I had to do was say yes. My parents would be ecstatic. Her family would be ecstatic. By the time her history became an issue, it would be too late. Yes, my parents would be mortified, but the reproach Bisma endured from them would be nothing compared to what I'd seen her father inflict on her. More important, she wouldn't be alone. I'd be with her. I could protect her.

Yet there was another part of me, the part that had been dreaming of Kaval for years, that didn't want to stop dreaming.

And a third part of me, perhaps the most sensible part, knew that the desire to be noble, to be chivalrous, was a bad reason to marry someone. The world was like a cheese board of misfortune made up of old Epoisses, moldy Camembert, and overripe Roquefort. It stank, in other words, and sometimes it gave people listeria. You could eat some of a partner's cheese for them, but ultimately, there was a strong chance you'd just be sick with them, and then two people would be miserable.

I pinched the bridge of my nose with my fingers. I was starting to get a headache.

It was all the thinking. I wasn't used to it.

I got on a train going to the City, because it was something to do.

I showed up at Remarquable. It was packed. A couple of waiters nodded at me as I made my way inside, pushing past the pleasant, low rhythm of customer conversations, past the tinkling melody of forks brushing against plates and glasses clinking, and stepped toward the kitchen, toward the savory, seductive smell of garlic butter and the primal call of perfectly roasted beef.

I couldn't remember the last time I'd used the front entrance, and for a brief moment, it felt like all the bustle in the clean, efficient clockworks of the kitchen paused, that everyone stopped to look at me, and then the moment was gone, though I saw a few more smiles than I'd spotted when I'd first come in.

Chef Brodeur marched up to me. She was not smiling, but she wasn't frowning either.

"*Enfin, vous êtes là,*" she said, and when I stared at her in confusion, she threw her arms up in the air. "What times I must live in that I see chefs without French. Took you long enough to get here."

"You were . . . expecting me?"

"Of course, *mon petit âne.* The only way to advance at Remarquable is to choose to be here when you don't have to be. When you don't have to cook, but need to cook, that is when you're a chef, yes? Now, go change into something worthy of your station and get to work."

))(

There is peace in the rapid motion of a sharp knife, in the surprising cooperation of a perfectly cracked egg, in the delicate perfection with which the sweet red of saffron infuses everything it touches with color and smell. In the chaos of a professional kitchen, among the shouting and the clanging of pots and the sizzling and the frying and the smoke, there is an astonishing amount of calm, if one knows where to stand and what to do.

That isn't why I love to cook, but it's a nice bonus.

A few hours in, Brodeur pulled me aside and asked, "Have you eaten?"

"Why?"

"Because you look hungry, of course," she said with more exasperation than seemed necessary.

"I haven't eaten, Chef."

Turning to the kitchen at large, she yelled, "Who's hungry?"

There was a pause, then a few timid hands went up. I counted seven.

"As am I," Brodeur declared, rounding to face me. "It is slowing down. Take a break. Make dinner."

"Uh . . . sure. What would you like me to make?"

"Surprise me," she said. "Something, maybe, that is not on the menu."

I would've thought this was some kind of ritual for the new guy on the night shift, if the other members of the staff weren't staring at the chef, obviously surprised.

"Okay," I said, trying to keep the nervousness out of my voice. "I'll . . . see what I can do, I guess."

I stepped away from my station, thinking about what to serve. I was cooking for a master of French cuisine. Anything I made would be judged by the exacting standards of Remarquable and probably found wanting.

I told myself it didn't matter. The first rule of cooking, in my opinion, is to make what you want to eat yourself, so that's what I decided to do. Just then, I wanted something comfortable, like my mother's *biryani*, but that would take much too long. Something quick and delicious and . . . there it was.

I rolled pici, a fat pasta, and went to work with Grana

Padano and black pepper that I crushed using a mortar and pestle. When it was done, I presented it to Chef Brodeur with Pecorino Romano on top, the cheese melting into the creamy pasta.

She stared at my creation, horrified. "What the fuck is this?"

"It's Cacio e Pepe. It's—"

"I know that, you idiot." She wrenched the fork I was holding from my hand and poked at the dish doubtfully. "It is not French."

"Not really."

"Then it isn't really food, now, is it?" She jabbed at the pici and shoved it in her mouth. She raised her eyebrows and gave a harrumph of . . . not approval, precisely, but tolerance. Then, with the air of someone doing me a huge favor, she said, "I will eat it."

"Thank you?"

"You are full of surprises tonight," she said, waving her fork around thoughtfully. "You came here when you were not scheduled, and then instead of overreaching with something complex, you made . . . this." Brodeur paused, then asked, "Who is she?"

"This isn't about—"

"A Frenchman doesn't make pasta unless he is thinking about a woman."

I raised my eyebrows and almost reminded her that I was not French, when I realized that she had just given me a high compliment. I was also pretty sure that what she'd said was ridiculous, but that didn't seem like the right thing to say either.

"It's complicated."

She shook her head. "And that's why you made something simple. A young person's mistake."

"I've got no idea what you're trying to say, Chef."

"I know," Brodeur said, almost sympathetically. "That's because you are a moron. It is all right. You can't help it."

"Are you going to explain it to me?" I asked.

She chuckled. "I do not have that much time. Get back to work."

The rest of the shift was relatively uneventful and passed quickly. As I made my way back to my locker, I realized that I was reasonably happy, which was amazing, given how awful the beginning of the night had been. Coming to work in a familiar kitchen, making food, had been exactly what I'd needed to recover after Mr. Akram's behavior.

I hoped that Bisma Akram had something similar in her life, something that could bring joy and light when all seemed dark.

CHAPTER SEVEN

I was totally planning to spend the weekend reading up on Churchill, but Saturday slipped by like a ninja, and Sunday I ended up taking the BART back to Remarquable unexpectedly. I'd gotten a super weird call from the maître d' claiming that there was a young woman asking after me. He had no other information, except that she'd said her name was Suraiya, but she liked to be called Suri for short.

I'd told the maître d' that I didn't know anyone by that name, which he'd said was fine, but the fact was that she obviously knew me, and she was waiting, so if I would be so kind, etcetera, etcetera.

When I got to the restaurant, I used the back entrance, washed my hands four times with industrial-strength soap to get BART germs off, and then made my way to the front.

I recognized the mysterious Suri instantly. It was Bisma's little sister.

She looked pretty cozy in an oversize heather-gray hoodie, reading a textbook at a table in the empty restaurant, sipping what I later learned was hot chocolate she'd prevailed on the maître d' to give her, even though we didn't serve hot chocolate, and Remarquable was closed.

She looked up and gave me a huge grin as I approached. "Hi," she said.

I sat down across from her. "Hey. What are you doing here?"

"I came looking for you. I heard you worked here."

"I figured that part out," I said with a smile. "Why are you here?"

"That," she said with an approving nod, "is a better question."

"Uh...thanks. Are you going to answer it?"

"I came to tell you," Suri said, drawing the words out slowly, then pushing the rest out as quickly as she could, "that I'm sorry about the other night and that shouldn't have happened and Abbu can be so awful and it's so unfair and that I think you should totally marry Bisma because she's so awesome and like no one gives her a chance because of one mistake and I think that's terrible and that you were kind of awesome too so you'd be good together."

I let her catch her breath, wondering if she'd go on.

She did. "And also that I don't want to live there anymore because I ran away from home and I told everyone at school that I'm living with you now so can I please live with you?"

"What?" I asked, my surprised shout echoing across the empty room.

Suri giggled. "That last part was a joke."

"Oh. You're hilarious."

"Totally hilarious," she agreed. Suri quickly bent down to reach for her backpack but hit her head on the table on her way back up. "Fuck, that hurt."

"Language," I said.

"God," Suri said. "Don't be such an uncle." She fumbled around inside her pack and pulled out a USB drive. It looked identical to the one that her father had offered me the other night. "I stole it from Abbu, and I'm going to destroy it. Unless...I mean, have you rethought his offer? It'd be really messed up if you did, but I guess you can have this if you're going to marry her."

"What? No. Dude, this whole thing is...so weird."

"Yup, it's totally fucked up," Suri agreed enthusiastically.

"Can you stop swearing? You shouldn't be talking like that. How old are you? Twelve?"

"I'm fifteen." She probably couldn't have sounded more offended if I'd said something blasphemous. She didn't look or act her age, though, so I'm not sure it was my fault I'd gotten it wrong. "Mostly."

"Anyway, I don't..." I took a deep breath. "There isn't anything wrong with Bisma. She seems lovely."

"She is."

"I just don't think we're a match."

"That's only because you don't know her yet," Suri insisted.

"Maybe, but—"

"So, I guess it's a good thing she's on her way here now."

I rubbed my hands over my face. This was a dream. A bad one. Wasn't it? Nope. Suri was sitting before me, looking at me with pitifully pleading eyes. "Look," I said, "I appreciate that you want your sister to be happy, but I can't marry someone because I feel sorry for her. That'd be stupid."

"It'd be totally stupid." Suri nodded, her tone cheerful. "Which is why I didn't ask you to do that. I asked you to marry her because she's the nicest, sweetest person ever in the history of people everywhere."

I started to say something, but she was not done talking.

"I mean, yeah, she did a stupid, stupid, stooooopid thing, but it's like totally our hang-ups, right? I mean, other people do it all the time, and like, isn't there a huge population boom problem in India and Pakistan? All those babies are coming from somewhere. People are drilling a lot of rods into a lot of holes, is what I'm saying, and Bisma's screwed for life because she didn't, like, sign the proper forms before she did it?"

"I—"

"And now she has to live with all this patriarchy

bullshit, while the guy who recorded her totally got away with it because Bisma and our parents didn't want to report him and make a big scene. That is such weak sauce."

"Do I get to say something soon?"

"No," Suri joked. At least, I think she was joking. "Just, like, have lunch with her or something, you know. What have you got to lose?"

That was a fair question, I guess.

Suri's phone rang. "It's her," she said, hopping off her chair and jogging to the front door. "Yeah. I'm going to let you in. No, I'm not coming outside. Danyal wants to see you."

I groaned and got to my feet. This was going to be awkward.

Bisma walked in moments later, saw me, and blushed prettily, looking away for a moment before glancing back. She was wearing a Wonder Woman T-shirt today, with a pair of jeans that highlighted her slender legs. "Hi," she said.

"Hey." I smiled at her, and then realized something was different. "You're not wearing your glasses."

"She wears contacts almost all the time," Suri said, "just not on *rishta* meetings. She thinks it's dishonest. Isn't that awesome?"

Bisma shook her head. "Yeah. I'm a paragon of virtue. Let's go, Suri."

"But I thought—"

"Suraiya." Bisma's tone was sharper than one of Chef Brodeur's knives. "Right. Now."

Suri gave a world-weary huff and stomped her way back to the table we'd been sitting at.

"I'm sorry about her," Bisma said. "This is really unfair to you. All of this has been."

"It's okay."

"No, it isn't. We're not awful people. Really."

"I don't think you're awful."

"He totally doesn't," Suri called from the table. "In fact, he wants to go on a date with you next weekend."

I turned to look at her, surprised, but Suri had a perfectly innocent expression on her face, as if all the truth in the universe was collected within her.

Bisma had apparently seen this look before. "Can you please not embarrass me any more than you already—"

"No," I said, "it's true."

I don't know why I said that.

Okay, I know exactly why. Because there was nothing else I could bear to do. I'd met Bisma all of two times, and I'd seen her go through more than I'd ever seen anyone else put up with. I didn't want our third meeting to be humiliating for her too.

Bisma stared at me, as if she couldn't believe I was really there. Then she shook her head. "No. Don't. Don't do that."

"What?"

"You know what. You're trying to be all noble and chivalrous, and just . . . I don't need to be rescued."

I held up my hands. "Not trying to do that. I just . . .

I had fun when we got coffee. We should hang out. Like friends. You seem like a cool person."

She narrowed her eyes at me, as if I were a pet store owner trying to sell her a weasel by telling her it was a cuddly little bunny rabbit. "Friends?"

"Friends. You . . . have friends, right?"

"A few."

"Then maybe you could use another one?"

Bisma crossed her arms and studied me for a galactically long time. It felt like my soul was being weighed by the scales of Libra. "Fine," she said. "But I'll pay for my own food."

"Sure. You can pay for my food too if you want. I'm pretty much always broke."

That made her smile, and Suri gave me a thumbs-up, and for like a second, it looked like this was miraculously going to end well, when Chef Brodeur stormed into the room, a scowl on her face, waving her toque in the air, as if trying to get rid of a particularly annoying bee.

"What is all this chatter? I am working on the books, Mr. Jilani. Do you know how much I hate account—" She saw my two visitors, and all of a sudden there was a wide, gracious smile on her face. "Ah, we have guests."

Of course, I thought. Did she think I was out here just talking to myself?

"Yes, Chef," I said.

She ignored me completely. "Lovely guests, at that. You are, of course, most welcome. Unfortunately, as you can see, we are closed at the moment. So, I can only assume that this imbecile let you in."

"We were just leaving," Bisma said. "I'm so sorry for our intrusion."

"Not at all," Brodeur said magnanimously. "I'm so entirely charmed to meet you, my dear. You are?"

"Bisma. This is my sister, Suri."

"So, you are the girl my chef was thinking about on Friday."

Bisma blushed and looked away.

"He made pasta because of you. I'm not a particular devotee of pasta myself. But given how unexpectedly well it turned out, I do hope that you make Chef Danyal cook for you all the time. And that his food gives you plenty of little deaths."

I stared at her. *Chef Danyal?* Where had that come from? I was a line cook. And *little deaths?* Wasn't that French for *orgasms?* She was asking Bisma if I'd given her foodgasms! I wanted to die.

"Chef," I begged, hoping she'd stop talking.

"What are you doing standing there?" she said. It was a bark more than a human noise, the good old Brodeur I knew and vaguely disliked. "Go make these girls something to eat."

"The kitchen is closed, Chef."

"I know that, you idiot. Open it."

"No," Bisma said. "Really. Thank you. We'll come back at a more convenient time. We were just leaving."

"And actually, I'm not scheduled for a shift today, so I'll just—"

"Go to the kitchen and start preparing for the day's work," she said.

I nodded. "Right. Absolutely. That's exactly what I was going to say."

A few days later, I met Bisma outside Powell Street Station. She'd put on a black leather jacket and black jeans. Today she'd worn her contacts and tied her brown hair up, and she looked really nice. She was wearing another superhero T-shirt, red with a yellow starburst pattern on it. I couldn't identify the symbol, but I stared at it for a little too long, trying to place it.

"Are you staring at my chest or at my shirt?"

My ears grew warm. How did she keep doing that? I straightened to my full height and said, "I'm not sure what the right answer to that question is."

"It's Captain Marvel."

"Oh right. Him."

"Her," Bisma said. "This date is not off to a good start for you."

"I thought it wasn't a date," I said.

"Did you?" She nodded at me, at my clothes actually, and my whole face felt hot now. So I'd dressed up a little. I was wearing my best button-down shirt, a Brooks Brothers one that I'd gotten in an amazing sale online, with gray slacks and Spanish leather loafers I'd saved up to buy. I'd also put on a maroon wool blazer, which it was still a little too warm for.

I stared down at my feet. "We agreed to go to dinner."

"Yeah. To like a falafel place or something. I didn't realize you were going to get all fancy."

"Sorry. We never actually talked about where we were going, though."

"It's okay," she said. "You look good."

"That can't be helped."

She shook her head. "There's that confidence again."

Without asking me where I wanted to go, she started walking, setting a brisk pace. I followed without complaint. The tall, glitzy shopping plazas around us vanished abruptly as we walked, entering a less-than-ideal-looking neighborhood.

The thing about San Francisco that surprises a lot of people is how sudden it is. You'll be in a perfectly nice area one second, and the next, everything is janky, and then things go back to being posh. The city is fused together in unexpected ways, like it wasn't thought out, which I suppose it wasn't. This makes it feel like an organic, living thing.

After a few minutes, Bisma slowed and came to a stop outside a small shop with a faded sign that had once been a deep blue, I suspect, but now was the blue of the sky on a clear day. The place was called Arab Food Restaurant.

"Creative name," I said.

"Accurate, though."

It took me a moment to realize that she was waiting for me to open the door for her, and I did, letting out a rush of air carrying the charred smell of overdone beef and the welcoming embrace of freshly baked bread. I followed her in and saw that the restaurant was basic, which I suppose is fairly typical of shawarma spots, with cold white walls and uncomfortable plastic furniture.

"Is the food here really good?" I asked.

"No."

I wanted to ask Bisma why we were here, then, and I almost did, but there was something in the way that she was looking at me, with those expressive brown eyes of hers, which made me realize she wanted me to ask that very question. For some reason, I didn't want to give her the satisfaction.

I ordered what she ordered, a combo plate that came with shredded beef, chicken, and lamb served on yellow rice—way too much food coloring, in my opinion—and some pita bread, along with a "salad," which was just lettuce, a couple of tomato slices, and a little radish.

And Bisma was right. The food was mediocre. She sprinkled a bunch of sumac on top of the meat as soon as it arrived, and with just one taste, I knew why. It was so terribly underseasoned that my resolve to not ask why we were here broke. "Is this a joke?"

"What?"

"This place. Taking the wannabe chef to a really bad restaurant, I mean."

Wordlessly, she slid the tray of sauces that we'd been given across the table. I tried the tahini, and it was really good tahini, without too much garlic, and the hummus was smooth and light.

"I like to come here," she said, "because it's like...a reminder, you know, that you can screw up everything you do, but if you do one thing right, maybe that redeems you. It's hopeful food."

I smiled at her. "I like that."

"Are you ever going to come back?"

"Never," I said.

Bisma laughed, and I was struck by how different she seemed when her guard went down and she just existed, without worry, without pain. It wasn't an infectious laugh, or very loud, or musical. It was just...pure.

I wished she'd laugh more, but people laugh when they have a reason to laugh, and people who have joy in their lives laugh more than people who don't.

I was taught that there is a Book of Destiny in which the details of our lives are written. When we will be born, how long we will live, and all that. Some people think that the details are specific. They'd say it was written that I would come with Bisma to eat this meal, and that every little moment leading up to this moment, and every moment spreading out from it, has already been plotted.

Others say that there was more freedom in one's life, like maybe Bisma and I had to come here, but what we ordered was up to us, and that choice, more than anything else, determined the quality of our experience.

Whether the Book is general or whether it is specific, the quality of the life we are given, I think, may not depend on how long it is, or how rich we are in it, as much as it depends on how much laughter is given to us.

"What are you thinking?" Bisma asked.

"You've got a pretty laugh."

She ducked her head a little, and I think she was pleased with the compliment.

I said, "So what's with the superheroes?"

"I'm a nerd."

"Lots of people are nerds. Not everyone wears Supergirl underwear."

"Hey. I don't—"

"Suri told me."

"That little... I can't believe she told you that." Bisma narrowed her eyes at me. "Wait. You're lying. She didn't tell you."

"You just did, though."

Bisma sighed and turned her attention back to her food. The way she ate annoyed me. She was eating quickly, efficiently, without joy or pleasure. I don't understand people who eat without taking time to appreciate their food. Then again, there wasn't a lot to enjoy here.

Just when the silence was getting awkward, Bisma made it worse. "I'm sorry about my father."

"Uh . . . it's okay."

"No. It's not."

I ran a hand through my hair. "It was worse for you than it was for me."

"I'm used to it."

"That's . . . rough."

Another silence.

"My father is a very angry person," she said. "He's been angry his entire life, or my entire life, anyway. He kind of hates me, hates us, so . . ."

I wanted to tell her that he didn't hate her, but what the hell did I know?

"You know what *watta satta* is?"

I did. It was a custom in some parts of Pakistan, a trade. You'd have two families, each with a son and daughter of marriageable age. The son from the first family would marry the daughter from the second family, and the son from the second family would, in exchange, marry the daughter from the first.

"Sure," I said.

"Well, my aunt—my dad's sister—there was trouble getting her married, I guess, though no one has ever told me why, and my mom's brother agreed to marry her."

"In exchange for your dad marrying your mom."

"Yeah. Anyway, my mom says that my dad was head

over heels for this other girl—can you imagine?—and he was heartbroken to have to marry my mom, but he did it for my aunt's sake."

The Love Story of Jaleel Akram. Who'd have thought?

"I think he's always resented my mom, though it wasn't her fault, and I think he also resents us—Suri and me—a little. The life he's living now, it wasn't the life that he wanted for himself. So, he's angry all the time, and it builds up inside him, and he has to let it out. I learned early that if I acted out, if I gave him a reason to scream at me, then he wouldn't take it out on my mom. She's a gentle soul. I felt like I had to protect her."

"Like a superhero."

Bisma smiled. "Yeah. It's stupid. I know."

"It's not stupid."

"Anyway, I'm like totally oversharing, but I thought, given everything, you should know why my family is so weird. My dad isn't like . . . a villain or something. He's just doing the best he can."

Was he, though? The guy had been in love with a girl and was forced to marry someone else. That totally sucked, but how long could he use that to justify being an asshole? Six months? A year? Not twenty years, that was for sure. Mr. Akram had held on to his anger way past its expiration date.

I didn't say that, though. It wasn't my place. If her dad's curdled frustration helped Bisma see him as a better person than he was, what good would come from disagreeing with her?

"Your turn," she said. "Tell me something you wouldn't tell a stranger. Something unusual. Don't think about it," Bisma said. "Just say the first thing that comes to your mind. Stop thinking. Just—"

"I'm a Renaissance Man," I said. It was all I could come up with on the spot, especially with her pressuring me.

She raised her eyebrows.

I explained the contest and told her how my father had reacted when I'd brought up Churchill. "I've done a lot of reading," I said, hopefully in a convincing manner, "and everyone believes that guy was awesome. Even Mr. Tippett, my history teacher, loves him. Which is incredible, because I don't think Tippett even loved his own mom."

Bisma smiled. "Well, you know, Churchill was big on the British continuing to rule India. And the Raj, despite how it's romanticized now, was terrible. So there's that."

I nodded. That made sense.

"Besides," she went on, "if you starve three million people to death, you deserve to be hated a little."

"Yeah, that's tru—wait. *What?*"

She frowned. "The Bengal Famine?"

"Right," I said, wondering if this was common knowledge. I've never been very good at knowing things, which can get embarrassing. "That."

Bisma looked at me closely and somehow saw through my act. "You have no idea what I'm talking about, do you?"

I scratched the back of my head, feeling a little sheepish. "Nope."

She explained it to me. Turns out that in 1943 or some time super long ago, there was a famine in the province of Bengal, and it killed three million people. During this time, Churchill diverted food away from India to places where it wasn't even needed, and he's reported to have said something like, famine or no famine, Indians will "breed like rabbits."

I shook my head, trying to comprehend it all. The meat and rice on our plates that had already been bad somehow tasted even worse now. I guess that's why no one talks about starving people at a dinner table. That's probably also the reason why there are starving people in the world.

This was the guy whose bust Tippett kept in his classroom? In fact, I'm pretty sure that in one of his lectures, Tippett had said that this man's statue was in the Oval Office.

Why?

"You okay?"

"What? Yeah. No. Totally. I just . . . didn't know."

Bisma nodded. "Anyway, that's a major reason Churchill is problematic. And it isn't ancient history. America became independent over two hundred years ago. For desis, the Raj is still in living memory. So, yeah, I get your dad's reaction."

That was . . . a lot. I wasn't sure what to think about it just then. I'd need time to process it. Besides, it was a pretty dark conversation to have while eating. "This isn't exactly a fun topic for a date, is it? I'm sorry. I shouldn't have brought it up. School stuff is boring."

Bisma blinked. "Um . . . when I said earlier that this was a date because of the way you were dressed, you know I was joking. Right? Because I don't date. You said we were going out as friends."

I held up my arms. "Sorry. I just—"

"I mean, don't take it personally, Danyal. It's not you."

"Trust me." I grinned. "There is absolutely no danger of me thinking it's me."

Bisma laughed. "Fair enough. Honestly, other than the pointless *rishta* meetings, I like my life the way it is right now, that's all. And my life, by the way, revolves around school, which is most definitely not boring. I kind of love it."

"Yeah, well, I don't. In fact, I'm pretty sure I'm going to have to read *whole books* for the first time for this Renaissance Man thing. Did you know people do that for fun? What kind of twisted—"

"Hold on. You're just now reading whole books? Aren't you a senior?"

"Yeah."

"Then how'd you get through English? They didn't make you read *Romeo and Juliet* or something?"

"Cliff notes." I offered her a sheepish smile.

"Ew."

"Hey, I passed."

"The point of school," she said, "isn't to pass. It isn't to get out so you can get to the real world. The point of school is to learn, about yourself and about other—"

"I get plenty of lectures at home, Bisma."

It was her turn to blush. "Sorry. I keep having to tell Suri about how important school is. It's become a habit, I guess."

I tore into my slightly soggy pita bread, but then decided not to eat it. That whole Bengal Famine thing had ruined my appetite. "Don't worry about it. It's cool that you like school. I mean, you know, it's not cool, exactly, it's just...fine, I guess."

"Just fine, I guess," Bisma repeated. "That's some compliment. I think I'm going to have to put that on a T-shirt."

"You should," I told her. "It would work on multiple levels."

"You're an idiot."

"Yes...but not all the time. For example, I happen to know that no one learns much of anything worth knowing from school or books. You have to, you know, live and stuff."

" 'There are more things in heaven and earth, Horatio, than are dreamt of in your philosophy,' " she quoted, "is basically what you're saying."

"Right," I said. *Romeo and Juliet.*"

A small smirk touched her lips, and I wondered if I'd gotten it wrong, but then Bisma said, "Exactly. Anyway, ready to go?"

We walked around the city mostly in silence once we left the restaurant. But it wasn't the kind of silence that made words seem urgent or even necessary. Her hand brushed mine accidentally, and even though it was totally innocent, and we apologized to each other, she slipped her hand into her jacket pocket, as if to make sure it wouldn't happen again.

The moon, a small and distant thing, was starting to become visible as the sun went down. "It's almost *Maghrib* time," Bisma said.

"I've always hated hearing that," I said. "Means the fun is over."

Bisma chuckled.

There was a common refrain desi Muslim mothers used to get their children home when it got dark: *Come inside or the jinn will get you.*

"I always thought it was super weird that jinn were just hanging around our backyard, waiting for the sun to go down so they could get me. It isn't like they can't stand sunlight, and they can easily just walk into the house uninvited.... Wait a minute. Do you think some old aunty just confused vampires with jinn like back in the day and now all the aunties are repeating what they heard from her?"

She shook her head, still smiling.

"I'm serious."

"You're not," she told me.

"It's possible."

"Maybe," she said. "It's probably just a way to warn kids that there are dangers in the world, especially where there isn't any light, and these dangers, these monsters, are less than human."

"I could just have Intezar ask his *pir*, I guess." When she didn't react, I said, "My best friend thinks that I should call this . . . they're like these holy—"

"I know what a *pir* is," she said. "I actually went to see one once."

"Zar thinks I should call his guy so he can pray for me to get good grades. Why'd you go?"

Bisma hesitated. "I wanted to know if there was a way to make someone happy."

"What did he say?"

We came to a stoplight, and she looked at me, a twist of lemon in her smile. "He said that he could teach me many ways to make someone happy, if I came by again at night."

"Gross," I said.

"Yeah. He wasn't great. Some men get like that when they find out about . . . what happened. A guy my parents introduced me to told me he couldn't marry me, obviously, but he'd . . . do me favors, if I wanted. Like he said, you can only lose your virginity once."

Sometimes it felt like God had just gotten bored with making decent people or had run out of ideas for them. "I'm sorry."

"Not your fault. Anyway, the *pir* did say he could make

an amulet that could make someone laugh. Make them laugh for the rest of their life, if necessary, but that there is no object in the world that can increase happiness."

"Ice cream?" I suggested.

"Very funny. Okay, so maybe except for—" She grinned when I pointed to the parlor across the street. "Sure. Let's go."

As we waited for the signal to change, I thought about what the *pir* had told her, that he could increase the laughter given to someone but not the joy, and I realized that I'd been wrong about the Book of Destiny. Back at the restaurant, I'd been thinking that if the life written for someone were full of laughter, it would be a good one. I hadn't realized that it was possible for someone to laugh a lot, to seem happy enough, but still be wounded on the inside.

CHAPTER EIGHT

Even though my father had tried to make nice over breakfast recently, I guess Mom didn't think he'd done enough because he decided to try again in front of her. As usual, he did this by spending money.

Ahmed Jilani could never bring himself to say he was sorry. So instead he went around and did nice things for people he wanted to apologize to or, more frequently, who his wife thought he should want to apologize to. He'd take you out for a fancy dinner, see a movie you wanted to watch, or buy you something nice.

The only problem was that he was incapable of buying people gifts they actually wanted.

It wasn't that he was cheap or had bad taste. It was just that he'd only ever get things for people that he himself wanted. As a result, I was the owner of a cricket bat, helmet, pads, gloves, elbow guard, stumps, bails, a cherry-red cork ball, and like fifteen posters of Imran Khan. Those things had never left my closet, and they never would.

That was why I couldn't help but make a face when my father walked up to me when I was watching TV in the living room, hands folded behind his back to hide his peace offering, and let out his "I'm sorry but I'll never say I'm sorry because I was raised old school and my concept of what makes a man a man is hopelessly outdated" grunt. The face earned me a scalding look from my mom, who somehow thought this aspect of Dad's personality was super adorable.

"It has been brought to my attention," he said, glancing at my mother out of the corner of his eye, "that I was too rough with you about your career and future. I'm not sure if you remember."

I raised my eyebrows at him.

"Anyway..." Dad held out the video game box he'd been hiding. "This is for you."

I think I managed to look excited about the gift. It was the *Ashes Cricket* game for Xbox One. Of course, none of my friends had an Xbox One, having pledged their loyalty to the PlayStation, and I didn't have a console at all. But it was the thought that counted, I guess.

"Uh... wow, thanks, Dad. This is... so great."

"All the British and Australian players are officially licensed," he said. "It says so on the back. Even the Muslim ones."

"Right. So, so cool. Thank you."

"You know," Dad said, "when we scold you or yell at you, it is for your own good. What of me? What of your mother? We're going to die soon."

I rolled my eyes.

"You'll have to deal with the world alone then, Danyal, and the world is a difficult place. Our job, as parents, is to give you a hard time now, so that when the hard times come for real, and they will come if you keep on with this nonsense of wanting to be a chef—"

My mother coughed loudly from across the room.

"Right. Anyway, you enjoy, okay? Enjoy the loose balls you're getting in these first innings of your life while you can, because in the second innings, after the pitch gets old, life is all toe-crushing yorkers and googlies."

"I have no idea what that means," I told him.

"You will. One day, I very much fear you will."

He turned to head toward the kitchen, and I should have let him go. He'd obviously been at the edge of another lecture, and I really didn't want to get any more gifts from him. I couldn't help myself, though.

"I learned about the Bengal Famine. I heard about what Churchill did, and how all those people died. That's why you called him a fu—" I stopped, glanced at my mom, and said, "That's why you called him what you called him when we had breakfast the other day. Right?"

My father heaved a huge sigh and faced me again. "Yes."

"Why didn't you tell me? You said to just write about Churchill like my history teacher wants me to, as if he were a hero."

"You need to pass your class."

"I know, Dad, but I've never heard you use that word before. I thought maybe this mattered to you."

He didn't say anything, but he didn't have to. I knew his face. It was one of the most familiar things in my world. It had been there, frowning, scowling, glowering, and occasionally smiling since I'd been born.

I could tell, without his telling me so, that this did matter to him. A lot.

"Why don't you want me to speak about it, then? I could—"

"It would change nothing, Danyal." Was my father speaking *gently* to me? It was strange. I found myself wishing he were yelling instead. That I could deal with. He took a deep breath. "Why would I ask you to do something this important? Yes, our people who died because of Churchill deserve a voice. But isn't it also true that they deserve better than you can give them? Have you even begun preparing for this contest yet?"

"Ahmed," Aisha Jilani warned softly.

He held up a reassuring hand to her. "It's okay," he said.

What was okay, exactly, I didn't know. Was this my father trying to be nice? I mean, I'd wished that he were nicer my whole life, but now that he was actually doing it . . . well, it sucked.

"You are not the kind of boy who will make a differ-ence in the world. I have accepted it. The dreams I had for you when you were born and I held you, those are all gone. Now I just want to make sure you can stand on your own two feet before I die, hmm? That cannot be too much to ask. Tell me it isn't too much to ask for you to just finish bloody high school. Please."

"Ahmed," Mom said again, more sharply this time.

He wasn't done, though. "There's no reason for you to fail history. And you can't do the story of the Bengal Fam-ine justice. So have mercy on our souls and tell everyone what they expect to hear about Churchill, pass your class, and matriculate."

"That's enough."

"Yes," he said, agreeing with his wife. "It will have to be enough."

"I wish your dad would yell at you more. It improves din-ner by a lot."

I rolled my eyes at Zar. I didn't feel like joking around, but jokes were what you got with him. Intezar was like a TV you couldn't change the channel on. It was Comedy Central day in and day out.

Not for the first time, I wished Sohrab wasn't busy with his mosque stuff. He was really more of my go-to guy when I was upset. Not only did he take things seriously— though he got too serious sometimes—the Sabsvari kitchen automatically made me feel a little better, no matter how bad a mood I was in. The possibility that I'd get to see Kaval was also always a nice bonus.

I'd come over to Intezar's and totally invited myself to both make and have dinner. His father was in town for a short while, and then he was flying out for another trip, this time to Melbourne. Zar would soon be on his own again.

He could've stayed with his mother, of course, during the long periods his father was out of the country, but he avoided that whenever he could. Seema Aunty was way more serious about Islam than Zar, so whenever he did see her, all she did was lecture him about praying more and thinking about girls less. There was a reason he'd chosen not to live with her after his parents had split up.

"He wasn't yelling," I said, "for once."

"I hate it when they don't yell."

"Yeah."

Zar looked at me for a long moment. "You okay, *yaar*?"

"Sure. It's just unfair, you know? People who aren't Muslim get through stuff like this by drinking and having special brownies. We don't get any of that."

"There's Pakola in the fridge."

I shuddered at his mention of the green, fizzy, super sweet Pakistani soda that he adored. I thought it tasted like diabetes. "I'm all right, thanks."

"If you were anyone else, I'd say don't bother cooking 'cause we were going to order in, but..."

123

I smiled. My friends had gotten used to my showing up at their houses to take over their kitchens when my dad became too much to handle. "Go play *FIFA* or whatever you were going to do. I got this."

"All right," he said, but instead of leaving, he went on. "Hey, listen, this probably isn't the best time to mention it, but Pirji had a vision—"

"Intezar. Dude, come on—"

"He saw you. He saw that you totally choked in Renaissance Man."

I rolled my eyes.

"I'm serious. I mean, he even described you, okay? He knew what you looked like from his dream. Explain that."

"Did you tell him my name?"

"Yeah, but—"

"Does he have Internet?"

Zar shook his head. "Whatever. Believe what you want. Just be prepared, okay? The contest is going to go really badly for you, brownther."

"Well...I'm glad I came here. You've cheered me right up after my dad's pep talk."

"Sorry, *yaar.* It's just what Pirji said. Besides, it's not just bad news for you. You know how Pirji was saying all these intense prayers and reciting Quran so I could get with Natari? He says it's not going to work out."

I stared at him.

"Did I not mention that?"

"No. Intezar, what are you doing? Just talk to Natari.

She seems really cool. You don't have to pay some holy guy to do magic for you—"

"It's not magic," Zar snapped.

"Whatever. Also, isn't the *pir* super religious?"

"Absolutely. That's the entire job."

"So how was he helping you get Natari?"

"I paid the sin surcharge."

"The... wait, you were paying him?"

"Of course, *yaar*. Pirji's gotta eat too."

"How much?"

My friend wouldn't look me in the eye. "That's not important."

"Dude."

Zar sighed. "You sound a lot like Sohrab right now."

"Hey!"

"Look, I'm only telling you this because maybe the reason you flopped at Renaissance Man in Pirji's vision is because you went after Churchill. Maybe your father is right. Just get through the paper and presentation and graduate."

"All right," I said, trying to keep the irritation out of my voice. I definitely didn't need Zar siding with Ahmed Jilani. "I'll think about it. Could you please go do whatever you were going to do? I've got food to make."

I understand the world less than I should. A lot of things just don't make sense to me, though they seem to be perfectly clear to everybody else.

People seem to expect that you'll just get algebra and mitochondrions and how gravity made the globe round. You're supposed to intuitively grasp that gerrymandering is a problem and understand why no one can fix it.

You'd think being awful at a bunch of stuff would bother me, but it doesn't. Not usually, anyway, because there is one thing in the world I do understand as well as anyone I've ever met: food. Always have.

Something in my soul recognizes the bright yellow of turmeric and the dull, grim red of ground red pepper. The sizzle of sirloin on a grill, the whisper of a swift, determined whisk were always familiar music. I simply knew the deep, alluring aroma of coffee and the quiet, rich scent of olive oil.

I can't figure out people who ask me why I cook. Why did Tennyson paint? No. That guy wrote plays, I'm pretty sure. Raphael painted, right? Who drew the creepy smile lady, the *Mona Lisa*? Definitely one of the guys named after the Ninja Turtles. Anyway, my point is that I cook for the same reason they pursued their craft, for the same reason Shakespeare wrote poetry. It's what was given to me. It's what I am—despite being inept at everything else—good at.

At least, that's true on most nights.

That night at Intezar's I decided to make chicken tikka masala, which everyone thinks of as an Indian dish, but is ridiculously inauthentic. Mom tells me it is more of an ABCD—American-Born Confused Desi—thing. A lot of people like it, though, and I can make a mean one.

I wasn't concentrating when I made the yogurt-based marinade, though. I just couldn't stop thinking about what Dad had said.

My first reaction had been that he was just a jerk face, but while definitely true, that wasn't what really bothered me.

It didn't sit well with me that he just assumed I would fail if I took on the Bengal Famine for Renaissance Man. Was he disappointed? It seemed that way, sure, but there had to be a different word for it, because I hadn't done anything yet. Saying my food isn't any good before you've tasted it isn't disappointment. It's doubt.

"You know," I told my perfectly butchered chicken, even though it seemed totally uninterested in my problems, "I don't think that's happened before."

You could say a lot of things about Ahmed Jilani—like more things than there are grains of salt in the world—but he'd never, ever assumed I couldn't do something before.

He'd made me try everything from Model UN to baseball to karate, even though I'd sucked at it all. Hell, my father had even done the usual desi parent thing and gotten me to volunteer at a hospital in the hopes that I'd develop a passion for medicine.

He'd hated seeing me fail, sure, and he'd yelled at me for it, but he'd actually believed I could do those things once.

"That was kind of nice," I said, "in an 'I made this steak for you, but with tofu' kind of way."

Tonight, though, for the first time, it seemed like his faith in me was broken.

"I shouldn't care. This is good, right? Maybe now that he understands that I'm no good at any of the things he wants me to be, he'll stop pushing me. I should be happy, really. I *am* happy. Honest."

The chicken, the only other one there, remained silent, being in no condition to respond, but it looked skeptical.

"Shut up," I muttered as I went to work on the tikka masala.

It didn't turn out great. It ended up more watery than creamy, and worse, the *botis* were overdone. I hadn't screwed up a dish this simple this badly in a long time. It seemed, in that moment, that I could do nothing right at all.

〰

"You should've gone to sleep, Mom."

Aisha Jilani marched up to me and took the Tupperware container I was carrying. "I wasn't waiting for you. I was waiting for your food."

"You didn't eat with Dad?"

She shook her head. "Come. Sit with me."

"Can I just go to my room? I'm really not in the mood to hear about how much he loves me."

My mother's answering smile had a little steel in it. I knew I had to follow her, and that it probably wasn't a good idea to make her repeat herself. I mumbled a complaint and shuffled like an exhausted zombie to the dinner table.

Mom remained unmoved by the display. She popped open the chicken tikka masala container and when she got some on her finger, tasted it. "Hmm."

"Yeah. It sucks. Can I go now?"

"What's your hurry? You'll have plenty of time to sulk."

"I thought I'd get an early start."

Shaking her head, my mother went to the microwave. "*Jaan*, you're going to have to make a decision about what you're doing with Renaissance Man."

I nodded. "Yeah."

"Your father isn't wrong about one thing. Passing history is important. If your teacher is a big Churchill fan... Danyal, you can't get held back again. Do they even let you go back into high school if you're twenty?"

That was a really good question. Given my current standing in Tippett's class, it was definitely something I should've already looked up. I sat in silence as my mother cracked a frozen naan into two so that it'd fit into our toaster. It wasn't long before she was sitting with me, a steaming plate before her.

"On the other hand," she said, "telling people truths they haven't heard is important too. You're in a tough spot."

"This is not a helpful talk."

"*Acha, baba*, fine. You can go to your room. Before you do, though... Did you know that Ahmed's father marched for independence from the British?"

"Really?"

"He was only sixteen, but it was the great struggle of his time, and he wanted to be part of it."

Sixteen? My great struggle when I'd been sixteen was convincing my parents to buy me a gaming console, which they'd promised to do if I could get my grades up.

That deal had not worked out for me.

"He marched and starved. His friends fought and bled. I know you never got to know your grandfather, but Ahmed was close to him. He grew up hearing stories about the Raj. *Sarfaroshi ki tamanna ab hamare dil me hai* and all that."

"Um . . . I don't know what that means."

My mother sighed. "That's our fault. We come to the New World and forget, I think, that the Old World still has things to teach us."

When I didn't say anything, she went on. "It's a poetry verse from back then that became like a slogan. It means 'the desire for revolution has seized our hearts, so let's see what strength is left in the arms of our murderers.'"

"Dark."

"Yes. Anyway, I'm just saying that your father isn't . . . he's not objective when it comes to the Raj or Churchill. I think he'd really like it if you wrote about the Bengal Famine. He just doesn't want you to risk your graduation."

"That isn't what he said."

"I know what he said, *jaan*. I was there."

"Why doesn't he believe I can do a good enough job to impress Tippett and talk about the famine?" When she

130

didn't answer, I took a deep breath. I didn't want my voice to shake when I asked the next question. It shook a little anyway. "Why doesn't Dad believe in me?"

"Well, they say that Allah sent anywhere from twenty-five to over a hundred thousand prophets to make people believe in Him."

"That's a big range."

"What I'm saying is that even God can't get people to have faith in Him. So maybe don't worry about yourself too much, hmm?"

I smiled despite myself. "Thanks, Mom."

"Also, Ahmed is only hard on you—"

I groaned. "Noooo. Don't say it."

"—because he loves you."

"Yeah, yeah," I said. "So you keep telling me."

After I escaped Mom, I went to my room and made things worse for myself.

I started reading about Churchill. There really was a lot of information out there.

I found out, for example, that he was bad at school, which was kind of my brand.

He had a sucky childhood because his dad was sucky. I could relate.

But then I found out he hated freshly squeezed orange juice and realized we could never be friends. What kind of person doesn't like fresh orange juice?

Nothing I found, however, mentioned the Bengal Famine.

So I googled that. Almost one and a half million results came up. A lot less than the almost billion hits I'd gotten when searching for Churchill, but still enough to switch to an image search.

That was a mistake.

I was not ready.

I wasn't ready for the complete devastation of the human form that was a famine. I wasn't ready to see what a lack of food does to a human being.

I saw, in black-and-white pictures, people who'd become walking skeletons with haunted, empty, mournful eyes. Their suffering was so raw that it cut me across centuries. I felt tears come to my eyes. Breathing got difficult. And fast.

I was not ready to believe that this was a world that had been. A world where you could count the ribs of every man and woman. A world where the skin on people's faces was pulled so desperately tight that they seemed like little more than skulls.

There was no dignity in these pictures. There was no modesty. People were naked and half-naked, lying broken on the ground or barely standing up, leaning against pillars or on sticks, no longer strong enough to bear their own weight.

Why had this been allowed to happen?

Why did the fact that Churchill had come to California

and hung out with Charlie Chaplin seem to interest historians more than the suffering his actions had caused in India?

What had really happened to my people?

And didn't everyone need to know?

CHAPTER NINE

There were only three days a year when Chef Brodeur broke out a set of small, porcelain, heart-shaped dessert dishes at Remarquable. I was good at setting hearts aflame, so it totally made sense that I was the one she asked to torch crème brûlée the night before Valentine's Day.

It was a holiday that Brodeur took seriously—how can it be a "holiday" if we still have to go to school?—but I didn't know if that was because it was good for business or because she actually cared about it. She did care about the special dishes, though, because she was on me like a hawk when I almost dropped one.

"You must pay *attention* to what you are doing," she snapped, pointing savagely down at the desserts.

"Sorry, Chef," I said.

She sniffed, obviously disdainful of both me and my

apology. I waited for her to say more, but when she didn't, I went back to work.

I love a good crème brûlée. Actually, I love custard. There's a simple purity about it. I don't necessarily like standing there with a torch, caramelizing the sugar on top. It can get to be boring if you do it over and over again.

Today, however, I was happy to be doing it. For one, the late-lunch crowd didn't really order dessert a lot. Second, watching the white sugar turn a lovely, crunchy brown felt like a satisfying middle finger to Churchill. Sometimes a little color is a good thing, Winston, so fu—

"You seem distracted tonight," Chef Brodeur noted. "But I suppose it is that time of the year for young people."

It took me a moment to figure out that she thought I was distracted because of a girl. It would have been a good guess, usually, but it had been a weird semester so far.

"Actually, I was thinking about Winston Churchill."

She raised an eyebrow at that. "I suppose there is no accounting for taste."

"What? *No*. It's just...I read some depressing things for school about the British Raj, and they kind of got to me."

"Ah," Brodeur said, her French accent suddenly becoming more pronounced, her tone a little sneering. "The British."

"You don't like the British?"

"Their empire was the greatest tragedy in the history of the world."

"Really?" I asked. "Are you interested in politics?"

"Politics? Of course not. Food, Mr. Jilani. All that matters is food, yes? Can you imagine if the French had taken India? What magnificent fusion of our two food cultures would the world have seen? Instead, the British got there, and all they came up with was"—she paused to shake her head in disgust—"chips and curry."

For the first time since I'd googled the Bengal Famine, I laughed.

She nodded. "Better. You must always smile when you are cooking, Mr. Jilani, otherwise your work, I have found, is not as good."

"But you never smile when you're working."

"This is true," Chef Brodeur agreed. "I am, however, much more talented than you. In any case, fools should always be happy. It is, you see, all they have."

I was pretty sure I'd been insulted, but I wasn't really sure how to respond. "It's just...did you know that there were a series of famines in India under the British, and the biggest of them, the Bengal Famine, killed like three million people or something?"

"I did not." Brodeur sounded more serious than usual, which I hadn't thought possible. "Nature is cruel at times."

"Not nature," I said. That sounded like a ridiculous thing to say, of course. It was hard to imagine that human beings could cause a famine. From what I'd read, however, scientists had somehow studied the soil and found that a lack of rainfall had not been a problem. "I mean, it was the

136

way the Raj handled things. What lives they chose to care about, what lives they didn't."

"What do you mean?"

"When they were trying to figure out where to send food, Winston Churchill said it was less important to feed Indians, who already didn't have enough to eat, than to feed sturdy Greeks."

She raised an eyebrow at me. "Sturdy Greeks?"

I shrugged. I wasn't the one who'd said it. "Also, the British totally looted Bengal, so the people there couldn't help themselves, and then they adopted policies that made everything worse. Churchill even had food that could have gone to Indian ports kept in some country called the Balkans—"

"That isn't a country."

"Oh. Okay. But still."

"Still," she agreed.

"Anyway, I'm sorry, Chef. I mean, I guess no one thinks it matters anymore, but everyone says Churchill is great and no one tells this part of his history. It just..."

"It bothers you." When I nodded, she smiled. Actually _smiled_. I didn't know her face could do that. I glanced around quickly to see if anyone else had seen it, but it didn't appear they had. No one would believe me if I told them. "Good."

"Good?"

"But of course. Maybe you'll be a chef after all, no?"

"What? I don't see how they're connected...."

"What I don't see," she said, "is how you can expect

137

to stand around talking and keep your job when there is work to be done."

I opened my mouth to protest. I wasn't the one who'd started the conversation. But then I stopped myself. I knew perfectly well that there was only one acceptable response, the two words I said most often in my life.

"Yes, Chef."

❞❞

"Hey, Danyal."

A lot of people have used my name in my life, and I must have heard it like a million times, but no one, ever, said it like Kaval Sabsvari. She made my name sound like it had been dripped in rich, creamy, melty chocolate. I don't think I was imagining it either, because her friends, who'd been walking with her, giggled and scattered, leaving us alone.

How were girls so good at that? I'd never managed to make Sohrab or Zar get lost when I'd wanted them to leave. In fact, just like they had at the Sabsvaris' basketball court, they tended to show up when they were least wanted.

"Happy Valentine's Day."

I swallowed. "Uh . . . yeah. You too."

I didn't really know what to make of that. Muslims and Valentine's Day didn't mix well. A bunch of people think celebrating romance runs counter to Islamic values. Saudi Arabia actually bans roses and everything in the shape of a heart on the fourteenth of February.

In Pakistan, there is a court ruling prohibiting Valentine's Day celebrations. I remember my parents laughing about it, wondering if it would lead to an underground market for suddenly dangerous flowers. Apparently, there is little a government can do to keep people from celebrating what they want.

Personally, I had never made a big deal out of the day because I'd never had anyone to celebrate with. I hadn't even thought to say something to Kaval, much less get her a card or whatever. I had no idea how she, or Sohrab, would react.

Anyway, I guess it didn't matter for this year, because she was already moving on to another topic. "How's the contest prep going?"

"Fine. I'm sort of having trouble coming up with a thesis."

She frowned. "What are you talking about? It's so simple."

"It is?"

"Sure. Tippett thinks Churchill is great. All you've got to do is list the reasons why. There's no way to mess this up."

"You'd be surprised," I muttered.

"I'm sure you'll be great. But if you're really worried, I did promise to help you. Why don't you put some notes together and I'll do the same. Then we can meet up and see what we have."

"Sure," I said, suddenly feeling a lot better than I had seconds ago. "That'd be awesome."

Just like that, I had a smile on my face. I was going to get a chance to spend time with Kaval, and I was heading to the one class where I could chill. In English, I could zone out, shut off my mind, and totally relax.

After all, there's no reason to worry when it comes to English. If you already speak the language, you're probably going to pass as long as you read summaries of the books you're given and hand in most of your essays. I'm pretty sure even the teachers don't expect you to pay attention. It's always an easy B minus or C plus.

This year it was even easier than usual because all we ever did was write a few paragraphs about stupid things no one cared about. Ms. Hart, our teacher, was on maternity leave, and the parade of subs we'd gotten in her place weren't really interested in preparing lesson plans. I liked them all.

Anyway, the topic of today's essay, which no one would read, was our perfect date. This, I thought, was unreasonable. How was I supposed to come up with a whole essay about that? The perfect date would be any date with Kaval. There. All done. One sentence. Boom.

I was just about to put my phone away and pretend to start writing—really, I was—when I saw Sohrab raise his hand.

The sub, who seemed obsessed with constantly checking to make sure her perfect bun of golden hair had not unraveled even a little, looked surprised. "Yes?" She glanced down at the seating chart. "I'm sorry, what's your name, please? Ah. So Rab, yes? How can I help you?"

"It's Sohrab, and I need a different essay topic. I don't date for religious reasons."

I rolled my eyes. *Come on.*

Someone groaned at the back of the class, loud enough for everyone to hear. The sub seemed tempted to do the same. "Fine," she said. "Why don't you write about what your *dream* date would be like instead?"

"I don't have a dream date. I don't date for religious reasons."

Dude, I wanted to tell him, *shut up.*

"Yes," the teacher drawled with exaggerated patience. "I got that the first time. I'm asking you to use your imagination."

"I'd rather not," Sohrab said.

Now the sub narrowed her eyes at him. "Fine. Write about something else."

"Like what?"

"Whatever you want. Write about your last birthday, or maybe about the best present you ever got."

"For my sixteenth birthday," Sohrab said, "I got a fragment of a spent American bomb."

Silence.

The sub stared at Sohrab, her brown eyes so wide, I was pretty sure they were about to pop out of her face.

"I guess I could write about the insidious illusion that

the United States military-industrial complex is a benign force for good in the world, when it is really just a soulless machine for the oppression, exploitation, and destruction of people who look more like me than you, if you want."

More silence.

Someone whispered, "Wow."

Then everyone was talking at once, and Sohrab was sent to Principal Weinberg.

After class, I hung out by the principal's office, waiting for Sohrab to be let out. What was his problem? Just write the essay, dude. It isn't going to get you slapped with a fatwa to imagine a date. It was his own fault he was in trouble now.

Still, I hoped the shit he was in wasn't deep.

A few people walked by, giving me curious glances and waving. I nodded back.

It was exactly twenty-eight minutes before Sohrab walked out. I know because I was on my phone, and the battery was about to give out. He managed a smile when he saw me.

"I should've known you'd be here," he said.

"What do you mean?"

"It's a very you thing to do."

I didn't know what that meant either but decided to let it go. He didn't look worse for wear, although he'd already looked kind of horrible that day, like he hadn't slept in a very long time. Now that I thought about it, though, he seemed to be a little more tired every time I saw him. "You look paler than usual," I said.

Sohrab brushed off my concern. "I'm fine."

"You in trouble?" I asked.

"I managed to avoid detention, though I have been asked to show some restraint when I speak up in class."

"That's fair."

"No," Sohrab said. "It is really terrible actually. They might as well put up a sign outside the school. 'Please refrain from voicing your opinions so as not to challenge how we see the world through the lens of our privilege.'"

"That's a long sign."

He nearly growled at me. "Not everything is a joke."

"Not everything is a fight either. It was just a stupid essay topic. There was no reason to say all that."

"If we're always silent, no one will ever see the world as we see it."

"Fair. But if you're always lecturing people, they just tune you out. Like Zar and I do all the time."

He made a face. "So how do I decide when to speak and when not to?"

"I've been thinking about that a lot actually."

"Really? You've been thinking? That's new."

"Look who has jokes now."

He grinned and I realized it had been a while since I'd seen him smile. It seemed like he was grim all the time now, and maybe that was a little on me. I always went to him when there was something big or weighty to discuss.

For fun stuff, like talking about girls or video games, I went to Zar.

So I decided to spare him all my confusion about Renaissance Man and my dad. It'd be good for him to just chill for a while.

"What are you considering speaking out about?" he asked.

"Don't worry about it. You want to go see a movie or something?"

"It's the middle of the day, Danyal."

"That just means tickets are cheaper."

"We have classes."

"What's your point?"

"I hate him," Intezar said. "He's dead to me."

I didn't say anything. It wasn't the first time that Sohrab had been dead to Intezar. It had been happening with increasing frequency over the years.

The increased tension between my two friends might have sort of slightly been a little bit my fault. I'd been flying high after convincing Sohrab Sabsvari, of all people, to skip class to catch a movie. In my excitement, I let slip that Intezar had a crush on Natari Smith and that I thought he should totally ask Natari out.

This had apparently led to Sohrab calling Zar later that night to explain to him exactly how doing that would land Zar in hell.

I should've kept my mouth shut, yes, but Sohrab should have as well. Honestly, if he kept getting himself killed in this manner, some day he might not be able to come back to life.

"Let's talk about something else," Zar said. "I've had enough of that guy."

I shrugged as Intezar and I looked around the cafeteria, searching for a place to sit. I would've rather just gone outside. The smell of stale meat loaf made me a little sick, but Zar liked to be indoors when he ate. It is the one principle he has in his life, so I put up with it without too much complaint.

The search for a place in the world is an awkward thing, and it's worse in a school cafeteria than anywhere else. There you aren't looking for a place among strangers. You're looking for a place among people you sort of know, and so you hope to be welcome everywhere but know that you're not.

We could have decided to sit with the Muslim Students' Association kids at the farthest corner of the cafeteria. I knew they'd make room for us. Sohrab waved at us from their table, like he did every day, though today he did so with some hesitation.

Zar wouldn't ever do it. He thought that the MSA judged him for having had girlfriends, and he was probably right about that.

We weren't close to any cheerleaders, unfortunately, and we weren't nerds. We were not in any clubs, or into any sports, and while we were friendly with a lot of people, we were really only friends with each other.

"We kind of suck," I said under my breath.

If he heard me, Intezar ignored what I'd said. Instead, he yelled "Dibs" and ran toward an empty table that opened up across the room, his food teetering perilously on the cheap brown plastic tray he was carrying. I followed with as much dignity as I could manage under the circumstances.

"So what did you decide about Churchill?" Zar asked, once we were settled.

"I don't know. It's rough. I'm still reading about the famine and, dude, I think I'm going to have to talk about it. It's like . . . I can't imagine not doing it, you know? I can't get the pictures out of my head. And there's the whole thing with my family stuff—"

"Tippett is going to hate it if you go after Churchill. That's his boy."

"Yeah. Anyway, can we talk about something else? I'd rather not think about the famine while we're eating."

Zar nodded. "Fine. You still have to tell me what happened with Sohrab in English. I keep hearing stories."

"I thought he was dead to you."

"We tell stories about people who're in the ground all the time."

I sighed but told him what had gone down.

"That's insane, *yaar*. He's starting to lose it. All those super intense books he's been reading have gotten in his head. Those crazy YouTube imam videos he loves aren't helping either," Zar said. "You should talk to him."

"He seemed better yesterday. It'll be fine. He's just getting more religious, that's all."

"You say that like it's a normal thing."

"Um...it is?"

Intezar shook his head. "It's not good, okay?"

"Isn't it the definition of good?"

"Not for everyone. Religion is like alcohol....Don't look at me like that. I'm going to explain it, *yaar*. Look, everyone has a tolerance level with alcohol, right? And everyone's tolerance level is different."

I had no way of knowing this and neither did Intezar, except that we'd heard about it on TV and in the movies, and as those were our primary sources of information about the world, I accepted his statement as true.

"Some people can take a lot of religion and they're fine. I mean, you know, they never have any fun, but whatever. That's their problem. They're fine. Other people, people like Sohrab, can't deal with it. They have a little bit of religion and it goes to their head and they end up throwing it up all over their friends and strangers and the world."

"That...actually does make sense."

"I'm basically the wisdom font."

"Have you ever found the wisdom font? I looked. It doesn't come with Word."

He shrugged. "I just use Times New Roman. Anyway, it isn't my theory. It's in the Quran."

"No, it isn't."

"Yeah. It says that the Quran is so heavy that if it had been revealed to a mountain, the mountain would've cracked under its weight. Some people crack under its weight too. Not everyone can handle it."

"Okay, but I already talked to him. Why don't you try?"

"Because I don't see dead people."

I rolled my eyes.

"Besides, he and I don't speak the same language anymore."

I didn't tell him it wasn't true, because it was, and I didn't tell him to work it out with Sohrab, because I didn't know how he could.

CHAPTER TEN

I hate sunshine. Despise it. I know that the sun is necessary for life on Earth and stuff, but if it could be a little less of a dick in the mornings, that'd be peachy. You know those weird people who wake up smiling, ready to face the day? Yeah. I'm not one of those awful, horrible, no-good people. I get up like a human should: mildly irritated and generally pessimistic about what will happen during the next eighteen hours.

That particular day, I was following my morning routine—cursing and covering my eyes with a pillow—when my phone rang. What kind of monster calls you in the morning on a weekend? It felt like only minutes ago I'd fallen back asleep after finishing the dawn prayer with my dad. I fumbled for my phone and answered without checking who it was.

"What?"

"Oh no. I woke you, didn't I?"

I sat bolt upright, forgiving the sun and the sky and all the stars instantly when I heard Kaval's voice. "Hey. No, it's cool. This is the best part of waking up."

"I'm not coffee, Danyal."

True, but you are brown and hot and make hearts race, so you're almost there. I managed not to say that, though. "Sorry. It's just early."

"It's ten thirty."

"Yeah. What's your point?"

"Nothing, I guess. Hey, I was wondering if you've got enough on Churchill to come over? I wrote you some notes. I don't mean to bug you about it, but I know the other picks are really buckling down and—"

"Yeah. Sure. I'll see you in an hour?"

"We live five minutes away."

"I know," I said. "But I've got to do my hair, and I've got my weekend skin-care regimen—"

"Uff. You're such a girl."

"I take that as a compliment."

Kaval laughed. "Just get over here when you can. I'll be home."

\(\wr\wr\)

What Kaval failed to mention was that she was going to be home *alone*. Was that why she'd invited me over? If it was, what did it mean, if it meant anything?

I gave an awkward little wave when she opened the door. Her hair was wet and undone, and she looked very different. It took me a moment to realize that it was because, for the first time in many years, I was seeing her without makeup. She still looked beautiful.

"You're early. I didn't have a chance to get ready."

"You look good," I said.

"Whatever. I've got nothing on."

"Except clothes. Unfortunately." I gasped as soon as I said that out loud. That thought had been just for me.

Luckily, Kaval giggled. "Get in here. Is it okay if we go up to my room?"

"Uh . . . yeah. Sure. Yes."

"You know where it is, right?" She held up a soaked lock of hair apologetically. "I'm going to go dry my hair."

I made my way through the sprawling, opulent Sabsvari home. I was very familiar with it, not only because I'd spent so much time at Sohrab's place growing up, or even because I came over so often to cook food Mrs. Sabsvari could take credit for, but also because the floor plan was pretty similar to my parents' house.

Of course, unlike my parents, the Sabsvaris actually had money, and it showed in the eclectic decorations on the walls, the handwoven rugs running the length of entire corridors, and the heavy, substantial nature of their furniture.

My mom got our furniture at IKEA, and my dad grumbled endlessly about having to put it together with my less-than-enthusiastic help.

Thinking about it now, I could understand why my mother was so reluctant to ask for Kaval's hand for me. Her life would be different in our house. Way different, actually, when I moved out of my parents' place. It wasn't something Kaval would care about, though, if we were in love. Mom was just old-fashioned in her thinking.

I got to Kaval's door and knocked for some reason before letting myself in. It was an awesome room, which smelled like cotton candy and peonies. On the wall by her bed, there was a huge poster of an old dude with weird hair and his tongue sticking out. Isaac Newton, I think. Or was it the guy who discovered gravity . . . Einstein? Did Newton discover gravity? Whatever. I know that there was an apple involved.

Next to the poster hung a massive television, and across from that was a giant collage of pictures of Kaval, obviously taken by a professional in a photo studio. Was having their picture taken and put up in their room something people did? Was it something I should be doing?

Anyway, she had a white desk with nothing on it but a MacBook Pro and a solved Rubik's Cube. I picked it up and messed around with it, then looked for somewhere to sit. It was weird to sit at someone else's desk. It was way weirder to sit on a girl's bed. I decided to plunk myself down on a giant purple beanbag that was lying in a corner.

I have to admit I got pretty absorbed in the stupid puzzle. I was just about ready to peel off all the little colored stickers and then put them back on so that it looked like I'd solved it, when Kaval said, "Hey."

I jumped a little, and the cube fell from my hands, rolling under the bed. "Sorry," I said.

"No worries. I'll get it later." She grabbed her laptop. "We have to leave the door open. If Sohrab gets home and we're in here with the door closed, he'll have a cow."

"Sure," I said. Honestly, I wasn't even supposed to be up here, open door or not. All the aunties in the world would freak out. Then again, from what I knew of Kaval, she'd enjoy that.

"Show me what you've got."

Kaval was smiling when I handed her my notes, but that didn't last long at all. Her brow started to furrow as she read more and more, and within five minutes, she was full-on scowling. "What is this?"

"Um . . . my notes for Renaissance Man?"

"You can't write this. Tippett doesn't want to hear about how the British treated Indian people." She looked down at the pages I'd handed her. "They stripped the wives of those who couldn't pay their taxes in public," she read, "and took sharp edges of split bamboo . . ." She shuddered. "You can't get onstage and say all this at school."

"I'm not," I protested. "That was before Churchill anyway. I was just taking notes about how Bengal got to be so poor in the first place. It was because the British looted everything, so there were no resources to deal with disasters when they hit. If I'm going to focus on the Bengal Famine—"

"That isn't Churchill's story."

"It totally is, though. It just isn't what we get to hear."
I got to my feet. I needed to make her understand how I'd
started to feel more and more as I'd read up on the Raj and
Churchill. For some reason, I needed to be pacing when I
made the argument.

Maybe I was restless because I wasn't just arguing with
her. I was arguing with a part of myself too. Kaval and
Zar and my dad were right. This wasn't what our teacher
wanted, and I needed to pass history. The easiest way to do
that was not to tell the story of the Bengal Famine.

And yet, I knew what I knew now, I'd seen what I'd
seen. The thought of going up onstage and pretending
Churchill was the gruff, old-school hero everyone thought
he was . . . well, it was unthinkable.

Okay, so not *unthinkable*, exactly, because I was thinking about it, but . . . pretty shitty.

"How is this not part of Churchill's story? How does no
one talk about the fact that three million people died on his
watch, under his rule. Slow, painful, brutal deaths. And do
you know what he said? Famine or no famine, Indians will
'breed like rabbits.' "

She bowed her head.

"Three million people. I googled it, and that's like half
of all the people in Denmark or Finland or Norway. Do
you think that we'd talk about Churchill the way we talk
about him now if he'd done that to three million Danes? Or
Finns?"

"No," she said.

"So where's the conversion table?"

"What?"

"In history. Like... you know, in math, we convert from feet to inches and centimeters and stuff. So, for historians, how many brown people are equal to one white person? Is there like a formula somewhere no one told me about?"

Kaval let out a deep breath and ran a hand through her hair. "Okay. You're right, but all this was a long time ago."

"Like all of history?"

"Yes. Look, you're not wrong, okay? But I'm just saying it doesn't matter now what happened back then. What matters now is that you do well in Renaissance Man. My parents are going to be there, Danyal. I need you to do well because..." She took a deep breath, like she was diving into deep, deep water. "I think you like me a bit."

Not going to lie. That threw me off. I sat back down slowly. "Uh... yeah. A little bit."

Her eyes were fixed on the notes that lay on her bed, all disarranged now. I found myself wishing she would look at me. Her voice was difficult to read. "There's someone coming to see me soon. A guy with his family for arranged marriage and stuff."

"Oh."

"He's a doctor. He's going to be a cardiologist. You... are not a cardiologist."

I wish I'd said something cool like *I don't mend hearts,*

I just break them or whatever. Instead, I just nodded. I felt like someone had taken a whisk and was whipping my emotions around, trying to make a meringue.

Kaval kept her eyes away from mine. "I think you're great. You're cute—really cute—you're funny, you're so sweet, and I'd trust you with...everything in the world."

She liked me. She liked me. Oh my God. Thank you.

I was sitting down. Why was I sitting down? Oh. Right. The cardiologist.

What did any of this have to do with Renaissance Man? What was going on?

"I'm...confused," I said. "You're saying you like me. Like *like*. Yes?"

Now she did meet my gaze, and I could tell that she thought my reaction was adorable. "A very little bit."

"Wow."

She grinned, and then just like that grew serious again. "But that's not everything, you know. Not in real life. My parents won't be cool with me walking away from a really good prospect because I like you. They're practical people."

"So you need me to do well in Renaissance Man?"

"I need you to win. You've got something of a reputation as not being...I mean, do you really want to be a cook, Danyal? That isn't exactly a viable career path. You can't raise a family off of that."

"Chefs have families."

"Not like ours."

I didn't know what that meant, but she went on without giving me a chance to ask.

"You're great. Okay? Just...this is your chance. You can win Renaissance Man. That would prove to my parents how much potential you have. I could talk to my dad, and he could get you into college."

"Kaval," I said, "I'm not going to college. Not with my grades."

"No. Listen. My dad has a lot of friends in Pakistan who can arrange for you to get into a school there. You can get a degree and come back. No one is going to care what your high school—"

"Pakistan?" I laughed. It was an odd thing to do, to laugh just then, but that's what we do when we hear absurd things, right? I couldn't believe what I was hearing. "Are you kidding?"

She shook her head.

"You want me to go to Pakistan?"

"Not forever. Just for college."

"What's the big deal with college?"

"What else are you going to do with your life?" Kaval asked.

I opened my mouth to answer, but then stopped myself. She already knew the answer to that question. She just didn't think it was a good answer.

"I don't need you to think," Kaval said. "Just do what I say, okay? It'll all work out." She hopped off her bed and walked over to a dresser. There was a printer on it that I hadn't noticed. "I made some notes for you. Write something based off of these. I'll help you polish it. Tell Tippett what he wants to hear. I'll stall the cardiologist."

"You're going to stall him?"

"My parents won't be happy if I say no," she said. "And besides, he's a good fallback. You know"—Kaval lightened her tone so I'd understand she was joking—"in case you screw everything up."

I'd spent a lot of time imagining the day that Kaval Sabsvari would tell me she liked me. I'd expected something magical, something wonderful, like those scenes in movies where love finally blossoms to rising music. This was . . . not that.

I looked down at the neat, color-coded, meticulous notes Kaval had handed me. It was obvious that she cared about me. She wouldn't have gone through all the trouble of writing this stuff out, of planning this crazy fantasy of me going to Pakistan and coming back armed with a degree, somehow capable of winning her parents' approval, if she didn't.

It wasn't what I'd wanted. But it was something, right? Kaval obviously believed in my ability to do well in Renaissance Man, which was more than I could say for anyone else.

It was enough. It had to be enough.

I smiled. It took some effort but I managed it. "I guess I should go read all this." I waved the sheaf of papers in my hand. "Thanks for these. And I'll think about everything else."

"What do you have to think about? I'm your dream girl, right?" She said it with a grin, which faded a little when I didn't say anything. "Just don't tell anyone what we talked about, okay? I don't want my parents to find out that I'm helping you with this. It has to look like you're smart on your own. Also, I don't think Sohrab would like it."

"Why not?"

"He wouldn't think you'd be bad for me or anything."

"Then what's the problem?" I asked.

"I'm pretty sure he'd think I'd be bad for you."

"What were you guys doing upstairs alone?"

Not. Good.

Sohrab had walked through the door just as Kaval and I were heading downstairs so I could leave. He didn't smile when he saw me, which was a bad sign. Everyone smiles when they see me. I'm the best bowl of ice cream in the world.

Worse, his tone was dark and full of suspicion, as if the mere fact that he had to ask the question meant that we'd been doing something wrong, which I suppose we had been. There is wrong, though, and then there is *wrong*. Just like there is real chocolate and white chocolate. You can't possibly get confused between those two.

"Hey, dude, we were just—"

"Having sex," Kaval said in the joyful but slightly faint

tone of a Disney princess who has just discovered talking animals. "So much sex. I think I'm getting a little pregnant just remembering it. I should go lie down."

With that, she spun around, leaving her sputtering, embarrassed, and speechless twin brother alone with me.

Neither one of us spoke for a moment.

Then I said, "I think I did pretty good. For my first time."

"I have told you before, haven't I, that you're not funny?"

"Yeah. No one believes that." More seriously, I added, "Listen, we were just working on school stuff."

"You know better than to be alone with her. She knows better too. That girl is out of control."

It seemed to me, honestly, that Kaval was in total control pretty much all the time, but I didn't think saying so would win me any points just then.

"Where were you?" I asked.

"At the mosque."

That was when I noticed the white cap on his head and the fact that his jeans were rolled up above his ankles, which I'd been told was protocol for prayer. He was also wearing a tee that said CAT STEVENS on it in big blue letters. I'd had no idea who the seventy-year-old British musician was until Sohrab told me he was a fan. If Stevens hadn't converted to Islam and started doing religious songs, though, I don't think Sohrab and his friends would be all about him. It was like Christian Rock, I guess, except, you know, not Christian.

"Aren't you going to roll your pants down?" I asked.

Sohrab shook his head. "The early Muslims wore their pants over their ankles all the time. I'm going to start doing it too."

Fashion had come a long way in fourteen hundred years, but whatever. I just wanted to get out of there and think about what Kaval had said. I hadn't come close to digesting it all yet.

I waved Kaval's notes in his face. "I have to go work on this stuff."

"Sure. Fine." Then, as I was almost past him, he asked, "Have you spoken to Intezar? Is he still upset with me?"

"Yeah. You're dead to him," I said. "But don't worry. With all the religious books you're reading, I'm sure you'll pick up some stuff about resurrection."

Sohrab shook his head but otherwise ignored my brilliant joke. "I just wanted him to know that he is contemplating a sin."

"He knows."

"Well . . . still, it was important that I tell him. Reminders, as the Quran says, are good for the believers."

"Yeah," I told him, "but so are friends."

CHAPTER ELEVEN

"*We have to* stop meeting like this."

Suraiya Akram looked up from the book she was reading and gave me a ridiculously hurt look, her eyes wide, her bottom lip stuck out like she was a little kid. "I thought you liked me."

I rolled my eyes and turned to Remarquable's maître d'. "Why do you keep letting her in?"

The older man sniffed in a superior sort of way. "Because it is personally inconvenient for you and I find that rather amusing." Then he smiled at Suri. "Another hot chocolate for the young miss?"

"No," I said. "Thank you."

"Rude," Suri said as the maître d' sauntered off. "And after I came all this way to thank you."

"Thank me?"

"Bisma was humming. After your date, I mean."

"It wasn't a date."

"Whatever," Suri said. "My point is that she never hums, which is why she was so off-key, I guess, but I'm just saying that you made her happy and that's super cool if you think about it because not everyone can do that for somebody, no?"

"Do you need to breathe at all when you talk?"

"Not usually."

I smiled, despite all her Suri-ness. "It's impressive."

"I know," she said smugly. Then, in a more serious tone, "Are you going to ask her out again?"

"I didn't ask her out the first time."

"Uff. Boys are so annoying about these things." Suraiya's phone rang and she grinned. "There she is. Behave. Or, you know, don't. Whatever."

I glanced around the restaurant as Suraiya answered the call and went to let Bisma in. At least it didn't look like Chef Brodeur was around today.

Bisma walked in, practically snarling at her little sister. "What do you think you're doing?"

"I just—"

"Shut up," Bisma snapped. "You do this again and I'm going to tell Abbu. You're going to get Danyal in trouble. This isn't his restaurant. Just stop trying to help me. I don't need your help."

Suri looked down, bit her lip, and nodded.

With a sigh, Bisma turned to face me. "I'm so sorry. I

had to come pick her up, but this won't ever happen again. I promise."

"No, it's cool," I said. "Actually, I invited her over."

Bisma frowned. "Really? Why?"

I had no answer to that. But I'd been yelled at so much by family—mostly by Dad—over the years that I didn't like seeing anyone else get the same treatment, even if Suri was being a little much.

"Yeah." Suraiya jumped in to buy me some time. "Really. Bet you feel pretty stupid, huh?"

"Not now, Suri."

Come on. Think. *Think.*

"I believe," Suraiya went on, "that I deserve an apology."

"Fine," Bisma said. "Oh my God, I'm sorry."

"It needs to be more abject."

Bisma crossed her arms. "Tell me what *abject* means."

"I've heard people use it. It's a word."

"You can't go around using words you don't know the meaning—"

"I wanted her opinion," I broke in, finally managing to put the time Suri had bought me to use. "So I called her."

"About what?" Bisma asked.

"I . . . There's a girl?"

Suraiya slapped the palm of her hand to her forehead.

Bisma raised her eyebrows. "A girl?"

Maybe I should've said something else, but aside from Kaval, there wasn't anything I could think of that I'd need Suraiya's advice on. "Yeah. I mean, you know, just a prospect."

"You called Suri for arranged marriage advice?"

"I mean... you never gave me your number, and I figured you'd come pick her up, and she likes the hot chocolate here...."

It was only after I'd said it that I realized I could've simply texted Suri for Bisma's number, and that the whole story I'd come up with made no sense.

"So you're asking me for relationship advice?" Bisma asked, her tone flat.

I nodded. "Sure. After all, what are friends for?"

⸎

Half an hour later, we were standing in line at Deli Board, which served my favorite hot sandwiches in San Francisco. Their pastrami melted in your mouth, and the corned beef was a thing of beauty.

"I'm not sure this is okay," Bisma said, concerned with keeping halal.

"We can totally eat here," I said. "This place is kosher."

"How do you know?"

"It said so in a review online. Therefore, it must be true."

Suri nodded, apparently in full agreement with me.

"But they serve bacon," Bisma pointed out.

"Obviously, the bacon isn't kosher," I said. "But everything else is. Probably."

"We could just ask them when we order."

"No, dude, come on," I said. "Don't ruin this for me. Ignorance—and the sandwiches here—are bliss. Just go with the flow."

"I just don't think," Bisma said, "that any sandwich is worth going to hell for."

"If you think God would send you to hell for eating a sandwich," I countered, "maybe you don't have enough faith in God."

"Oh. That's deep," Suri said appreciatively.

Bisma gave us both a dirty look, but she ordered "A. Stud," which was a good choice. The jalapeños went well with the house-made sauce and the Romanian pastrami.

Suri leaned over and whispered, "Giving away what she's thinking about with that order, isn't she?"

"What?"

Suraiya didn't have time to explain before she got called up to the counter, and soon we were sitting at a table outside. My sandwich was a mess of steaming salami, roast beef, and melting cheese on a nicely crunchy roll. I took a bite.

"I'm in heaven," I said with my mouth full.

"For. The. Moment," Bisma replied. Then she took a tiny bite, her eyes widened a bit, and she drew back to look at the sandwich with a great deal more respect. "Wow."

"Right. Told you."

"I don't even care if I'm going to hell," Suri said. "This is fucking amazing."

"Language," Bisma and I snapped at the same time. Suri groaned.

"Anyway, tell me about your prospect," Bisma said. Then, perfectly casually, asked, "Is she pretty?"

"Yeah," I said. "She's beautiful."

Suri shook her head, her face a Wikipedia entry for *dismay*.

"Oh. So..." Bisma waved her hand in a motion indicating that I should get on with stating whatever the problem was.

I gave them the short version of what Kaval had said about her feelings, about Renaissance Man, about her parents, and about the cardiologist she had coming over soon.

"What a bitch," Suri declared, way too loudly.

"Language," Bisma said again, though with a lot less heat than she'd said it before.

I, on the other hand, stared at Suri, surprised. "What?"

"She's a total..." Suri trailed off, glanced at Bisma, then finished, "*kuttiya.*"

I wasn't sure how saying "bitch" in Urdu was any more polite than saying it in English. "She gave me notes on Churchill. That was nice of her."

Suraiya rolled her eyes. "She's just trying to get what she wants. It's totally obvious that's all she's about."

"What does she want?"

"I mean...well, you. Which we totally get 'cause you're super cute, right, Apa?" We both looked at Bisma, but she didn't say anything. She seemed intensely focused

167

on her sandwich. Suri turned back to me. "Guys are usually the ones trying to use girls for their looks. But I guess it's different for you 'cause you're a pretty face."

"Hey." I pointed an indignant pickle at her. "I'm more than a—"

"It's like she's only interested in your body, dude. Wake up and smell the poop."

"Gross," Bisma muttered.

"Come on, Apa, you agree, right?" This time Suri didn't wait for a response before going on in her usual rambling way. "This girl is totally not interested in who he is because she doesn't want him to write what he wants for that project of his and she doesn't want him to be a chef. All she cares about is making him into something she wants. It's like plastic surgery for his personality. You marry that girl and she'll have you working in like an *office*," Suri said, as if it were the worst thing in the world, "just to make money to take home."

I looked at Bisma when her little sister paused to gasp for breath to see if she agreed with what Suraiya was saying. She gave me no clue as to what she was thinking. "She never mentioned money," I said, quick to pounce on a fact that I could use in defense of Kaval.

"Oh?" Suraiya asked, before continuing in what was meant to be an impression of Kaval, I guess, but it just sounded like Minnie Mouse had inhaled a bunch of argon—no. Helium? Hydrogen? Whatever. "You have to be practical and have viable goals in life and I'll just hang on to this assologist as a backup in case you don't go to college and never make something respectable of yourself."

"She never mentioned money." I repeated it to Bisma this time, because Suri obviously wasn't listening. And it was the truth. Kaval hadn't. Had she? I mean . . . she'd kind of implied it, I guess, when she'd said chefs couldn't support families.

I continued looking in Bisma's direction so long that she figured out I was waiting for her to say something.

"I've never really had occasion to admire anyone practical," she finally told me.

I frowned. What did that mean?

"Why do you need advice about this girl, Danyal?"

"Yeah, Danyal," Suraiya said. "It's obvious what you should do."

"Is it?" I asked. "I mean . . . what she's saying isn't wrong. If you and I, Bisma, had . . . you know, if we were doing the whole arranged marriage thing, you would've been okay with my wanting to be a chef?"

She didn't hesitate. "Of course."

"Even if that meant we would struggle?"

Bisma shook her head as she picked up a pickle. "Why would we struggle? I'd work."

"What?"

"I'd work. I mean . . . obviously." Bisma sat back, looked at me, and laughed. "Wow. That didn't even occur to you, did it?"

"No," I admitted. "I didn't think . . . I mean, yeah."

"You do know what year it is, right?" Suri asked.

"Maybe you should mention this revolutionary concept to your prospect," Bisma said.

"No. He shouldn't. He should never see her again. Why would he want to marry someone so...calculating?"

"He wouldn't be asking for advice if he didn't like her." Bisma wiped her hands on a napkin. "You guys ready to go?"

"Go?" I asked. "You're barely halfway through your sandwich."

"I'm full," Bisma said. "This thing is huge. Suri and I could've split one."

"You're a disappointment," Suri told her sister, still munching away. "I'm not done."

Neither was I, so we stuck around and talked about nothing much, until the conversation circled back to Renaissance Man.

"I'm really not sure what I'm going to do at this point," I admitted. "I know what Kaval wants me to do. I know what my teacher wants and what my dad wants....There's a lot to think about, and I haven't even decided what direction to go in. I'll probably screw this up pretty badly and that's going to suck."

"I could help you," Bisma said.

Suri whipped her head around to look at her sister. "Really?"

"Really?" I echoed.

"Sure. Like you said, what are friends for?"

CHAPTER TWELVE

It was picture day for the contestants of Renaissance Man, and my tie wasn't sitting right. I'd gone with a half-Windsor knot, which seemed like a good middle road between the casualness of a four-in-hand and the fuddiness of a full Windsor. The problem was that while I knew a lot about the knots in theory, having watched a gazillion YouTube videos on how to tie, this was the first time I'd worn one in real life. It looked a little lopsided and kept drifting to the left.

Don't get me wrong. I looked awesome in my deep blue suit, but even though I got a ton of compliments from all the other kids at school, I couldn't stop fussing with the tie.

It was Sohrab, ultimately, who noticed. He gestured for me to give it to him. "My father makes me tie his every day. Has since I was ten."

"Why?"

"For days like this, I suppose."

I watched as Sohrab looped the silky snake around his own neck and began twisting it. It looked like he was doing exactly what I'd done. The task gave him the perfect excuse not to look at me as he said, "I am sorry about the other day, when you were talking to Kaval. I should not have...I shouldn't have said anything."

"It's cool," I told him. I'm really good at letting things go. People screw up. I get it. I screw up all the time and I forgive myself pretty much right away. Seems only fair to do the same for other people. "Just admit that you were wrong about me not being funny, and we'll call it even."

"You know how I feel about lying," he said.

I rolled my eyes.

"I meant what I said at the party at our house. No one likes you because you're funny. They laugh when you tell your little 'jokes' because you want them to, and they want to do what you want—"

"Because I'm gorgeous."

He shook his head. "Because you're true."

"What does that even mean?"

Sohrab didn't answer. He was done with the knot, so he forced the tie over his own head and handed it to me. I put it on and tightened it. The knot was perfect.

"You look good," he told me.

As if I didn't know.

"Have you seen Zar?" Sohrab asked.

"Have you thought about when you want to stop asking me that and just talk to him yourself?"

He looked away and smiled a bit. "A little."

"You know how sensitive he is about the fact that he dates—"

"He's sensitive about it because he knows it is wrong. Deep in his soul, he knows he is dooming himself to eternal torment."

"Um...yeah. I don't think that's it."

Sohrab folded his arms across his chest. "Sometimes it surprises me how little you seem to know about Islam having been a Muslim all your life."

"Sometimes it surprises me how little you know about Intezar, you know, having been his friend all your life."

That seemed to take the fire out of him. "That was clever," he said.

"I know, right? Now, if you'll excuse me, I have a camera to dazzle."

As I walked away from him, I couldn't help but wonder if I should have said something more to my old friend but decided that I'd been right to keep my mouth shut. Just like Intezar was touchy about anyone challenging his decision not to practice Islam, Sohrab would be touchy about his decision to embrace it. My friends were, strangely enough, more alike than either one of them would admit.

By the time I walked into Mr. Elridge's class, where

the photographer was setting up, everyone else was already there. Six faces, sour as *umeboshi* plums, glowered at me. Natari alone smiled and came over. She was wearing a full-length red dress that highlighted her dark hair. "The man of the hour," she said. "We were just talking about you."

"You were?" I glanced at the others while trying to look like I wasn't looking at them at all.

"We all think it is ridiculously unfair that our pictures will go up next to yours. Maybe try to not look great, so we'll look okay?"

"I would, if that weren't impossible."

Natari chuckled.

"You look nice, though," I told her. Then, without thinking about it, added, "Which I'm sure I'll hear from Zar."

Her cheeks went a little pink, but she looked pleased. Then she started to say something, but the photographer spoke up. He told us we'd do individual portraits, which he thought parents might be interested in buying, and we'd do a few group shots.

"So," the photographer said, clapping his hands, "who wants to go first?"

"Jilani should go first," Alan Rhodes said, "in honor of the fact that he'll finish last."

That drew some chuckles.

"Come on, Jilani," Rhodes went on. "Show us how it's done."

I didn't want to think about what Bisma and Suri had said about Kaval. One of the problems with trying not to think about something, of course, is that it always fails. You can't help but think about the thing you're trying not to think about. I mean, people say that the human mind is incredibly complex and all, but it has this very serious and basic design flaw which no one talks about.

It'd be like a web browser that only takes you to websites you don't want to go to. What's even the point?

Anyway, one thing Bisma had said did make sense. There was no reason for me to get a degree or a respectable job, as my father would put it. Kaval could do that. There's no reason for two people in a couple to be respectable. That'd just be boring.

I don't know much about relationships—not that Kaval and I were in a relationship or anything—but I've always heard that communication is key. That sounded like something that was true.

Of course, my parents had been married for like twenty-three years or something, and they never seem to really talk at all, but maybe they were the exception that proved the rule.

Anyway, I decided to discuss all this with Kaval, and I found her at lunch in the cafeteria. She was, unfortunately, sitting with a bunch of her friends, Cindy, Maria, Galina, and a few others. I sighed. There's something about a group of girls together that I find a little scary. I'm super smooth and suave one-on-one, of course, but something about a battalion makes me a little nervous.

Still, as one of the books I'd read about Churchill said, I girded my lions—what the heck does that actually mean? What's a gird? And why do people do it to lions? Why do people even have lions?—and made my way over to their table.

"Hey, Danyal," Cindy said, twiddling her fingers at me. "I like your shoes."

I glanced down at my caramel-colored dress shoes. "Thanks. Hey, Kaval—"

"Yes?" she asked, pretty frostily, which caused all the other girls to start snickering.

"Can I talk to you for a second? Alone."

That drew a series of suggestive *oohs* from the table.

Mercifully, Kaval nodded and followed me to the hall outside.

"What?" she demanded, turning to face me as soon as there was no one in earshot.

I frowned. Her eyes were narrowed, her arms were crossed, and her lips were pressed together in a tight line. "Wait, you're pissed at me?"

"Yeah, genius. I'm pissed at you."

"Why?"

Kaval threw her arms up in the air. "I gave you an

opening, and you didn't take it. After you've been drooling over me for years, by the way. You wanted time to *think*. Seriously? That is so insulting. I can't believe you didn't realize I was mad."

"Um...sorry?"

She tossed her hair back over her shoulder with a forceful jerk of her head. "Fine. Whatever. What do you want? I assume you've finally decided to agree to what I was saying."

"Actually," I said. "I was thinking—"

"You shouldn't do that, Danyal. You'll sprain something."

"Okay. Look, Kaval, I do really like you, but..." I paused. I didn't want to be the first one to mention money. She hadn't technically done it. It felt...I don't know.... Maybe Bisma and Suri had been wrong. Maybe Kaval didn't care about being wealthy and I'd just misunderstood her. If so, I'd definitely offend her by bringing it up. "I wasn't clear on what you meant."

She crossed her arms. "I literally told you what to do. How could I possibly be any clearer? Use my notes. Do well in Renaissance Man. Impress my parents. Go to college. Get a degree. Then we can be together. What part of that, exactly, is confusing you?"

"I understand what you want me to *do*." I held up my hands to show that I wasn't trying to be difficult. "I just don't understand why. I mean, when you said that chefs can't support their families..."

177

"I meant that you won't make any money flipping burgers for the rest of your life."

"Oh. Well...so, I was thinking that there might be another solution to the whole...financial aspect of our... agreement." I shook my head. "Is this weird? This is weird, isn't it? That we're talking about money and stuff, at our age, instead of being in—"

"I'm being practical," Kaval said. "Nothing wrong with that. What's your idea?"

"You could work," I told her.

"What?"

"You could work. I mean, you know, I could still do what I want to do, and you could work if you think that I wouldn't make enough—"

"Danyal, did you miss the part about how my parents have got a doctor lined up?"

"Uh...no."

"And even if I pass on him, I'll get other offers. I mean..." She waved her hands vaguely at herself, pointing out that she was obviously too desirable to stay on the market for long. "If I go with any of them, I wouldn't ever have to work. How is your offer better?"

"Well...I mean, there's me."

"Tempting," Kaval said, "but that's not the life I want. I mean, if I wanted to get a job for like fun or something, sure, but I don't want to *have* to work. Not when I have the option not to. I want a traditional marriage. I want someone to take care of me."

"I thought this was a good compromise."

"It's not. Look"—she reached over and touched my arm—"I'm sorry, okay? I know this sounds...uncool or whatever, but I've thought a lot about it, and I'm telling you, my way is the only way this works. Just trust me. Don't worry about anything but doing well in Renaissance Man. Say how great Churchill was—"

"He wasn't. Not all the time."

She sighed and let her hand slide away from me.

"I want to talk about the Bengal Famine, Kaval. I want to write about it. It's important."

"It's not," she snapped. "Okay? It'll change nothing. Those people will stay dead. Even if you totally thrash him, everyone will still laugh at Churchill's jokes and keep thinking of him as a hero. All you'll manage is to piss off Tippett, you'll fail history, and we'll still be exactly where we are."

"What if I did a really good job, though?" I asked. "What if I wrote such a great paper on the famine that I impressed everyone? Tippett, my dad, your parents. It would work, right? Everyone would get what they wanted."

"You really think you could pull that off? Even if it were possible, Danyal, you wouldn't be able to do it without help. And I'm not going to help you if you won't listen to me."

I looked away from her.

"This is a chance for you to change who you are, okay?

It's a chance to change how everyone looks at you. Don't waste it."

I told Zar what Kaval had said, and I could tell that he wanted to say *I told you so*. It was written all over his face. After all, he'd warned me that Kaval was out of my league with his weird egg theory. Instead of rubbing my face in it, however, he just handed me a video game controller and started up a first-person shooter.

I didn't usually agree to play shooters with Zar. It scared the shit out of me because he randomly liked to freak other players out by bursting into bouts of loud, nonsensical Arabic in a threatening tone. Sometimes he'd scream out stuff like "Die, infidel dogs!" as he attacked the opposition.

I was pretty certain that the government was going to come for him—and maybe me for being around him—one day. But the more urgently I pleaded with him to stop, the more he laughed, and the more he did it.

Today, however, we played pretty much in silence until he asked, "Did it hurt?"

"What?"

"When Kaval said those things to you at school."

I shrugged. Then, when Zar didn't seem to want to move on, I nodded.

"Do you think she knew it would hurt you? Do you think she cared?"

"What's your point?"

"I think you should forget her, Danyal. She's a bitch."

"No, she's not."

"*Yaar*, come on. Don't tell me you're going to defend—"

"What did she do wrong? I've been thinking about it, and yeah, okay, it super sucked in the moment for me, but...I mean, she's allowed to want things, right? She knows what kind of life she wants, and she's demanding it. There's nothing wrong with that. She should be happy."

"You're a better person than I am," he muttered.

"This is true," I said.

He elbowed my ribs, but without much force.

"And maybe she's right about everything," I added.

"No," Zar said. "She's not. You're allowed to want things too. You've wanted to be a chef since we were kids and that Courtney girl used to come over."

"Oh yeah. Whatever happened to her?"

"Her family moved to like Phoenix or Jersey or something. Dude, watch out for—"

"I see him," I said, having my character duck behind a car for cover.

"Anyway, yeah, I tried to look her up, but I couldn't remember her last name."

I thought about it and shook my head. "I can't either."

"Funny, isn't it? How someone can seem so important to your life, and the next thing you know, it's thirteen years later, and you can't even remember her name."

I glanced at him. "You trying to tell me something?"

"Nah," Zar said with a grin. "What could I possibly be trying to tell you?"

We made our way through the streets of Karachi together in silence for a while, streets that we'd never walked, but where our parents had lived, and loved, and known joy. I wondered if they, all these years later, knew the city as well as I did, though it had once been part of their everyday reality, and I was only ever virtually there.

"I really like her," I said.

"Everybody knows."

"And I could do it. Like everything she wanted. I could go to school in Karachi, come back, become what she wants me to be. She basically said she'd wait for me if I did."

Intezar let out an irritated sigh but didn't say anything.

"Isn't that what love is? I mean, aren't you supposed to compromise and change for the person you love?"

Zar groaned and paused the game. I couldn't remember the last time he'd ever stopped a game for anything other than nature or nourishment. He went to the quit option.

"What are you doing?"

"I'm done being on the same team as you. Let's play a game where I can punch you in the face."

I laughed despite everything that was happening with Kaval. Zar had that effect on people.

"Can I tell you something?"

"Yeah," I said. "What?"

"I wouldn't say things like that to you, not ever, just

to get something I wanted but you didn't. I'd never make your life about me. Do you know why?"

I shook my head.

"Because I love you."

What he wasn't saying was obvious. Kaval Sabsvari didn't love me.

I was pretty sure he was right, but I didn't know what to say in response. We sat together, staring at the menu screen before us, asking us if we really wanted to stop playing. Finally, I said, "Natari looked good today, right?"

"I know," Zar practically squealed. "That dress. *Mirchain, yaar.*"

I wasn't sure if a dress could be spicy, exactly, but it certainly had been the color of ground red pepper. "She's great."

"I've been telling you."

"I know," I said dryly. "It's just that she's been really nice to me about Renaissance Man, even though Alan and the others seem to hate me. Anyway, we were talking today, and I may have told her you'd like her outfit."

Zar's mouth dropped open, and he shoved me so hard that I nearly fell off the couch. "No. *Way.* What? *Why?*"

"Calm down. It was fine. She seemed...I don't know, happy to hear it. You should ask her out."

"But Pirji told me his thoughts and prayers weren't working," Zar reminded me.

"Maybe that just means it's time to do something yourself."

CHAPTER THIRTEEN

I stared at images of the people who'd lived through the Bengal Famine on my computer screen. It should've been easy to make them go away. One little click, and they'd be gone. I wouldn't have to see their silent suffering captured forever, forever ago, again.

Instead of talking about these people, I could get up onstage and praise the man who had helped bring them to this state. I could ignore them, as history had done. I could pretend that Churchill hadn't championed their oppression, through the racist and brutal enterprise of colonialism, which had ultimately resulted in their deaths.

It was the smart thing to do.

There was just one problem with that, though.

I wasn't known for doing the smart thing.

Unfortunately, if I went in the opposite direction, the direction that my heart pulled me to go, and spoke up about the Bengal Famine, I'd have to do a great job. It wasn't just about passing history, and it wasn't just about showing my father and Kaval and Zar and everyone else that I could do it. It was bigger than that.

These nameless people, who had sold themselves and stolen and begged and sacrificed for the smallest morsel of food, they deserved more than my best. My dad had a point when he said I might not be able to do their story justice.

Like Kaval had said, I couldn't do this without help. Was it weak to admit that? I don't think so. A man should know his limitations. Anyone who has ever seen desi uncles trying to dance at a wedding knows this is true.

"Were you serious?" I asked Bisma as soon as she answered her phone.

"Probably," Bisma said. I could hear the smile in her voice. "About what?"

"About helping me with Renaissance Man? I have this idea that I really want to present, but if I'm going to do it, I need to be good, okay? I can't get crushed. It's important. Will you please help me?"

"Of course. Do you want to meet somewhere today? I'll be at the Fremont Library."

"The library," I repeated slowly. "Sure."

"It's on Stevenson. You can google the address."

"Hey," I said. "I know where the library is."

"Do you really?"

"I have, you know, a general idea," I lied. "So do I like need cash for a cover charge at the door or will they just let me walk in and pay them later?"

؟؟

"Let me get this straight," I said. "You're like a Netflix for books."

The woman at the information desk nodded. "Yes. I suppose that's one way to look at it, except we don't charge anything."

"So you'll let me walk out with any book I want. And then you'll trust me to bring it back."

"It's a little more involved than that," she said, "but basically, yes."

"And this works?"

"We've had a pretty decent run of it," she told me. "Don't you have a library at your school?"

"I mean, sure, but I've never been in it. It's kind of a nerdy place to hang out. No offense."

"Don't worry. I made my peace with being a nerd a long time ago. Tell me, what brings you to . . . Bookflix?"

"I'm looking for a girl."

"We have some great ones here, but I'm afraid they're all fictional."

"Very funny," I said. "No, seriously, I'm meeting—oh, there she is."

"Bisma?" the librarian asked, looking back to where I was waving. "Well, you should've just said so."

"You know her?"

"Oh sure. She and her sister are here all the time. I don't know her that well, but she seems like a real sweet girl going through a hard time."

"What makes you say that?"

"If you read enough books, you figure out how to read people too."

"Really? Can you read me?"

The librarian frowned. "You're too young. Your story is still being written."

"I'm the exact same age as Bisma."

"Except, you're really not. And you're lucky for it."

Bisma had a bemused look on her face when I finally joined her at her table, a stack of books about the British Empire by her side. "You met Joanna, I see."

"She's interesting," I said.

"Spending time in a library will do that to a person."

"Sounds horrible. Let's get out of here as soon as possible."

Bisma laughed. "What's going on with your contest?"

"I've decided to tell the truth about Churchill."

She raised her eyebrows. "That's not going to impress that pretty girl you mentioned."

"Yeah. It'll also probably make me fail history and I'll end up disappointing my father yet again—"

"I know a little bit about that," Bisma said with a smile.

"It's just...my ancestors were willing to die for this. What's another F?"

"Another F? How many of those have you gotten?"

"Is that really relevant?"

She shook her head. "I guess not. All right. Show me what you've got on it so far."

I fished around my backpack and pulled out all my notes. Bisma frowned as she flipped through them. "Who wrote these?"

"Why?"

"They don't seem to be in any kind of order."

I frowned. "What is order?"

Bisma looked at me for a long moment, probably trying to decide if I was joking, then just said, "Give a minute to read these over?"

I nodded and sat back as she flipped through what I had researched so far. Her face changed a little, subtly but distinctly, as she sank deeper into the pages before her. She seemed at peace. Content.

Someone in a mosque once told me about the water behind people's faces. This water, he said, changed depending on what you did and what you believed, and as you got older it began to freeze. The kind of life you led, whether your heart was full of love or joy or shrewdness or bile, all of this changed the nature of the water and, therefore, the look of your face. In this way, your face told the story of your life.

Bisma's face, especially at that moment, was a calm lake

under a gentle sun. You could tell that she was a kind person, someone who cared about other people deeply, and who was capable of extraordinary love.

Maybe I'd been staring for too long, because she looked up. "What?"

"You have a very nice face pond."

"Thank . . . what?"

"Don't worry about it. You're welcome. So." I nodded at the notes in her hand. "What do you think?"

"There is some good stuff here. Honestly, though, presenting Churchill as an agent of dehumanization and injustice will be challenging. Are you sure you want to do this? Writing about him as a hero is the easier and probably wiser path."

"I avoid being wise whenever I can," I said, "as a policy."

She grinned. "I can respect that."

"So you'll help me? I've got to come up with an awesome pitch that will sell Tippett, my teacher, on letting me go against Churchill."

"Yes," she said without hesitation. "But I don't think you should write about the Bengal Famine."

"Um . . . what?"

"I just don't think you'll win Renaissance Man by writing about it. Aren't you going to go up onstage and present this paper to a big crowd? You're going to have to do a speech, yes?"

I nodded.

"That's what I meant when I said this will be hard to present. You can't go up there and talk about how many tons of shipping capacity Churchill and his war cabinet had at their disposal," she said, pointing to the numbers I'd copied out. "Or what quantities of rice and wheat he had, and where he chose to stockpile it. That's all too technical. You're going to lose your audience. You have to figure out a way to make it interesting. You need a little masala."

"Masala," I said, "I'm good at."

"I don't doubt it," Bisma said. "Let's see if we can figure out a way to play to your strengths."

⟨⟨

"Stay after class, Mr. Jilani," Tippett said, just as the bell freeing us from the clutches of history rang. I groaned and sank back into my chair. Normally, I'd have gotten sympathetic glances from my classmates. No one wanted to spend more time with our prickly teacher than absolutely necessary. Because they thought it was about Renaissance Man, however, I got jealous glares instead.

I sat where I was for a while, waiting for the old man to speak, but he just stared at me in silence. Eventually, I realized that he wanted me to go up to him. I grabbed my backpack and practically dragged it to the front of the class.

"What?" I asked, probably not in the nicest way possible.

"I was wondering how your Renaissance Man project is going. You have not been your irritatingly effervescent self recently, so I assume that you are preoccupied with thoughts of your imminent humiliation in front of the entire school."

"I'm fine," I said.

He folded his thin arms across his chest and gave me a look that said he didn't believe me.

I sighed. "It doesn't have anything to do with school. It's just...it's a girl."

"You seem to spend an inordinate amount of time thinking about the fairer sex."

"I'm nineteen."

Tippett raised an eyebrow. "A valid defense, perhaps, but thankfully, none of my concern. Tell me you've made some progress toward your thesis for Renaissance Man."

"Progress?"

My teacher grimaced. "Movement. Headway. Momentum. Tell me your work on this project is moving forward."

"Yeah," I said defensively. "It's moving."

Tippett made a derisive sound. "And toward what destination is it headed? At some point, you're going to have to tell me what you plan to say."

Okay, so I totally wasn't ready to do that yet. Given that Algie here would be hostile to any attempt at beseeching Churchill—no, that wasn't right...besotting, maybe? Besmirching? Yes. That one. Where was I?

"Mr. Jilani?"

"Yeah. No. I'm here."

He sighed. "I'm aware. What is your thesis?"

"I'll get it to you soon," I said. "I promise."

"We've entered March. You only have two months left."

"I know. I got this. Trust me."

"You may have noticed, Mr. Jilani, that I am a big believer in history. My history with you gives me little reason to extend you the benefit of the doubt." He paused, then shook his head. "Then again, I suppose I have little choice. I'd give you a deadline, but I know you will likely not honor it. At some point soon, however, I expect that you will brief me on your plans for the contest."

"Yes, Mr. Tippett. I won't disappoint you."

"I know you won't. To be disappointed, you see, one must have expectations."

〰

"Does your shirt say 'Rat Queens' on it? Is that like a band or something?"

Bisma looked up from whatever she was working on— she had a bad habit of actually doing her homework—and shook her head at me, as if I'd said something super disappointing. "You're a philistine, Danyal Jilani."

"I'm American, actually."

She smiled one of her half smiles that were becoming familiar. "*Rat Queens* is a comic," she said, "and it's only the best thing since sliced bread."

I don't know why people say that. You know what's better than sliced bread? A loaf. Bread that comes presliced for you is generally always inferior to bread you have to slice yourself. The world is full of weird expressions . . . and weird comics, apparently.

"What's their superpower?" I asked.

"Not every comic book character has superpowers."

"Seriously?"

Bisma nodded.

"Then what's even the point?"

"Well . . . it's about this team of women who have adventures in a fantasy world. There's a dwarf, Violet, who shaves her beard against the traditions of her people, and then there's an elf, Hannah—"

"Really? The elf is called Hannah?"

Bisma narrowed her eyes at my remark, and I couldn't help but smile. "Aren't you supposed to be reading up on Churchill?"

"I am." It wasn't exactly a lie. I was skimming. Lightly. There was a ton of information out there about Churchill and most of it was *dull*. I didn't care about how he and his wife had separate bedrooms, or how he ran his house or whatever. It wasn't even history, if you asked me. It was just stuff that happened. There's a difference, or at least, there should be.

Bisma went back to her other assignment. I flipped through a couple of pages, then looked up around half a minute later, totally bored.

When Zar had learned Bisma was helping me, he'd asked what she was like. I hadn't really been able to tell him. She was so . . . average, and yet, I don't know, there was something about her that made me feel like she was kind of spectacular at the same time.

There is a time in every desi boy's life, if he's growing up in a traditional, arranged marriage type family anyway, when his parents ask him what is absolutely, without doubt, the most awkward question in the world: "What kind of girl do you want?"

I definitely hadn't described Bisma Akram in answer to that question.

When my parents had first asked around a year ago, I'd just described Kaval. My mother had rolled her eyes. My father had taken notes, which seemed weird, but maybe he didn't want to forget what I'd said. First time that had happened, I was pretty sure.

Kaval was easy to describe. She was consistent. She and her friends pretty much always looked the same, like they got up every morning and a super advanced machine helped them put their perfect faces on. I'd only seen Kaval without makeup once in the last forever.

Bisma was random. I never knew what she'd look like when I showed up at the library to meet her. Some days she wore makeup, but sometimes she didn't. She wore contacts when she felt like it, and when she didn't, she wore her rectangular nerd glasses. There were days her hair was up, and days her hair was down. The days she dressed nice weren't about anyone but herself, and the days she looked like a bit of a slob weren't about anyone but herself either. She was very . . . self-contained.

194

My point is, no one tells their parents they're looking for a self-contained girl, and even if someone did, his parents would have no idea what their kid was talking about.

After a while, Bisma sighed, put her pen down, and looked up at me. "What?"

"This book is *so* boring."

"And looking at me is not boring?"

"It really isn't."

There was that little hint of a smile again. "You're an idiot."

"A lot of people say that."

She frowned. "I didn't mean it the way they probably meant it."

"I know. Come on. Let's get out of here and do something."

"Like what?" Bisma asked, almost cautiously.

"I don't know. What do you do for fun?"

Bisma held her arms out to her sides, like she was embracing the whole library. I rolled my eyes and reached for my backpack. "That's sad."

"It's okay to be a little sad," she said. There was no smile this time. It almost sounded defensive.

"Yeah...but that's more than a little sad. You like Zareen's, right? Let's go there."

"Who's Zareen?"

"*Dude.* It's just a Michelin Guide Pakistani restaurant right here in the Bay. How do you not know it?"

"Michelin? Like the car tires from the commercials?"

I stared at her, too stunned to speak.

It must have been some look, because Bisma started to laugh, which drew irritated stares from the other people in the library, who'd already moved away from us because we hadn't exactly been silent till now. "We've got nothing in common, do we?"

"I can think of one thing."

"What's that?"

"We're both going to Zareen's."

Bisma looked around the small restaurant, eyes bright. It was a little depressing actually, because these few moments when her guard was down made me realize that this girl was living in a constant eclipse.

"This place is awesome," she whispered as we stood in line.

A strange thing to say about a restaurant before you've even tried their food, but she was talking about the decor. Zareen's had been decorated by someone who loved books. They dangled from the ceiling from tiny ropes, and there was a shelf where I think you could take a book if you left a book. The walls, a burnt-orange color, had comments from customers handwritten all over them with dark pens and markers.

"It's like you and I came together and became one." She turned a little pink when I raised my eyebrows, then bumped my arm with her elbow. "With the books and the food and everything, not..."

She seemed so ridiculously embarrassed, I had to let it go, though it would've been a perfect moment for me to show off my world-class funnies. "Do you know what you're getting?" I asked instead.

"You can order for me. I trust you."

I whistled. "I don't even trust my mom that much."

"I'm a sweet girl."

"I know you are."

"Stop it." Bisma grinned. "I meant I'm a sweets girl. I like desserts."

"Your favorite?" I asked.

"Anything chocolate." She nodded toward the cashier. "They're ready for us."

Zareen's serves the closest thing you'll get to Karachi street food in the Bay Area, so they have some really awesome menu items, but there is nothing they do better, in my opinion, than *gola kababs*. I ordered two plates of those, along with *sheermal*, which is kind of like a naan, but the slightest bit sweet, with a kiss of saffron. The soft but crusty ghee-infused bread went perfectly with the velvety beef of the *kababs*. It was really something.

I ate while Bisma told me more about *Rat Queens* and some other comic book called *Saga*. Then she started in on superheroines.

I'd never really appreciated how many superheroines

there were until then. Everyone knows the major ones, obviously. Wonder Woman and Black Widow and Batgirl. But there was also a girl called Violet Parr, who Bisma was especially fond of, and another called X-23, and so on.

It dawned on me that there were entire worlds Bisma knew about that were foreign to me, and she obviously liked to talk about them. So I listened without interrupting, except to ask a question or two, because I liked her voice, and I liked how much she enjoyed the topic.

"Sorry," she said eventually. "I know you don't care about that stuff. I just—"

"It's cool," I said. "Not every conversation can be about food, right?"

"I guess not. But you were right. The *kababs* were really good."

It was an understatement, but not enough of one to call her on. "Better than your Arab food place?"

"Yes." She laughed. "Less poetic, though."

We went to Tin Pot for dessert. On the short drive over to the creamery, Bisma fiddled around with the radio, found nothing that she wanted to hear, and shut it off. Then after looking at me for a while like I was a math problem she was trying to figure out, she said, "You never told me why."

"Why what?"

"Why speaking up about the Bengal Famine is so important to you."

I shrugged. Truth be told, it was more than important to me. It haunted me. But I hadn't figured out why, which felt weird. People should know themselves. If I couldn't understand me, then who could?

My first thought was to come up with some way to dodge her question, except there was something about Bisma that made me think she'd like it if I were honest about how I felt. And I wanted her to like me. Her regard felt like it was something worth earning.

"I don't know," I said. "Maybe it was the pictures I saw. I can't get them out of my head."

Bisma nodded, but she didn't seem satisfied with the answer.

"It doesn't bother you?" I asked.

"Of course it does," she said. "But, honestly, I've seen the pictures too, and I don't think I would risk failing a class just to give a speech about them. It almost seems... personal to you somehow."

"It is. Somehow. Did I tell you that my grandfather fought for independence from the Raj? That could be it."

I drove in silence for a while. Then Bisma said, "Maybe. Or maybe it's the food."

"What?"

"Those people who died, they were denied food. I think, maybe, that's why you can't... Maybe that's why it's touched you so much. You love food more than anyone I know."

I felt a light bulb flicker and then, reluctantly, go off in my brain. What had Brodeur said when I'd told her about the famine?

Good. Maybe you'll be a chef after all.

I shook my head. Why couldn't she have just said it like Bisma? Maybe she'd wanted me to figure it out myself, but that never would've happened. I have zero curiosity about what goes on in my own brain. It was kind of awesome that Bisma got me, though.

"You don't think so?"

"No, I think you're right," I said. "When you understand what food is, the idea of shipping it away from hungry people... it's monstrous. Food is a miracle. It is life. I mean like... *literally*, you know? And one of the guys responsible for it all gets to be a hero? It isn't right. And I've got to do a good job explaining why to everyone."

"You will," Bisma said. "I promise."

《〈

A croissant looks like it's easy to make, but it isn't. Making one perfectly requires a lot of patience and skill. It's worth it, though. When it's just right, its delicate, crunchy outer shell collapses effortlessly into smooth, flaky layers of divine deliciousness.

I love croissants. Unfortunately, I'm not all that great at baking them.

This isn't entirely my fault. Chef Brodeur is partly to blame.

Remarquable isn't a patisserie, so we don't usually have croissants on the menu. Every once in a while, however, Brodeur will reluctantly use them to make sandwiches for lunch specials, while complaining bitterly about having to cater to American tastes.

No one else who works here seems to have a problem with their croissants, but I'm sure that is only because they get to use a machine, while I have to make them entirely by hand. It is, I've been told more than once, critical for my development.

Making a croissant takes three days, which is why some people say that croissants aren't made; they are grown.

You begin with a poolish, which ferments and bubbles nicely. Then you make the dough, let it rest, and add a large slab of butter. After that you have to stretch the dough out really far to get layers. That's where my troubles start.

We have a sheeter that everyone else uses but I'm not allowed to touch. I have to use a rolling pin. That gets painful. I complained once, a while back, and Brodeur responded by keeping the sandwiches on as specials for a month. By the end of it, my hands were *bruised*.

I'd finished with the rolling pin yesterday, so that part of the process was over. Today, I cut the delicate dough into triangles and began to shape it with my fingertips. The process felt familiar and repetitive, which was a good sign.

My mind drifted to Sohrab, because I always thought about Sohrab when I was making croissants. He'd suggested once that it wasn't proper for Muslims to eat them

201

because, apparently, some seventeenth-century Polish baker had created their crescent shape to celebrate a Christian victory over Islam.

As I put the croissants—which I was definitely going to keep eating no matter what Sohrab thought—in the proofer, I literally crossed my fingers. I was going to get it right this time. I was. It had to happen eventually, right?

The saucier saw the gesture and chuckled, patting me on the back as he went by. I smiled. One reason I loved being in a professional kitchen was that you were surrounded by people who understood food was important to you because it was important to them. No one else ever seemed to get that.

Except for Bisma Akram, I guess. She'd figured out that the Bengal Famine mattered to me because of my connection with food, which was amazing. She'd understood something about me that I hadn't understood about myself.

Best of all, she believed I could do well in Renaissance Man and take on Churchill at the same time. I couldn't remember the last time someone had believed that I could succeed, in the contest or in life, by doing what I wanted to do.

Once the first batch of croissants was ready, I brushed on egg wash and baked them. For all the slow, careful steps that it took to get to this stage, the end was fast. You had to bake croissants at high heat or they didn't rise.

The kitchen was flooded with a warm, buttery smell

when Chef Brodeur came by. She looked at my work, which was exactly the right shade of golden brown. When she picked one up and broke it open, it shattered, steam escaped, and the insides looked beautifully delicate and soft.

Brodeur gave an appreciative nod, then took a small bite. "*Bien*," she said a moment later.

I waited for the hammer to drop. "But?"

"But nothing. It is well done."

I grinned, trying really hard not to pinch myself or break into a victory dance in front of Chef.

I'd done it. *I'd done it!* I'd . . . done it?

"Really?"

The woman who was both my mentor and tormentor seemed irritated by my surprise. "I do not have time to stand here and reassure you of your own competence. I notice, however, that today you did not grumble as you usually do when making these. That is probably why they turned out well. You know, of course, what the most important ingredient in French food is, yes?"

"Butter?" I ventured.

Brodeur sighed. "No, Danyal. It is but a touch of love, and it makes all the difference."

The last few weeks had convinced me that asking Bisma to help with Renaissance Man was one of the best decisions

I'd ever made. Yes, I was losing out on time with Kaval, but she'd said she wouldn't help me if I decided to write about the Bengal Famine, so studying up on Churchill and the Raj with her wasn't an option.

I'd asked everyone I knew for help with schoolwork before. Well, everyone except for my dad. He'd volunteered. But his attempts to teach me usually ended up with him yelling. Mom was way nicer, of course, but she mostly just patted my head and told me not to worry about the answers I was getting wrong. When you're getting almost everything wrong, that is more aggravating than reassuring.

Sohrab always ended up going on about how memorizing the Quran improved one's memory and I should do more of that. Zar just handed me a controller so that we could play one game before hitting the books, which we never ended up doing. He was my favorite, and least effective, study buddy.

Bisma was different. No one had just let me talk like she did. They tried to discipline me or soothe me or teach me or distract me. But maybe I just needed to be frustrated for a while. Maybe I needed someone to see how difficult it was for me to do stuff that seemed so much easier for other students.

Bisma never tried to fix me. She didn't even interrupt when I started to vent. She just let me complain until I asked her, "So what do you think I should do?"

That was when she'd say something like "Let's come back to it later, Danyal," or "You just need some distance."

A lot of the time she was right. If I went back to an argument after a day or two days, I could see its flaws more clearly. Connections that I'd missed became apparent. Sentences I'd written that had looked perfect suddenly sounded awkward. Even typos became easier to spot. It was amazing.

"You're doing that thing where you just sit there and look at me again," Bisma said.

"Sorry. I was just thinking about..."

She waited for me to figure out how to explain myself.

"Don't worry about it," I said. "It's going to sound weird if I say it out loud."

"I like weird."

I tried to find the right words. "It's just...I like hanging out with you. It's like you know I'm stupid, but you're cool with it, and that makes me feel less stupid."

Bisma frowned. She didn't like it when I called myself dumb. It wasn't allowed in our study sessions.

Before she could scold me, I went on. "I feel good about myself when I'm around you. Whatever. Like I said, it's weird. Can I go back to reading now?"

"Now, there's a sentence you don't hear Danyal Jilani say every day."

I felt my face do that thing it did around her, where it got all warm. I decided to pretend that the last two awkward minutes had never happened and went back to my research.

After a moment, Bisma said, "Hey, Danyal?"

Oh God. How was this conversation not over? I mean, I'd totally embarrassed myself as much as possible already, right?

"Yeah?"

"I like hanging out with you too."

CHAPTER FOURTEEN

At our next study session, Bisma looked up from whatever she was working on, obviously surprised by the question I'd asked her. I guess "Have you ever been in love?" isn't the kind of thing you expect to be asked in a library.

"What? Where'd that come from?"

"I was just thinking about this friend of mine—Intezar—who won't shut up about this girl he likes. That's why I was almost late today. He says it's love. I think it's spring fever. That's a thing, right? It's hard to tell the difference."

"Maybe you should stop trying to tell the difference and think about Churchill instead."

"Not an answer to my question."

Bisma sighed. "No. I haven't." Then she paused, and I

was sure she was going to tell me to focus on the project, but instead she said, "What about you?"

I shook my head. "I don't think so. I mean, you know, I've been in *like* with people, like that girl I told you about...but nothing like in the movies. I mean, if you're going to be in love, it has to be epic, right? Like the girl's hair starts blowing in slow motion and lightning strikes from the sky. I haven't ever felt that."

Bisma laughed. "I don't know about all that, but...I think it'll happen for you. I'm sure of it. You'd be easy for a girl to fall in love with."

What did that mean? "Well...thank you. I should start working, I guess?"

"Sure," Bisma said. She didn't move, though. Instead she looked at me like...I don't know, really. My mom watches this show where people bring their super old stuff to get priced, to see if it is worth something. Sometimes the things they bring are worthless; sometimes they're really valuable. The way the hosts on that show looked at the antiques was the way Bisma was looking at me then. "Can I ask you something?" she asked hesitantly.

"Sure."

"Suri told me..." She glanced away and then leaned forward. She whispered so softly that I had to lean forward too, until our noses were almost touching across the library table. I could see my reflection in her light brown eyes. "Suri told me she stole...the tape and gave you another chance to take it."

"She said if I married—"

"I know. She's an idiot. What I'm saying is that you could've taken the drive from her and never followed through on the second part. Most guys, I think, would have. Why didn't you?"

I didn't think she was right about that. In fact, I didn't know anyone who'd behave that way.

"I'd never do something like that to you. Or anyone."

Her eyes were bright, shining at me, and she shook her head a little. Her light brown hair grazed my cheek.

"What is it?" I asked.

"Nothing. It's just . . . you're brilliant."

I had to laugh at that, library rules or no library rules. "No one I know has ever said that about me."

"Well," Bisma said, "I think they've all been wrong."

I was about to sit back down, but she leaned farther forward suddenly and kissed me on the cheek. I stared at her, and she blushed furiously, cleared her throat, and said, "So, like you were saying, back to work."

"What?"

Bisma grinned. "Back to work, I said."

"Right. Sure. Yes. That . . . is why we're here."

I stared at the book in front of me without reading it. It seemed like Bisma was doing the same, but I couldn't be sure.

After a few minutes, she said, "By the way, I was talking to Maddy—Professor Madeline Okpara—and your name came up."

"It did?"

"I told her about Renaissance Man and what you're working on. She thinks it's super interesting. She'd like to talk to you."

"A history professor?"

Bisma shook her head. "Psychology."

"That's random."

"She'll give you stuff you can use. Trust me. And I found a place for us to meet her that you're going to love."

"It's another library, isn't it?"

She just smiled at me. "Are you interested?"

"Yes," I said. "Absolutely."

We met Dr. Madeline Okpara the next day at The Cheese Board, which is a perfect little spot in Berkeley. It is a cheese shop and bakery, but they're known for their pizza. There is a set menu, so you can't pick your toppings, but the crust is beautifully thin, the vegetables always fresh, and the hot green sauce they drizzle over the pies tastes like Jesus made it.

It's a cilantro base with, and I'm pretty sure I'm right about this, serrano and jalapeño peppers to bring some heat. There's a little garlic kick, and some lime to cut everything, and . . .

Bisma elbowed me, and I snapped to attention to see Maddy—that's what she wanted to be called—smiling at me.

"Sorry," I said, realizing that I'd been crushing on my lunch so hard that I'd missed what the professor was saying.

"Not at all. It is always nice to see young people passionate enough about something to be transported by it. Bisma tells me you're a chef?"

"I work in a kitchen around chefs. I'm still learning."

She nodded. "Well, I think it's wonderful. Anyway, as I was saying, I'm really interested in how technology impacts the human psyche, and I think history is a particularly interesting field where that is happening."

I glanced at Bisma, to see if she knew what her professor was talking about, and she said, "Social media."

"I assume you are familiar with the maxim that history is written by the winners?"

"Sure," I said.

Maddy paused to take a sip of water. "There is a corollary to that maxim, or at least there should be. The present, you see, is also written by the winners. When the Romans sacked Carthage, the Roman populace was insulated from Carthaginian voices. This has been the case for most of human history."

"You don't even have to go back that far," Bisma said, as if I had any idea how far back the professor was reaching to pull Carthage, whatever that was, out of her hat. "Even Desert Storm happened in a very different world than we live in now."

"This is true," Dr. Okpara agreed. "The communal

psyche of the conqueror has never before been persistently challenged by the narratives of the conquered in real time. It is an entirely new phenomena in human history, made possible, of course, by the Internet."

"Okay," I said, and took a deep breath. Bisma was always telling me it was okay to take my time before responding to a question or an idea, instead of rushing to say whatever seemed right. Time, she said, brought clarity, or at least the possibility of it. "So nowadays people who are wronged can actually speak up while they're being harmed, which is different than how things were before. This makes it harder for governments oppressing other people to sell that oppression to their own population?"

Bisma gave me an encouraging nod.

"That's cool and everything, but I'm not sure what it has to do with Churchill."

"It doesn't have anything to do with him," Maddy said with a shrug. "It does, however, have something to do with your project. You see, colonialism wasn't sold to the British populace as an enterprise of conquest. It was sold to them as a moral enterprise by which they were 'civilizing' the world and stewarding races who couldn't take care of themselves. Improving them. Trying to get them to live the kinds of lives that the British approved of."

"As Conrad points out in *Heart of Darkness*," Bisma told me.

That sounded like a heavy metal band. Maybe Conrad

was the lead singer or something. "Right. Conrad. Darkness. Totally got it."

"Anyway," the professor went on, "that kind of fiction is a lot harder to perpetuate now for any significant period of time. The truth is more difficult to suppress, in this age of lies, than it has ever been."

"Like the claim that Iraq had weapons of mass destruction in the second war there," Bisma supplied. "That came apart fast."

"Not fast enough," I said.

"In terms of history," Bisma insisted, "it happened very quickly. There isn't going to be any book written that will say those weapons existed."

"She's right," Maddy said. "You see, the way the history of our time is written will be different than the way history has ever been written before. The narrative and the counter-narrative will have to learn to exist at the same time. It is remarkable, if you think about it."

I frowned, trying to figure out how Bisma thought this would help me with Renaissance Man. I'd thankfully never come close to drowning before, but I imagined this is what it felt like. I was surrounded by information and it was getting a little difficult for my brain to breathe. Still, I tried.

Having awesome pizza helped. It was something real, tangible, and delicious that I understood completely.

"So," I said after I was done with my next bite, "what

you're saying is that the British were able to let the Indians starve because they didn't see things, didn't see the Indians even, from the Indian point of view?"

"Precisely." Dr. Okpara wiped her hands on a napkin, having finished her slice. "In order to justify oppression of the Other, one has to believe, and has to get all participants in that oppression to believe, that the Other is somehow fundamentally different. Do you think that the people who put my ancestors on boats and ripped them away from Africa believed that black men and women were just as human as they were?"

"No," I said, "they thought they were better than the Africans."

"And the British thought they were better than the Indians," the professor said. "I believe future history will be different, though, because these narratives of superiority will be challenged by narratives of equality. The way we remember the world as it is will be entirely new."

"That sounds wonderful, Dr. Okpara—sorry, Maddy," I said, "but what about right now? I mean, racism is still a problem, even when everyone has a voice. People still aren't equal. Why is that?"

"An excellent question. I would suggest to you that what is happening now is not the purview of historians." She glanced at Bisma and smiled. "It is, rather, the domain of renaissance women. And, one supposes, all other genders as well."

I didn't say anything for a while, thinking about what the professor had said. There was something important here. I just had to figure it out.

Maddy smiled at Bisma. "Always a delight to see a mind at work."

"Sorry," I said.

"Not at all. I was being perfectly sincere."

"Thank you, Professor. It was super nice of you to speak to me."

"It was fun. Besides, Bisma is an excellent student. I always make time for those when I come across them."

"Still," I insisted. "Thank you so much."

"My pleasure, Danyal." Then, turning to Bisma, she said, "I can see why you like him."

"I swear to God," Bisma said as we walked away from The Cheese Board, "I didn't tell her that I liked you. Obviously. She just assumed."

"So you're saying you don't like me? That's a kick in the nuts."

Bisma, who'd just stopped blushing, started going a little pink again. "No. I mean, yes. I just . . . you know, entirely platonically—"

"Bisma?"

"Yes?"

"I'm messing with you."

She exhaled.

"Thank you for setting that up."

"Not a problem. So what did you think?"

"She's awesome."

"But was it any help for the contest?" Bisma asked. "The question she raises is interesting enough to be your thesis."

"What question?"

"Would Churchill, or the British, have acted differently if Indians had a voice and could have forced the British to see them as their equals, with lives that had the same value as their own?"

I scratched the back of my head. It sounded good. I didn't think Tippett would go for it, though. He'd say the same thing that I'd said to Dr. Okpara. If white supremacy exists in our world, where everyone can potentially find their voice, then why would it have been any different for Churchill or the Britishers who set up the empire before him?

"It's not enough to have a voice so you can speak up for yourself," I said. "You need something more."

"Like what?"

I shrugged. "I don't know. What I do know is that Tippett will expect me to figure it out."

Bisma's hand brushed mine, like it had when we'd gone out together for the first time, but she didn't pull away like she had then. I have to admit that I stopped thinking about Renaissance Man for a second.

She didn't. "Well, at least we know to make the canvas

bigger now, right? You can talk about . . . You've stopped listening to me, haven't you?"

"Yes," I said. "Sorry."

"And what shiny object caught your attention this time?"

"You."

"Oh." We walked in silence for a while, then she said, "What about me?"

"I just realized, you know, you're helping me a lot, and there really isn't any reason for you to. And I was just thinking I never said thank you. So—"

"It's okay. This is what I do for fun."

"Hang out at the library with dudes you've turned down for arranged marriage?"

She laughed. "Whatever. I didn't turn you down. You turned me down."

"I never turned you down."

Bisma raised her eyebrows at me.

"I mean, okay, so I did. If I hadn't, my mom was going to start making inquiries. I didn't think you'd want her digging around in your past."

She started to nod, then she shook her head.

"What?" I asked.

"I don't know. I think my life would've been a lot different if I'd met you—someone like you, I mean—earlier. I think I could've been happy."

"There's still time to be happy, Bisma."

"No," she said softly. "I'm not sure there is."

217

Sohrab texted to remind me that I'd promised to attend a lecture at the mosque by a big-time speaker. Honestly, I couldn't remember making such a promise, but he insisted I'd done so earlier in the semester. His word was good enough for me.

I never did catch the name of Sohrab's famous speaker, but that was because I arrived late. It wasn't entirely my fault. I just went to the wrong mosque. When I finally got to the right place, finding parking was a pain. The lot was packed.

There is a cult of personality that builds up around Muslim preachers. They're a lot like rock stars, with huge numbers of YouTube followers, lectures that sell out auditoriums, and devoted fans who dote on their every word. This guy, whoever he was, was apparently no different.

I tried to find Sohrab, but it was impossible. Eventually, I gave up and just decided to sit in the back.

The speaker was a slender, charismatic man, probably just over forty, with a habit of making dad jokes that, somehow, everyone around me seemed to find hilarious. He was articulate and engaging, and even though I didn't really want to be here that much, I found myself actually paying attention. At least for around ten minutes, which I'm pretty sure is a personal record for me.

He was speaking about something called *qalb-e-saleem*, which can be translated in a few different ways: "A Sound

Heart." "An Unstained, Pure Heart." "An Undamaged Heart." It was a spiritual state that Muslims were supposed to aspire to, because on the Day of Judgment, according to the Quran, nothing would save people except for having a heart like that.

The rest of the lecture was a discussion about the practical applications that led to such a spiritual state, and I admit I zoned out, until the call to prayer was given, and the congregation rose to answer it.

Afterward, I found Sohrab leaning against a wall in the mosque's courtyard, staring up at the night sky. The moon was dying and hoping to be reborn at the same time.

"How's it going?"

Sohrab seemed to think about it for a moment, then let out a shaky sigh. "I don't know. It is frightening to think that Allah will look at our hearts one day and know the darkness within. The things we did. The things we failed to do. We'll be able to hide nothing from Him when the Final Judgment comes."

"Well," I said, "He's like . . . All-Knowing, right? So it isn't like we're hiding anything from Him now."

Sohrab looked at me out of the corner of his eye, then began to laugh. It echoed around the emptying mosque and became a horrible sound as it folded upon itself, carrying on after he had fallen silent. "It's amazing how simple wisdom can be, isn't it?"

I frowned, unsure if I'd just been insulted. "I guess."

"It'll be different, I think, to stand in front of the

Creator, and to have Him ask you why your heart wasn't pure, why you fell into sin. Don't you agree?"

"I don't really think about that stuff."

"What do you think about?"

"Food. Girls. Music."

He shook his head. "All of those are dangerous."

"And God created them all."

Sohrab didn't take it as a joke. "As a test, you know, not as a diversion."

"I've never been very good at tests," I said, and then attempted to change the topic. "Hey, I've been meaning to ask you, was it true what you said in English that time? About getting the fragment of a bomb that had gone off for your sixteenth birthday?"

"Of course. I never lie. Remember when we went to Pakistan a couple of years ago?"

A whole summer without any Kaval Sabsvari sightings. Hell yeah, I remembered. It had been brutal, and not as hot as usual.

"Anyway, my mother's father lives in Afghanistan. Kaval didn't get to go, but I went north to visit him. When I had a birthday, my cousins gave me a piece of a spent bomb. Every boy there gets one when he turns sixteen."

"That's weird."

Sohrab let out a sigh. "It's a joke. When there is a drone strike, and the Americans end up killing a bunch of people along with the person they were actually aiming for, they just say any boy or man of fighting age that died was an enemy. That way when dead civilians are counted, the numbers look better."

"Really?" I asked. "Why would we do that?"

"Because Americans care about perception more than they care about the truth."

"That's not true."

"No? Have you heard of Khataba?"

I shook my head.

"It's a village near where my grandfather lives. American soldiers thought that a party celebrating the birth of a newborn baby was a terrorist gathering or something. They stormed it. Killed five people, two of them pregnant women, one a teenage girl. So what did they do? The soldiers took knives and dug the bullets out of the women. They said that the men they killed were bad men. That the women had already been tied up and dead when the Americans got there. They tried to make their own victims seem like monsters. Do you know why?"

"No," I admitted softly.

"Because they only care about what things look like, not what things really are. They tell stories that make them look noble and innocent, because if those are the only stories people hear, then those are the stories they will believe."

I stood beside him for a while, staring at the deepening night. Then I said, "We. Us."

"What?"

"You kept saying 'they' when you were talking about

Americans. We're American too, you know. It isn't 'they' and 'them.' It's 'we' and 'us.' "

Sohrab nodded and placed a hand over his heart, his tired eyes fixed again upon the unlit heavens above.

〜

I groaned as I got into my van and turned the ignition. How did Sohrab get through life with a head so full of heavy thoughts all the time? I didn't want that much truth in my life. I just wanted to be happy, and people who know a lot of stuff can't be happy. That's why they say ignorance is bliss. It's in the Bible.

No, seriously, what tree was it that Adam and Eve were forbidden to eat from? That's right, the tree of knowledge. I'm just saying, that's worth thinking about. Just, you know, not too much.

The problem with thoughts, though, is that they're contagious, and even though I didn't want them, I'd caught them from Sohrab. It'd be a while before I was cured again.

So I sat there, brooding on my way home, trying to figure out how to help Sohrab, because my friend did need help. Unlike Zar, I didn't think that his being religious was, by itself, an issue. The real problem was that religion was the only thing Sohrab ever seemed to think about anymore, and nothing anyone said that wasn't connected to Islam seemed to get through to him.

Some people, even if their beliefs were outdated or

imbalanced or just wrong, seemed to be unable to appreciate the validity of other experiences.

I could tell my dad over and over that it was okay to be a chef.

I could tell Kaval that going to college to get a high-paying job wasn't the only way for a man to be worthy of her.

Bisma could tell all her marriage prospects that her past didn't define who she was.

None of it would matter because the people we were trying to convince could only hear one story, which seemed perfect to them.

That's why it wouldn't have mattered to Churchill if the Indians had possessed a voice. That's why it didn't matter to racists today, to bigots today, that there were black and Muslim and queer and other oppressed voices. They just embraced the narrative they'd always embraced. The existence of other narratives didn't change anything.

The evil that let three million people starve in the Bengal Famine wasn't that different from the evil that was with us still. It was the same evil that had led those soldiers to lie about the people they had murdered in Khataba. That evil was the inability to recognize the humanity in experiences that were not your own, in experiences that seemed alien.

So, in a way, Kaval had been right. She'd asked me why it mattered what Churchill had done almost a century ago.

By itself, it didn't. Whether Churchill was a hero or a monster was not a problem we really needed to face.

The problem we had to face was that the story that allowed Churchill to be monstrous—the colonial mind-set, the mind-set of supremacy based on race and nationality—was still alive.

This was not about Churchill the man. This was about Churchill the legacy.

Parked in the driveway of my parents' house, I called Bisma to tell her that I had a thesis.

CHAPTER FIFTEEN

Now that I'd figured out what I was going to say in Renaissance Man, I made an appointment with Tippett to see if he was cool with it. I mean, I was going to say what I wanted anyway, because it was too important not to say, but I wanted to know if it meant I was going to fail history again.

He'd asked me to come by early, so I was standing outside his classroom half an hour before his lecture usually started. But now he appeared to be running late.

"Hi."

I looked up from my phone, surprised, to see that Kaval had stopped in front of me.

We hadn't spoken since our argument outside the cafeteria almost a month ago. We'd seen each other in classes, of course, but I hadn't had anything to say to her, and I guess she'd felt the same way.

"Hey."

"This doesn't count," she said.

I frowned. "What?"

"This conversation. I don't want you to think it means we're cool."

"Um...okay."

"All I'm saying is that if you finally decide to get serious about Renaissance Man and come to me for help, we'll talk about our deal then."

I was tempted to tell her about all the work I was putting in with Bisma, but that would just confirm for Kaval that I wasn't going to fawn over Churchill in my essay or speech like she wanted. If she was upset now, that would probably make things worse.

Besides, it seemed like she had something else she wanted to talk about. Best to just focus on that. "Everything okay?"

"I'm worried about my brother."

I stood up straight and slid my phone in my pocket. "What happened?"

"Relax," Kaval said. "Sohrab is fine. I mean...you know, he's not fine, but he isn't hurt or anything. We talked about this before, about how he's getting super strict about religion. I know he cares about that stuff, but—"

"It's all he talks about now."

"Right. And, you know, when he isn't up late at night

reading or praying, he's either listening to the news or he's at the mosque. Yesterday, at dinner, he gave Mom and me a lecture about how we should be wearing hijab. I swear to God, if he doesn't stop, he's going to get hurt."

"Like fall asleep while driving because he's so tired or something?"

"What? No. I mean I'm going to fucking murder him in his sleep."

"Fair," I said.

"He said you guys are coming over soon to watch a movie. Something about making peace with Zar?"

"I hadn't heard."

"Well . . . whatever. Will you talk to him? Please."

"Look, I'm worried about him too. He's been kind of extra lately. But why me? You could talk to him yourself. Or have your parents talk to him."

"We've tried."

"Then what makes you think he'll listen to me?"

"It's worth a shot."

"Yeah. I guess it is."

Kaval nodded like someone saying the conversation was over, and she was leaving now, except she didn't leave. She just stood there, like she was waiting for me to say something.

Finally, she broke the silence herself. "You're really not going to apologize?"

"For what?"

Her eyes got wide. "You know what? Forget it. Just so

you know, though, the cardiologist we talked about is coming by to see me again soon, and if you don't—"

"I do hope you're feeling well, Ms. Sabsvari. I had no idea your heart was in distress." Kaval and I turned around to see Tippett walking toward us.

"Hi, Mr. Tippett," Kaval chirped, suddenly brighter than a full moon. I just waved at him half-heartedly as she continued. "It's not like that. It's just...a personal thing."

Our history teacher glanced at me, very briefly, before shuffling past us and fumbling with his keys as he tried to open the door to his classroom. "All matters of the heart, in my experience, are personal, Ms. Sabsvari. Now, if you will please excuse us, I have an appointment with Mr. Jilani and am looking forward, therefore, to being absolutely dazzled by his brilliance."

Kaval and I looked at each other for a moment, then she whirled and marched off. I turned to follow Tippett. "Are you really expecting to be dazzled by my brilliance?"

"Of course not," he snapped, making his way to his chair. "It was sarcasm. You have heard of sarcasm, have you not?"

"No. What is it?"

His sharp green eyes looked up at me with surprise, and I grinned.

"Very amusing. Now, can we please get to the business at hand?"

He reached into his desk drawer, and pulled out the thesis proposal I'd submitted. I held my breath a little. I really didn't want to have to explain to my parents that I was going to fail again, almost on purpose this time.

Tippett held the papers out to me, and I took them. Even as I did, I could see that there was a lot less red on the first page than I was used to. I exhaled. I'd have to remember to thank Bisma.

"Astonishingly, this is not a complete disaster."

"Really? Thank you. I was a little worried you wouldn't like me criticizing Churchill's handling of the Bengal Famine. I know you like him, and everyone says revisionist history is uncool—"

"Anyone who knows anything about history"—Tippett paused significantly before continuing—"and anyone who has been paying attention in my class, knows that all history is revisionist. First in time is not first in truth."

I nodded. I was a little taken aback, but what he'd said made sense.

"As for Churchill, I continue to admire him, but I think we should tell the truth about our heroes, don't you?"

"I do."

"There are no flawless people, Mr. Jilani, and to perpetuate myths to the contrary is not history or biography, but rather hagiography, which may be useful for nation building, but that does not hold my interest."

"Right," I said, having absolutely no idea what he meant. "Totally. It's not interesting."

Tippett looked at me with some suspicion. I think he figured I didn't entirely get his meaning, but he moved on.

"Using Churchill as a jumping-off point to discuss broader themes is a good idea. That is what the Renaissance Man is all about, after all."

I blinked. "Really?"

"Why else would we name it that? You are to use one subject to show mastery in all subjects. I do believe that Ms. Smith is going to use geography to discuss climate change and the politics that comes with it." Tippett gave me a wintry smile. "But you knew that, of course, having looked into what your competition is working on."

"Uh... yeah. I did that. Obviously."

Except, of course, I hadn't done that. Trying to figure out what other contestants were up to hadn't even occurred to me.

Then again, what did it matter what anyone else was doing? As long as I did my own project as well as I could, I wouldn't get laughed off the stage. Probably.

"This is still a significant academic risk," Tippett warned. "I decide whether you pass my course, not judges in a talent show. And, you realize, that I like colonialism."

I frowned. "You do?"

"Not colonialism, precisely, but yes, I think it resulted in a great deal of good for the world. We would not have this great country if it weren't for colonialism. Eventually, of course, we threw off the shackles of the Empire and claimed our independence. For a former colony, I would say we did very well for ourselves."

"How did the Native Americans do?"

Mr. Tippett's eyes widened. Mine did too. That was an unusually quick and sharp answer for me. Maybe I'd been spending too much time around Bisma.

"Mr. Jilani," Tippett finally said, his hand going to the flag pin he always wore on his lapel, as if to shield it from my question. "As an educator, it is generally my policy to encourage the intellectual development of young minds. I must advise you, however, that you are exquisitely annoying just the way you are. Develop a wit, young man, and you'll be perfectly insufferable."

〰️

I got to the library super early to catch Bisma before she settled in. I couldn't wait to tell her what had happened with Tippett. I was practically bouncing. She smiled when she saw me, and I grinned back. She had the kind of smile you had to respond to, a smile that proved Newton's third law of motion. For every action, there is an equal and opposite—well, okay, the opposite of a smile wouldn't really be a smile, so that doesn't work. Applied sciences aren't my thing.

"How did it go with your teacher?" Bisma asked.

"Awesome," I said. "He called me perfectly insufferable."

"That's...good?"

"It is only the nicest thing any teacher has ever said

about me," I told her. "Let's skip the library today. We should go celebrate."

Bisma laughed. "Okay, where do you want to go?"

"Where I want to go," I said, "is to Sam's in Davis, where you will find the best shawarma plate in California—"

"We don't have time to go to Davis."

"I was getting to that. Since we can't go there, let's get something fun here. I know this place that sells cotton candy."

The look on her face was proof that she thought Mr. Tippett's faint praise had made me a little crazy. "Seriously?"

"You don't like cotton candy?"

"I don't know. I used to. I just haven't had it in a long time."

"Think about it for a second. Remember all that soft, fluffy sugar. Remember when you got your hands on some when you were a kid. How did it make you feel?"

"Just . . . happy, I guess. But, Danyal, just because something made you happy when you were four doesn't mean it'll make you happy now."

"You're right," I told her. "But it'll refresh a memory of happiness. That's worth something, I think."

"Hmm."

"What?" I asked.

"You're surprisingly deep sometimes, but only about stupid things."

"Thanks," I said. "I like to stay on brand."

I was at Remarquable, making chocolate mousse. Everyone I work with thinks it's boring, because there really isn't much to it, technically speaking. You melt the best dark chocolate you have, you beat egg whites until they're frothy, add sugar, and gently mix them together. Simple.

So when Brodeur assigns you to make it, you're not learning, advancing your skills, or being challenged. I don't care. I think it's relaxing. Maybe that's because it doesn't feel like work. It feels like . . . falling in love for the first time. Simple. Easy. Effortless.

What I'm saying is that I'd had a pretty good day at work, when I got a couple of texts from Bisma.

Can't make it to the library today.

Some friends are going to Ocean Beach for a bonfire.

Oh. That sucked. I'd been looking forward to seeing her.

I totally got it, of course. She had her own life, and I was just some guy she was helping with his homework, after all.

In fact, we didn't even really have to meet anymore. I mean, she'd already helped me with my Renaissance Man outline. I had to, unfortunately, write the paper myself. She'd said she'd review it afterward, and we'd come up with a presentation together, but until then, I didn't need to see her. Not for Renaissance Man reasons, anyway.

I thought about what to text back. Just saying "okay"

seemed too . . . I don't know, it was like I didn't care. At the same time, I couldn't be all like "I'll miss you," because that'd just be weird.

My phone buzzed as another text from her came through.

You in?

I grinned. "Yes. Definitely."

Then I realized that she couldn't hear me, and texted her back.

The problem was that I wasn't exactly ready for the beach. I'd been dressing up a bit for the library lately, and so I had on my best pair of jeans, a nice button-down, and Killshots that, at ninety bucks, were the nicest sneakers I owned. They were not going to the beach.

The awesome thing about San Francisco is that you can find clothes pretty much anywhere, and I was able to get a casual outfit and flip-flops on my way over. The possibility that you'll be able to wear flip-flops outside in April, by the way, is one of the reasons California is awesome.

Anyway, that was how I came to meet Bisma wearing a Captain America shirt over khaki cargo shorts. Her sheer voltage of smile when she saw me froze me in place. Literally. I was walking toward her, she turned, and then . . . I wasn't walking anymore. She jogged up to me instead, her brown ponytail trailing in the wind behind her.

"Hey. A Muslim Cap. Very political of you."

I scratched the back of my neck. "Umm . . . actually, I just thought you'd like it."

"I know." She grinned. "You look good. Yes, yes, that can't be helped. Come on. I'll introduce you to everyone."

There were a few fires going, and she took me to the highest one. It crackled, sizzled, and hissed as it ate wood and fed on the wind. There were around ten other people there, all of them Bisma's classmates, she explained, who'd decided to take a break from lab work.

"Bisma almost never comes out with us," a guy named Andre Soumare said. "Always hurrying home to you, I guess."

"She hadn't even mentioned you," a girl named Abigail Winters said with a smirk. "So private. You know, Akram, no one's going to steal your boyfriend if you bring him around."

I waited for Bisma to correct them, but she didn't. Instead, she took my arm—*she took my arm!*—and said, "He isn't the type who lets himself get stolen."

I looked down at Bisma, who flushed, let me go, and, turning to her friend Andre, asked, "If you aren't playing right now, maybe Danyal could?"

"Sure, yeah," he said, gesturing grandly to a guitar case resting by his side. "By all means, sing to your girl."

"I definitely don't sing. How'd you even know that I play?" I asked Bisma.

"You told me the first time we met."

"I can't believe you remember that."

There were a couple of *aww* noises. Andre had a simple

starter acoustic Yamaha. I picked at the strings experimentally. My fingers felt a little stiff and out of practice, which made sense since I hadn't played in forever. I cracked them as Bisma sat down cross-legged across from me.

I started strumming a little, going through the chords, letting the memories of my fingertips come back, and then played an old song that I figured none of them knew. They seemed to like it, though, or at least they were nice enough to say so when I was done.

"What was that?" Andre asked. "I'll have to check it out."

"It's an old one. My mom taught it to me. It's called 'The Book of Love.'"

"His mom taught it to him," Winters repeated. "Where did you find this guy?"

Bisma shrugged.

Her friends were cool, and time passed quickly. I kind of wished I had a hoodie or something as the sun started to go down. When it comes to weather, San Francisco will always betray you.

I was standing close to the fire, just watching Bisma, when Andre came up to stand beside me. She was laughing at something one of her friends had said, and lit by the orange glow of the flames, in the sand and by the sea, she seemed, as she so rarely was, perfectly herself, unburdened and alive.

"I wish she was like this all the time," I said, forgetting for a moment that I wasn't alone.

Andre looked at me sideways. "We've all noticed that she's been happier than usual. We were wondering why. So, whatever you're doing, keep doing it."

"I'm not doing anything."

"Even better."

I didn't get a chance to ask what that meant, because Bisma ran up to us. "Hey," she said. "You want to go for a walk?"

"Sure," I said, turning to Andre, who shook his head. "You guys have fun."

Bisma and I strolled along the edge of the water, our feet mostly staying on dry sand. "That's amazing that you can do that."

"What?" I asked.

"Just, you know, make music by touching something."

You can do it too, I thought, remembering how the rhythm of my heart had changed when she'd wrapped her arm around mine. "Thanks. I'm not as good as I used to be."

"No one is," she said, obviously not talking about the guitar anymore. "Hey, I'm sorry about telling those guys we're a couple. I just thought it'd take too long to explain and—"

"I didn't mind."

She smiled. "Well...thanks for coming out."

"I was glad you asked." I hesitated before saying, "I would've missed going to the library."

I didn't give a single fucksicle about the library, of

course. It was her.... But that isn't the kind of thing you just come out and say to someone.

"I'm glad you've come to appreciate it."

"I know, right? It's crazy. Like ... who even am I anymore?"

"You'll figure it out. I believe in you."

"Why?"

"I don't know. I just do."

"Um ... thanks," I said, because what else was there to say? "You want to head back?"

She looked back over her shoulder to the blaze where her friends were standing. It was almost the only fire still going. It had to be getting close to nine, when the flames would have to be put out. Then she looked forward, to the darkness stretching out in front of us.

"I'd like to keep walking," she said, "if you'll walk with me."

"Yeah," I said. "I will."

$$\text{〜}$$

"What are you guys watching?" Kaval asked, walking into the den to find Sohrab, Zar, and me collapsed in our usual spots on the super soft leather sofas in the Sabsvari house. At least, they used to be our usual spots, back when the three of us hung out more and hogged Sohrab's parents' epic home theater to watch movie after movie. Now we rarely got together like this, because Intezar got irritated every time Sohrab made us take a prayer break. So I guess they were our *un*usual spots now.

Kaval had been right. Sohrab did want me and Zar to come over for a movie marathon. It was a good peace offering, and I'd talked Intezar into it.

I tried to catch her eye and give her a friendly smile. Things had been kind of frosty between us lately, but maybe they'd thaw out, now that it was almost spring. She didn't look in my direction, though.

"The *Taken* series," Zar answered with an excited grin. "With Liam Neeson. So much killing."

Kaval rolled her eyes. "Boys."

"It's just pointless violence," Intezar said, defending his pick.

Sohrab folded his arms across his chest. "Actually, it isn't pointless. It is an affirmation of the idea that any amount of bloodshed is acceptable in the defense of—"

Zar groaned. "Dude."

"What?" Sohrab asked.

"Why do you have to ruin everything?"

"Seriously," Kaval agreed. "You need to chill." She looked at me then, and I knew she was asking me to chime in and support her.

Sohrab looked at me too, and I shrugged. "You have been kind of intense lately."

"Well, in case you people haven't noticed, the world is an intense place these days."

"Everyone knows," Zar told him. "You're not helping by going on about it all the time."

No one said anything for a long while after that, then Kaval asked, "You guys want some popcorn?"

"That," Intezar said, "is the kind of talk you want to hear *before* a movie starts."

"Danyal, do you want to come help me with it?"

"Uh...sure, yeah. Yes. I can do that."

"What do you need him for?" Zar demanded.

"He cooks," Kaval said.

"It's just popcorn, though."

I was pretty sure Zar didn't want to be alone with Sohrab, who was still sulking because no one was interested in his sociopolitical analysis of *Taken* and its bloody sequels.

"I'll be right back," I said.

Zar gave a sigh fit for the end of the world but didn't say anything else as Kaval led me to the kitchen in silence. It was only when she was pulling gourmet deep purple and ruby red kernels out of the pantry that she said, "We didn't get a chance to finish talking at school. Tippett interrupted."

"I remember."

"Why were you meeting him? He hates your Bengal Famine idea, doesn't he?"

I shook my head. "He doesn't, actually. In fact, he liked it a lot."

"Oh." She bit her lip. "Well...okay, that's good. Do you still need help with the paper?"

"No, I got this. Thanks, though."

Kaval dug around for a pot big enough to serve everyone. She didn't look at me when she spoke. "You think I'm shallow, don't you?"

"No—"

"It's fine. I think you're shallow too."

"Uh . . . okay. Wait, not canola. Unless you don't have coconut oil, I guess."

Kaval, who was pulling a large container of oil from the pantry, roughly shoved it back. "I don't care about the fucking popcorn."

"Sorry."

"You're just like me, Danyal. Why do you even like me? Have you ever thought about that?"

I had, in fact, thought about that quite a bit over the years. "I like that you're fierce. You do what you want. You don't take crap from anyone. And . . . well, I like the way you look."

"I like the way you look too," she said, with a little less heat. "See? We're the same. Shallow. Your judging me for wanting you to have a decent career is bullshit."

"I'm not judging you, Kaval. Seriously. You should have the life you want."

"So you're going to do well in Renaissance Man?"

"I am."

That earned me a smile. "And you'll go to Pakistan and go to college?"

I took a deep breath. I'd been crushing on Kaval for so

long that I'd kind of gotten in the habit of telling her what she wanted to hear just to make her happy. There was a part of me that still wanted to do that.

But, weirdly, in that moment, Churchill and the British popped into my head. They'd tried to make India what they'd wanted. They'd changed it, claiming that they were improving it, but war and suffering had followed. It wasn't until India was free that it had started to become something like itself again, and even now, it remained broken, divided into three countries.

I meant what I'd told Zar. Being in a relationship with someone meant compromise. You gave up things you wanted because your partner needed you to. I'd seen my parents do it for each other for years.

What he'd been trying to tell me, and what I saw now, was that there were some things you couldn't compromise on. The things that were part of you, that made up who you were, had to be appreciated by the people who claimed to love you. Otherwise, they were just trying to make you what they were.

That's not love. That's colonialism.

I shook my head.

"You should have the life you want, Kaval, but I should have the life I want too."

"You can't have the life you want without me. I'm all you've ever wanted."

With that, she turned on her heel and left the kitchen,

so I never got a chance to answer her. That was fine. I wasn't sure what I would've said to her anyway.

As I made popcorn for the guys, I couldn't help but wonder if there had ever been a time when what Kaval had said had been true. I didn't think so. Obviously, I'd imagined a future with Kaval, but I'd always had other dreams as well. How had she not seen that before, and how could she not see it now?

I walked back to Sohrab and Zar. They were sitting on opposite ends of the room, looking frustrated with each other. I sighed. Whatever. I was over trying to get them to make nice. I hit play on the movie, and we watched it in silence.

Well, we watched around half of it. About an hour in, Intezar got a text reminding him that he was supposed to drop his father off at the airport for his latest business trip. Predictably, our friend had completely forgotten.

"We can watch the rest of it with Zar another time," I said, after he'd gone.

"Sure," Sohrab said, in an "as if that's going to happen" tone. "Was there something else you wanted to do?"

"We don't have to do anything. I'm very good at that."

He smiled and reached for the popcorn bowl again. "I like the *garam masala* in here. It's a nice touch."

I nodded. "Thanks."

He studied me for a moment, then he said, "What did you and Kaval talk about in the kitchen?"

"Nothing." I hated lying to him, but there was no help for it.

He clearly didn't believe me, but it wasn't like he could call me on it.

"She did ask me to talk to you." That was the truth, at least. I didn't really feel like talking to Sohrab about his getting super religious just now, but it was better than the path this conversation was going down.

"About what?"

"What you've been reading."

Sohrab gave me a confused look. "Really? Al-Ghazali *is* fascinating—"

"Read anything not so Islamic lately?"

He frowned but nodded. "Sure, I read this book about the end of the Soviet invasion of Afghanistan and how that war has shaped—"

"Something fun?"

"What do you mean 'fun'?" He asked it like I was a babbling idiot.

"You remember what fun is, right?"

Sohrab ran both his hands over his face, obviously frustrated. "Look, we don't have time for fun, Danyal. I don't know how you guys can't see that. Zar is off doing whatever he wants with any girl who will go out with him. You're cooking or whatever. I don't know how you guys do it. In this world—this messed-up world that is so cruel to people like us, that would crush you and crush me and everything we love if we gave it a chance—how can you let yourself be happy?"

I didn't have an answer. I'd never thought that I needed permission to live my life. I just did it.

Sohrab got to his feet. There was fire in him again, the one that had been there when he'd gotten into it with the sub in English class. It was the quiet, burning anger that I'd seen at the mosque, when he'd spoken about that village where innocent people had died. "What's happening in this country? In this world? Do you even know what the Saudis are doing in Yemen? What about what's happening in Myanmar and Sudan? What's happening at the borders of our own country? There is hatred in so many hearts. And you guys want to have fun? That's insane."

I sank back into the couch, wondering what I could say, wondering what he needed to hear, wondering how long he would go on if I let him, wondering if this fire inside him would eat up everything that made my friend my friend.

Sohrab looked at me, a plea in his eyes, as if begging me to understand. "We're Muslims and we're brown, man. This is the darkest time there has ever been to be those things. We're going to have to live serious lives—"

There it was. I saw it. Suddenly I understood what Sohrab had gotten wrong. Maybe it was because I'd been thinking about history a lot more than I usually did, but I saw the flaw in the story he'd started to believe, and I hoped he would listen when I pointed it out.

"It's not."

"It's not what?"

"It's not the worst time ever to be who we are." Sohrab tried to interrupt, but I pressed on. "We went to the same Sunday school, dude. We read the same stuff."

He gave me a look that could, if you were being kind, be described as skeptical.

"Fine. I didn't read anything, but I did have to sit through the lectures and I was even awake for some of them. Do you remember people who were thrown out of their homes for their beliefs? Exiled from their cities? Chased across deserts? Hunted and stoned?"

"You're talking about the Prophet Muhammad," he said quietly.

"Sure. And his companions. And the other prophets. Moses fled Egypt and wandered the desert, right? And Jesus...and don't forget regular people. Not just Muslims either, but like...everybody. It's always been serious times, and through it all people have had fun. They went to work, they told jokes, they listened to music, they made the best food they could. They hung out with their friends, fell in love, got married and had kids and all that. Zar and I and everybody, we're just living our lives as best we can despite everything, like people always have."

"And what good has come from any of it?"

"Well...you're here. And I'm here."

Sohrab exhaled, shook his head, and sat down. "So, what are you saying? I shouldn't fight?"

"Not all the time. I mean, sorry, but it's been kind of exhausting just being around you. I can't even imagine what it's like *being* you."

Thankfully, he didn't seem offended. "You're saying that we have to be human before we're anything else."

That sounded good to me. Sohrab had always been good with distilled wisdom. "Yeah. So just relax every once in a while. You're the best of us, man—"

Sohrab snorted and waved dismissively.

"You are," I insisted. "You're going to be . . . awesome. Important. You'll make a difference. I know you will, but not if you burn yourself out by stressing over things we can't control."

We were quiet for a long time, both of us staring at the screen that had gone dark. Even though there was nothing on it, it still put out a dim glow.

"That's kind of my thing, you know," Sohrab finally said.

"What?"

He smiled. "Giving out good advice. That's my thing you just stole."

"Sorry," I said. "It won't happen again."

CHAPTER SIXTEEN

"*How is the* Churchill project going?"

I looked up from my mom's *khichri* reluctantly. The mixture of long-grain basmati rice, ghee, and *daal* was one of life's simplest pleasures. Talking to my dad was . . . well, the exact opposite of that.

"Fine," I said.

"Isn't it impressive how much time he's been spending in the library these last few months, *haan*? He's there all the time," my mother said proudly.

That drew another Ahmed Jilani grunt. This was the "I want to believe what is happening, but I don't really" kind.

"What? Just tell us what else he has to do to make you say something nice about him."

My father broke the back of a *papar*—which a lot of

people call *papadum* for some reason—and for a moment it seemed that the crackling noise was going to be his only response. Eventually, however, he said, "Danyal knows very well what he has to do to make me say something nice. Don't you?"

"Fawn over Churchill," I said, "and graduate."

A small, bitter smile from Dad. "Yes. Also, just as important, you must learn a lesson from this experience. To be successful in life means to compromise. You cannot always speak your truth or live your fantasies. You can't have unrealistic goals like opening a restaurant—"

I was about to interrupt, to ask him how, if life was compromise and dreams were worthless, his father and others like him had stood against the largest empire in the world and won their freedom at the price of their heads.

That had not been realistic. It had not been a compromise. It had not been practical.

Practical people doubted and mocked poets, writers, philosophers, musicians, artists, and revolutionaries, and told them that the shining world they hoped for would never come to be. But who did history remember? Who did it revere?

What was it Bisma had said?

I've never really had occasion to admire anyone practical.

Before I could say any of that to my father, however, Mom cut in. Which was fine. Ahmed Jilani would see he was wrong when Renaissance Man came.

"*Acha*, enough, okay? I just want you to know, Danyal,

that we are very happy to see you putting this much work into something. Whatever happens, *beta*, you are a Renaissance Man in my book."

When she fell silent, my father cleared his throat pointedly.

"Except," she went on, "there has been some talk."

Crap. Talk was never good.

"Yeah?" I asked.

"We have verification," my father said, "that you have actually been going to the library—"

"Verification?"

"Now, Danyal, don't raise your voice. *Baba*, we're just saying, you know, people have seen you there. It is just that . . . they haven't seen you there alone."

I groaned. "Seriously? Don't your friends have anything better to do than spy on me?"

"Don't be silly, *beta*," Mom said soothingly. "Our friends don't go to libraries."

"But their children do," my father put in.

"Not that their children are spying on you either," my mother hurried to add. "You know how it is, *jaan*. People talk."

"And we don't like it when people talk," Dad told me. "At all."

"Being talked about is one of the great tragedies in the world, you know. That's a quote."

"Right," I said. "From *Othello*."

My parents exchanged a glance.

"Sure," Mom said. "So, anyway, our sources...not sources, you know, but...we haven't been able to identify the young lady in question, and we were wondering if you would like to tell us who you've been spending so much time with."

"And don't worry," my father said. "From what we've heard, you really have been studying. Not engaging in... the wiggle waggle."

"The wiggle waggle?"

"It's what kids are calling it nowadays," Aisha Jilani said with more confidence than any parent should ever feel about slang.

"Must've missed that memo."

"Danyal, it is just that—"

"It's not a big deal. I asked Bisma Akram to help me with the Renaissance Man project."

This time my parents exchanged a longer glance. Then they both smiled that disturbing "look what we did for our kid, aren't we awesome, we know him so well and should make all decisions for him for the rest of his life and maybe our grandchildren's lives too" smile.

I sighed.

"What a lovely girl she is," Mom said. "I told you, didn't I, Ahmed? Lovely girl, that one. Maybe we should call her mother—"

"No," Dad and I said at the same time.

My mother frowned. "Why not?"

"Let him focus on his schooling. For once in his life,

he is seriously studying. After graduation, there will be plenty of time to deal with the rest of this business."

"Right," I said. "What Dad said."

Aisha Jilani sighed. "Fine." Then she pointed a warning finger at me. "But I think it only fair to warn you that if you screw this up for me, Danyal, you won't have to answer to your father. You'll have to deal with me."

"Which," Dad said, "is a kind of pain you, my son, have never known."

〜

As much as I hated getting up early, I'd agreed to come out for a run after dawn, because Bisma had mentioned that it was something she did. It seemed like a chance to show her I was good at something.

That was before I'd realized that she ran pretty much every single day. I mean, I was in good shape. I worked out at a run-down little gym every once in a while, and did cardio and everything, but Bisma was a machine.

"You okay?" she asked. "I thought you said you ran."

"I do," I gasped, breathing hard, bent over with my hands on my knees. "Just not, you know . . . wow. You're a beast."

"I run whenever I'm angry," Bisma said with a grin.

"You must be angry all the time."

She laughed. "Come on. There's a bench over there. Let's sit down."

"I'm fine," I panted, still sucking oxygen.

She raised her eyebrows.

"I will be fine," I corrected.

"I'm not going to judge you if you sit down, you know."

"You won't?"

"Of course not. I've judged you already."

I made a face at her and headed for the wooden bench she'd pointed out. It was a nice morning. Bisma sat down next to me. I noticed that she was also out of breath and sweating. Maybe she'd been pushing herself more than usual too.

I'd been to Coyote Hills Park before, but never on the Red Hill Trail. Bisma had chosen it, and it was more challenging than I'd expected, especially when you were running flat out. It was a beautiful spot, though, green, with some pretty cool-looking rocks breaking up everything, and a bay that filled the horizon. It looked like we'd just missed seeing the sunrise from the hill.

"I'll miss you," Bisma said, out of nowhere.

"Are you going somewhere?"

"No. You are, though, right? Your contest is getting closer and soon . . . well, you won't have a reason to come to the library anymore."

"Will you be there?"

"Yes," she said.

"Then I'll have a reason."

She refused to meet my gaze, but I could tell from her smile that I'd said the right thing. Then, just as quickly as it had come, it was gone.

I nudged her shoulder with mine. "Where'd you go?"

"What do you mean?"

"Just then, you were thinking something." *That made you lose your smile*, I didn't add, because . . . I don't know, it didn't feel right.

"It's just . . ." She stared out over the water; at what, I couldn't figure out. "I feel like we know each other sometimes, and then I remember that you've been too nice to ask me about what happened with the . . . tape."

"Do you want to talk about it?"

She shook her head.

"Then we don't have to talk about it."

Bisma sighed. "The world isn't that simple, Danyal."

"It can be. Mine is."

"Must be nice."

"It is." I'd meant it as a joke, but when she didn't react, I tried to explain. "You know how people think the moon is beautiful? Well . . . it's not perfect, is it? There's like spots on it and stuff—"

"Craters."

"Be less of a nerd for like two minutes."

Bisma held up her hands. "Sorry."

"I'm just saying that those craters are part of the moon's past. The moon has a history, and I don't know it. No one knows it, really . . . but we can still love the moon. It's still wonderful. It still lights up the dark. You know what I mean? So . . . we don't ever need to talk about anything you don't want to talk about. You are who you are and that's more than good enough for me."

Her eyes shone in the growing light of the new sun. "I think I'd kiss you now if I could."

"Oh...wow. Dude. Being Muslim sucks so hard sometimes."

She laughed and got to her feet. "Come on. Let's go. It's getting late."

"I think maybe, young man, you could be working faster, *haan*?"

I looked up from the sandwich I was making and frowned at the rando uncle who'd come along to criticize me. "Sorry?"

"It is just," the old man said, waving a hand over the perfectly aligned, beautifully arranged sandwiches on my table, "that if you didn't spend so much time making everything pretty, you'd be more productive."

I frowned at him. For a long time.

The uncle seemed to get uncomfortable. He fidgeted a little and tugged at his beard. "After all, what does it matter what food looks like? It is going to end up in the same place, *haan*?"

Allah, give me patience.

All of the Fremont mosques had gotten together and, with an unusual amount of coordination, put together a joint event. It was Saturday morning, and my family was in the courtyard of the Lowry mosque, making food for the homeless. Sohrab, who'd texted me like five times to make sure we'd be there, had said I was assigned to a group putting together sandwiches.

Of course, I wasn't just slapping the ingredients onto white bread and stuffing everything into Ziploc bags. I had standards to maintain.

When I kept staring at him, the uncle nodded emphatically, as if I'd agreed to do exactly what he asked, and wandered away. I sighed. There was no chance that was the last time that was going to happen.

I wondered if I'd get in trouble if I suggested all the uncles get beard nets. Brodeur would flip out if she saw this much uncovered facial hair around food. I decided it was worth pointing out, even if I ended up getting a lecture about how beards were awesome or whatever. You don't make compromises on food hygiene. It's sacred.

I asked around to see who was in charge today, expecting to be sent to one of the imams. Instead, I was told to talk to Sohrab Sabsvari.

I found him with Intezar, whose arms were full of loaves of bread.

"What are you doing here?"

Zar tried to shrug as best he could. "Sohrab asked me to help and I thought . . . it just sounded cool, *yaar.*"

"It is," I agreed.

There was a weird silence. I don't think any of us knew what to say.

Then Zar cleared his throat. "I should get this bread where it's supposed to go. So...yeah." He nodded to Sohrab. "You did a good thing, brownther. This is really great."

As Zar fled the awkwardness that was just begging for a heart-to-heart—those really weren't his style—I asked Sohrab, "You did this? I heard you organized everything."

He laughed in that way he had when he was trying to be modest. "No, not really. I just came up with the idea. Actually, I didn't. You did."

"Sounds like something I'd remember."

Sohrab chuckled. "You said we should be human before we're anything else." I hadn't actually. If I remembered it right, he'd come up with that on his own. "I figured this was what being human looked like. Your obsession with food became my inspiration."

"You do look better. More human and less zombie." I clapped him on the back. "So how come you didn't tell me you had all this going on? I would've helped."

"I figured you were busy with the Renaissance Man. Besides, I had Zar."

I grinned and my words came out hopeful and bright. "You guys good now?"

Sohrab held his hand out before him and shook it in

a "meh" gesture. "It isn't like before, you know... but maybe that's okay."

"That isn't the answer I wanted."

"I'm sorry," he said. "We're different people now, and... don't look so disappointed, Danyal. At least Zar and I are making an effort. Besides, we'll always have you to make sure we hang out, right?"

"Always."

"Then we'll be fine. Come on, let's get to work."

"Really, Intezar? A new PlayStation. That would be your super *dua*?"

After the food drive at the mosque, I grabbed Zar and Sohrab and drove us all to Falafel Corner, a halal burger place. If they were getting along again, even a little bit, it was worth celebrating.

Besides, it had been a while since I'd been to a burger joint, especially one with an open kitchen. There's something cozy and comforting about the sizzle of a fresh patty hitting a grill and the rising smell of charred beef. It sang to the American in me, I guess.

It was exactly the kind of place you came to celebrate healing friendships.

"Whatever, *yaar*," Zar said. "What else would I ask God for?"

"Forgiveness?" Sohrab suggested.

"For what?" Intezar demanded indignantly, but then

he wilted a little under Sohrab's even, unblinking gaze. Seriously, Sohrab can go without blinking for a very long time. It's freaky. "Fine, so my super *dua* could be for forgiveness," Zar admitted, "but that's boring. It's not a fun game if everyone gives boring answers."

"What about world peace? Or an end to poverty?" Sohrab suggested.

Zar groaned and stuffed his face with a massive bite out of his triple-patty, double-beef, bacon, extra-cheese burger so that he could get out of the conversation.

Sohrab shook his head and turned to me. "What about you?"

"I know what Danyal wants," Zar tried to say with a full mouth. At least, that's what I think he tried to say. Obviously, he was talking about Kaval.

Zar was wrong, though.

A *dua* is just a prayer. Something you ask God for. Sohrab had heard that when you went to Mecca and saw the Kaaba for the first time, whatever *dua* you made was guaranteed to come true. He'd dubbed this the super *dua*.

I wanted to say that my super *dua* would be to get an infinite number of super *duas*. Everyone knows to wish for more wishes.

The thing was...I knew that if I went to Mecca and my eyes fell on the famous black mosque at the center of all I'd ever been told was holy, there was one thing my heart would ask for before anything else.

I'd wish for Bisma Akram to be happy.

She was awesome and she deserved joy. It bothered me that the society we lived in, and the families we were part of, would never really let her move on from her past, despite the fact that she just wanted to live her life.

The whole thing with the sex tape haunted her, not because she was unable to let it go, but because the people around her couldn't let it go. That was bullshit.

Her own family, her own community and people, were the restraints on her smiles, the checks on her laughter.

And for some reason, the fact that the light in her world had been dimmed hurt me. I couldn't explain why, but I was increasingly sure that I'd never be happy if Bisma wasn't happy.

So if Allah promised to give me one thing, I'd ask Him to give her a beautiful life.

I didn't want to tell my friends that, though.

And, just in case Allah was taking an interest in the conversation, I didn't want to lie about it either. That'd be a bad look.

"Close your mouth when you chew your food, man," I said, mostly to change the subject.

When Zar opened his mouth to answer, however, he started to gasp and choke on the giant bite he'd taken. A waiter rushed over, worried, and a few customers muttered to themselves with concern.

Sohrab and I looked on unmoved.

"He's fine," I told everyone.

"This happens about once a week," Sohrab put in.

Zar had, by this time, recovered enough to croak, "I hate you guys. I could've died."

"If you were meant to die just then," Sohrab said, "nothing we could've done would have mattered. You'd be dead. How long we live, how well we live, all that is written by God. There is no changing destiny."

"If that's true," I asked, "then what are prayers for?"

CHAPTER SEVENTEEN

You're out of time.

The cardiologist is here.

Need your answer.

Kaval's texts felt like they came out of the blue, but to be fair, she'd mentioned that her heart doctor was coming to see her again. I just hadn't known it was happening this soon.

The messages came just as I was walking into Remarquable for a shift. I stopped by the door, trying to figure out what, if anything, I should say. Brodeur, who was walking by, made the choice for me. She plucked the phone from my hand, turned it off, and handed it back.

"Station," she ordered.

"Yes, Chef," I said with a sigh. Fine. Whatever. I went to the back, put my phone in a locker, and changed. Then

I washed my hands with bright pink soap that smelled like nothing except chemicals and went to work. Brodeur had decided to serve a dessert based around an orange cake, and for that she needed me to zest and cut oranges.

As for Kaval, I had to come up with a good reply.

If I told her no, then I'd always be the one who walked away from "us."

If I told her yes, then...

The truth was I didn't want to say yes. And not just because of the life she'd demanded of me.

It was because of Bisma.

I didn't know when I'd started to feel this way, and I didn't know what it meant, but I knew that it would hurt more to lose Bisma's company than it would hurt to lose... whatever it was that Kaval and I had.

That didn't mean I *liked* liked Bisma, of course. Not in the way that I liked Kaval.

Did it?

Sure, I flirted with her sometimes, but that was because... well, it was my default setting when I was around girls. Right? I mean, every Bollywood and Hollywood movie I'd ever seen had taught me that I was supposed to be bowled over when I liked a girl, that it was supposed to hit me like a bus and shatter me like Sub Zero's frozen hammer. It wasn't like that with Bisma.

I wasn't overwhelmed by her. I was just... overtaken.

Unless there was more than one way that love was supposed to feel, and no one talked about the other kind, the kind that didn't set fire to the sky or shake the earth but just existed, like the shade from a redwood tree on a hot day.

I gave a little cry of pain as I pulled my finger instinctively away from the cutting board I was using. The oranges I'd been slicing . . . well, they were blood oranges now.

"*Qu'est-ce que tu fais?*" Brodeur screamed from across the room. One of the other line cooks handed me a clean towel, and I pressed it against my finger, which was really starting to hurt. I wanted to smile to thank her, but my face was stuck in a grimace.

Brodeur's glare was sharper than the blade I'd cut myself with as she gestured for me to go to the back office, where schedules were made and menus decided. She followed me, cursing all the way there, cursing as she pulled a first aid case off the wall, and then cursing as she examined my bleeding finger.

"I'm sorry," I said, trying not to sound as pathetic as I felt. It wasn't the first time someone had hurt themselves in the kitchen, of course, but it was the first time I had done it. Worse, I'd done it because I'd failed to focus because of that text from Kaval, which felt really stupid. She was probably chatting up her cardiologist right then.

"Why shouldn't she? I'm not going to give her what she wants," I said out loud.

"Pardon?"

My ears started to burn. "Sorry. I . . . was thinking about a girl."

Brodeur's face softened just a little. "The girl who visited you here?"

"Bisma? I mean, not really. It's someone else."

She chuckled. *"Vraiment?"*

She seemed to expect an answer, but I had no idea what she'd said. When I didn't reply, she harrumphed and went about cleaning the cut with gauze and iodine. "It is, I think, not so bad."

I tried to flex my finger. It stung, but it was definitely bearable. "I'll be fine."

She perched herself on the edge of the desk, folded her arms across her chest, and looked down at me. "A kitchen is a place for concentration, yes?"

I nodded.

"Do not forget in the future. Food has to be the most important thing in your life when you are creating it. The world should be as nothing to you."

"Yes, Chef."

She took a deep breath. "And pick one jam for your little brioche. It'll make for a simpler life, I assure you."

"It isn't like that. I'm not with anyone. Bisma and I—"

"You do not like the girl? She was, I thought, most charming."

"She's great," I said. "But this other girl—"

"Someone to whom you cannot give what she wants, hmm? I know nothing of it, of course, so I must say nothing. Very well. Go home."

"I'm fine. I can go back to my station."

She jabbed a finger against my forehead. "This is not working, so you are no use to anyone here. You're done for the night. Walk. Think, if you can manage it."

I sighed. "Yes, Chef."

As I got up to leave, I heard Brodeur sigh. "Wait," she said. She pulled off her toque and tossed it on the desk, then ran a hand over her blond hair. "I am not, I fear, very wise. There are two things I know, and perhaps they can be of benefit."

Before I could ask her what she was talking about, Chef Brodeur raised one finger in the air with an extravagant flourish. "First, you will never regret cooking for a beautiful woman, yes? That one, I think, is self-explanatory." She picked up her hat and clutched it tightly in her hands. "I used to make simple things for the girl I loved. Just an omelet, maybe, or a fig tapenade."

I smiled, trying to imagine the dictatorial chef in love. "Really?"

"Second," she went on, raising the index finger on her other hand in exactly the same style with which she had raised the first, "you will never regret asking that girl to dance. In fifty-four years, only those things I've found to be true, and they are the only things I've regretted not doing more."

))

Walking in San Francisco always surprises me. It's easy to forget sometimes, because it can feel so big, how small the city is. After Chef Brodeur told me to go home, I walked under the red lanterns of Chinatown, past the delicious and awful smells of the Tenderloin, and headed toward Union Square, the most expensive part of a very expensive town. The streets were lined with stores so pricey that I never even bothered looking at their displays.

It was all very pretty to walk toward, all glittery from over the hill, but then you got close, and you noticed hidden nooks with badly painted rusted pipes running along them, and saw people begging for help as the world passed by them, and there were children crying, and tourists lost, all in the fading light of a falling sun.

Kaval felt like that. The closer I'd gotten to her, the more I'd realized that she wasn't perfect. In fact, she had flaws I hadn't seen before, and that wasn't Kaval's fault. It was mine.

After all, there's no such thing as a perfect person. It's naive and unfair to think that just because you're infatuated with someone, they're somehow better than everyone, somehow more than human.

The reason Kaval Sabsvari and I couldn't work wasn't because she had imperfections, just like everyone else. It was because her imperfections made it impossible for her to accept mine. She needed a different partner, with different failings than the many I had.

Bisma Akram, on the other hand...

I pulled out my phone. The texts from Kaval were still right there on the screen. I cleared them away, and then dialed the only person I wanted to speak with just then.

"Hey," she said, "aren't you supposed to be at work?"

"Hi," I said. "I'm Danyal Jilani, and I'm not very bright."

"What's happening right now?"

"I'm letting you know that I'm not perfect, just so you aren't disappointed later."

Bisma laughed on the other end. "Okay. Well, you'll have to pick a different weakness to share. You already told me you weren't bright."

"I did?"

"Yeah. The first time we met. In your van. Remember?"

I smiled, but of course she couldn't see that.

"Danyal?"

"Hmm?"

"What's going on?" Bisma asked. "You sound sad."

"No," I said. "No. I was just thinking. That always makes me a little sad. It's why I don't do it much. Hey, listen, let's not meet at the library next time. Let's have dinner instead."

She hesitated.

"Please?"

"Okay, I guess. Where do you want to go?"

"There's a young, up-and-coming chef in Fremont that I know. I hear he's pretty good...."

CHAPTER EIGHTEEN

A few days later, I was staring into Bisma's brown eyes, which she quickly cast down. "Danyal?"

"Hmm?"

"We've been standing here for a while."

"We have?"

Bisma nodded.

"And?"

"Maybe you should let me in."

"Oh. Sorry." I stepped back, and she walked into Zar's apartment, nervously tucking a strand of her hair that had escaped her high ponytail behind an ear.

Uncle Inayat was on yet another business trip aboard, and Zar had agreed to be exiled, so we had the place to ourselves. Sohrab, of course, had been kept in the dark. If he knew Bisma and I were alone together outside a public space, he'd...I don't know what he'd say, but it'd definitely involve the suggestion that I grovel before Allah to ask for forgiveness.

Anyway, I realize that freezing at the very beginning of a date isn't the smoothest move in the world, but in my defense, there is nothing sexier than a *shalwar kameez* that fits a woman just right. All the fashion designers in the world can come at me if they want.

Bisma was wearing a plain sunshine-yellow *kameez* over a white *shalwar*—she hadn't bothered with a *dupatta*—and it was simple and classy and flirty all at the same time. It looked like it had been custom stitched for her, which it probably had.

Even so, I don't think it would've stopped my world from spinning if anyone else had worn it. I was just so used to seeing her in superhero tees and beaten-up jeans that it caught me completely off guard.

"I like your outfit."

She ducked her head in that awkward, embarrassed way she had of accepting compliments. Then she looked around. Inayat Uncle's post-separation home was nice enough, but it was really bare. There was a TV and console, a leather couch, and a wicker patio table on which he and Zar ate dinner. There were no pictures or paintings on the walls, no embellishments of any kind.

"It's...nice."

"Hopefully," I said as I made my way back to the kitchen, "the food here is better than the decor."

"I'm sure it'll be great," Bisma said.

"You're early, though."

"Sorry."

"It's totally fine. I just, you know . . ." I picked up a chef's knife and gestured at the ingredients I was still working with. "You want to sit down?"

She shook her head. With her arms crossed behind her back, she peered over the counter. "I'd rather just watch you. Hey, what happened to your finger?"

I waved off her concern and turned my attention to the onion I'd been chopping when she'd knocked. "It's nothing."

"Need help?"

I chuckled. "Thanks. But this is my library."

"That . . . doesn't make any sense."

"Yeah, it sounded cooler in my head. The kitchen is my happy place, is what I meant."

I started dicing an onion. I wasn't as fast as usual, because of my finger, but Bisma still seemed impressed. I had to slow down even more when she drifted into the kitchen and stood next to me, and her arm grazed mine. Chef Brodeur's warning about focus was fresh in my mind, as was the sting from the cut on my finger. "Do you like to cook?"

Bisma shook her head. "No. I mean, you know, I do it when I have to, like an obedient desi girl and all that. It just isn't fun for me."

"Really? I think it's awesome."

She laughed. "I know."

"The first thing I remember, ever, is this time we were at a fancy restaurant—must've been some special occasion for my parents or something—and this man walked up to a table with a plate of food and *whoosh*, there was a ball of fire, and everybody started cheering."

"That's a great first memory."

I looked over at her. "What's yours?"

She wrinkled her nose at me. "Having to throw away one of Suri's really stinky diapers."

"Gross."

"Yeah," Bisma said. "Speaking of Suraiya, I'm starting to worry she has a crush on you or something. She talks about you all the time. You've made quite an impression."

"Happens to everybody," I said. "Even I've got a crush on me."

"There's that confidence again." Bisma laughed. "So... everybody, huh?" She turned away and studied the video game stickers Zar had on his fridge. Her voice was quiet when she asked, "Do you think I have a crush on you too?"

The knife in my hand stopped for a moment. Then I pressed on. "Well, if you don't, you will once you've had my food."

"Ah. So all this is an elaborate ruse."

"Yup. I'm going to seduce you with my grandmother's *khatti daal* and *keema*."

Bisma, who'd been tracing the N7 logo for *Mass Effect*

with a delicate touch, spun around. "Wait. Seriously? You invited me over for *daal* and *keema*?"

I got why she was surprised. It was a staple food in Pakistani households all over the world. It wasn't for special occasions. It was like going to someone's house and being served chicken soup or spaghetti.

Hopefully, she wasn't too disappointed. "I can make something else if you want."

"No, it's cool. I was just...I mean, you—"

"You were expecting something fancier. It isn't too late. I can make something like that for you." I'd decided to listen to Brodeur's advice and gone with something simple, because I'd figured out why she'd told me to do things this way. "I just think that if you're going to cook for a friend, you shouldn't make something that you'd make for a stranger. It should be personal."

Bisma smiled as she stepped away from me a little, putting some distance between us. "Makes sense."

We both went quiet for a while.

Leaning against the wall farthest from me, she started examining her fingernails, as if she'd discovered something really interesting about them. "By the way, Suri was asking what happened with that prospect of yours. The one you were asking advice about."

"That isn't going to work out."

Bisma looked up. "You finally realized she isn't good for you, did you?"

"Told you I was slow."

"I thought you meant with school and stuff."

"No. I'm just generally an idiot."

She tapped her fingers against the wall she was leaning on. "I wish you'd stop saying that. You're not an idiot, and you're not slow. You've just got other interests. That's actually really great. How many brown doctors or lawyers or engineers does the world need anyway?"

"You know," I said, using the edge of my blade to pile diced green chilies into the bowl that held my onions, "we've never talked about what you want to do. I mean, I know you're studying microbiology, but what comes next?"

"A master's, maybe? I picked microbiology because it's kind of like the study of how really small things can have really big consequences. I know that sounds like I picked it because of what happened in Portland with the tape. And maybe that's a little true. But it's actually awesome. What's fascinating about microorganisms..."

I'd always thought that nothing was fascinating about microorganisms. Actually, that's not true. I hadn't really ever thought about them at all. Bisma, on the other hand, had a lot to say about the life around us that we couldn't see. I listened to her speak, ignoring for once the sizzle of the ground beef on the stove, searing, turning a rich brown. When the smell of cumin and garlic threatened to overwhelm the cherry blossoms and pears of her perfume, I moved a little closer to her to keep them at bay.

Soon I was done with my *keema*, and I set rice to boil. The *khatti daal* I'd already made last night, and according to Zar—who'd been impossible to keep away from it entirely—it had turned out almost perfectly, though he'd thought it wasn't sour enough. I could've gone with more tamarind pulp, I guess, but when it comes to food, I opt for subtlety.

So far, I'd followed Brodeur's advice and things were going well. There was, however, a second part to what she'd said I should do, and that made me kind of nervous.

"You're super quiet all of a sudden."

"Me? No. Really? No. I'm good. Fine. Great, in fact."

Bisma raised her eyebrows.

"There's...I think there's something I need to ask you."

"Go ahead."

I took a deep breath and said something I'd never said to anyone before. "Do you want to dance?"

Bisma stared at me like...well, like I'd done something completely unexpected, which I supposed I had.

What had Chef Brodeur said? *You will never regret asking that girl to dance.*

That was a lie. I'd just realized it about a millisecond too late. Obviously, you're totally going to regret asking a girl to dance if she says no and then you've made everything super awkward.

"What?" Bisma finally asked.

"I'm supposed to ask you to dance."

"Supposed to?"

Crap. I'd never told her that I'd gotten advice about today from my head chef. It didn't seem like information I could just break out now.

"Um . . . yeah, it's part of the code."

She narrowed her eyes. "What code?"

"The code of the . . . kitchen?" I said. "If you invite a girl to watch you cook, you have to ask her to dance."

"And this code is written down somewhere?"

"Not everything important is written down."

"Kind of is, though. Danyal, you're not allowed to touch me, so—"

"Is that your rule or God's rule?"

Bisma, thankfully, smiled, and the painful tightness in my chest that I hadn't even realized had come on loosened a little. "You'll respect it if it's mine?"

"Of course."

"But if it's God's . . ."

"He won't mind if we bend it a little."

She gave me a skeptical look. "Really?"

"He's super forgiving and stuff. I've heard He wrote a few books about it. They did pretty well."

She laughed.

"Trust me," I said.

Bisma bit her lip and looked at me for a long time. It was the same look she'd given me in the library a while back, the day she'd kissed me on the cheek. "I do," she told me in a tentative voice and, very slowly, held out her hand.

Bisma was ridiculously hot.

I don't mean . . . what I mean is that she was literally hot. When she stepped close to me, her body almost touching mine, and looked up at me, it felt like I'd gotten close to a gentle star. I placed a hand on her waist, and she put an arm around my shoulder.

Heat came off her small frame in waves. I'd never been this close to a girl before. Warmth radiated from her, like she was the world's prettiest piece of magnesium. No. Wait. Plutonium?

As I looked down at her I noticed things I'd somehow managed to never notice about her before. She had a few light freckles around her nose, but they were really hard to see because they were almost the same color as her skin.

I could see a vein in her neck pulsing a little, betraying the secrets of her beating heart.

There was a slight upturn to the corner of her mouth that somehow made her lips very kissable. I wished she'd smile at me, because her smile was everything, but she wasn't smiling. She was just staring back at me, studying my face, and her breath had lost its natural rhythm. Maybe she was finding air as difficult to draw in as I was.

The same stubborn lock of her wavy hair that she'd tucked behind her ear freed itself again. It swayed gently beside her cheek, and I couldn't help but reach for it. My fingers trembled a little as I carefully pushed those soft strands back. She closed her eyes when my hand touched her cheek.

She stepped closer to me, and if there was anything left of the world aside from the feel of her and the smell of her and the pull of her, I didn't know and didn't care.

Bisma buried her face in the space between my shoulder and my neck, and we gathered each other up and just stood there. We didn't move and there was no music that anyone else could've heard.

Then, suddenly, she pulled away. "I'm sorry."

"What? No, Bisma, it wasn't just you. I—"

"No, Danyal. I'm sorry, but your rice is boiling over."

I managed to salvage the rice. There was no harm done, except to my pride, I guess. As I sat down across from Bisma at the wicker table, I realized I'd forgotten to give her any cutlery. Apologizing, I started back for it, but she stopped me.

"Are you kidding? We're not eating *daal* and rice with spoons."

I didn't usually eat with my hands. I had to admit, though, that there was something...I don't know, true about eating my grandmother's food the way she would've eaten it.

Bisma took a bite and let out a happy whimper-sigh-moan, her left hand going to her chest. "Uff. This is so good, Danyal."

"It's nothing," I said. "Just everyday food."

"Everyday food? Oh my God, you have to marry me."

I choked on some *daal*. It wasn't graceful.

She gasped, and her face flooded with color. "Oh... sorry, that totally isn't... I didn't mean... It's just so good that I meant—"

"It's cool," I said. "I know what you meant."

"Thanks. I don't know why I'm so awkward."

"And I don't know why I'm so smooth. Can't be helped either way."

Bisma rolled her eyes, but she seemed to relax, which was exactly what I'd been going for. She ate in silence for a while after that, and I'm not sure if it was because she was afraid of saying something embarrassing again, or if she was just enjoying her food.

"I'm surprised you didn't make *lassi* to go with this and *gulab jamun* for dessert," she finally said.

"*Lassi* isn't hard. I just like to elevate it with saffron and crushed pistachios, and I don't have those right now. Still, I can—"

Bisma laughed. "No. I was kidding."

"Dessert, unfortunately, is not desi. Our people never really mastered sweets like the French did."

Bisma's response was dripping with disbelief. "I can't believe you just said that."

"I mean, it's true."

"Whatever, Danyal Jilani. *Gajjar ka halva. Kheer. Anday kay lauz. Badam ki jalee.* And *double ka meetha*?"

I gave her my best unimpressed face at the list of dishes.

"I'll fight you," she warned.

I held up my hands. "I'm just saying that if you keep making—and your people keep buying—*chum chum*, no one is going to take you seriously about desserts."

She sighed. "Yeah. *Chum chum* I can't explain. So what did you make?"

"You told me chocolate was your favorite."

"When?"

"At Zareen's."

"That was months ago."

I grinned. "Well, I hope you haven't changed your mind, because I made you a Scharffen Berger chocolate torte, with a very light dusting of paprika, caramelized hazelnuts, and Chantilly cream."

She stared at me like I'd just parted the Red Sea.

I took a little bow, which was hard to do gracefully since I was sitting down.

"I can't believe you."

"I'm pretty unbelievable."

"How many girls have you done this for?"

"What? I mean . . . just you."

Bisma shook her head. "Then you've missed out. Your life could've been the story of a lot of very satisfied women."

"What do you mean 'missed out'? It's not too late."

Bisma looked away from me and smiled a little, in a way that told me that even though she wasn't going to say it, she was pretty sure that I was wrong.

And then, in a flash, the smile was gone, and the light

in her eyes dimmed, and I wanted to ask her what had happened, what she'd thought of to cause that change, but I didn't know how.

〜

"This was incredible, Danyal. Thank you."

"Another dance before you go?" I asked.

"No," she said with a chuckle. "You're a terrible 'dancer.'"

"Actually, I'm an awesome dancer. I was just getting warmed up before."

She walked up to me. "I'm serious. This was..." She raised her shoulders in a half shrug. "It was the nicest thing anyone has ever done for me. I'll never forget it."

"I'm happy to kick Zar out of his place any time you want to come over for dinner."

"We...can't do this again. I can't."

But she'd just said that she had a good time, that everything that I'd done was great. So what was she talking about?

She must've seen the confusion on my face. She put a hand on my chest, her long, thin fingers drumming a beat on my heart. "I'm sorry. You have to know that when I'm around you I feel like, maybe, in my personal life I'm allowed to be happy—"

"That's good—"

"But this isn't real, Danyal." Bisma pulled her hand away and shook her head. "Tonight was amazing, but your mother is going to find a nice girl for you soon, and then all I'll have left is...You're just...you're so easy to hope for, and when I start to hope, it feels like glass in my veins. And I know that glass is going to break and cut everything inside me to pieces. Do you understand?"

"What if it doesn't have to break?" I asked. "What if I don't care about what happened before?"

"Your parents will care. Won't they?"

They would. Of course they would.

"Don't make me promises you can't keep. I like you so much. You're one of the few people in my life I...I don't want to end up hating you too. Please."

I sighed and stepped back to give her room to go past me, but she stepped up to me again and stood on tiptoe to kiss my cheek before walking out into the dark.

CHAPTER NINETEEN

"*You seemed rather* out of sorts again today, Mr. Jilani," Tippett drawled, having kept me back after class again. "Over the last two years, I have gotten so used to your airheaded joyous apathy, it rather throws things off to not have it present. Your troubles, whatever they may be, are personally inconvenient to me, you see."

"Sorry," I muttered.

"Trouble with your paper?"

"No. It's a girl."

"Young man," he said with a chuckle, "this girl, whoever she is, certainly does steal away more of your smiles than seems ideal."

"What?" I asked, confused for a second. Then I remembered that we'd had a similar conversation before, when Tippett had demanded to know my thesis. I'd been worried about Kaval being upset I wasn't taking her advice about Renaissance Man then. "No, it's another girl."

"Really?" Tippett asked. "Aren't you just a regular stamp collector."

"That isn't . . . that's not what it's like, okay? It's complicated."

"More complicated than the Battle of Waterloo? Than Carrhae? Than the Siege of Malta?"

I shrugged. "I have no idea."

I suddenly wondered if I should tell him about Bisma. I mean, he was hecka old. You don't grow old without growing wise, right?

So without mentioning any names, I told Mr. Tippett about Bisma's tape, what her father had done, and what had happened up till now.

"She's a special girl. I really like her. But my family will never allow it. It's an honor thing for them, same as it is for her father."

"Ah. I see. That old gem-encrusted bowl of applesauce, hmm?"

"What?"

"It's an expression," my teacher said placidly.

"If you say so."

"There is a curious phenomenon in this world, Mr. Jilani. For some reason, when it comes to the sexual habits of women, all of a sudden, men become very concerned with their honor. I don't mean to sound rude or politically incorrect, of course, but I would suggest that the Muslim

284

community should have more significant worries than a personal decision a young girl made."

"I don't disagree with you, but it doesn't solve the problem. My parents still—"

"Well, in that quarter, I fear, no one can help you. You will, as the kids say nowadays, simply have to grow a pair of testes."

"No one says that."

"They most certainly do. In all your reading about Churchill, did you happen to see the definition of *manhood* that is misattributed to him?"

I shook my head.

"A man does what he must, Churchill is said to have remarked, in spite of personal consequences, in spite of obstacles and dangers and pressures—and that is the basis of all human morality."

"Okay," I said slowly, "but that just says to do what you must. It doesn't tell me what I should do in this situation."

"A fair point. Perhaps knowing what you have to do is the part that makes you a man in the first place."

Tippett had said that a man ought to know what to do in tough situations. Well, I knew a smart guy who always seemed to know what to do. Sohrab.

Under normal circumstances, faced with a problem like this one, I would've already asked him for advice. Lately, however, he'd had so many worries on his mind that I hadn't wanted to burden him further. I'd also been intent on protecting Bisma's secret. I hadn't even told Zar about it.

But surely Sohrab could be trusted. I needed help, and he was the one person with whom I'd always found it.

So, even though it was just before midnight, I texted him to see if I could come over, saying that it was super important.

Text me when you get here. Don't ring the bell. Everyone is sleeping.

That was perfect, I thought, as I crept outside to my van. I really didn't want to run into Kaval.

I hadn't responded to her texts telling me she was meeting her cardiologist again, and we hadn't spoken since. I felt guilty about that. I should've said something. I just had no idea what, though, and I didn't want to hurt her.

Anyway, so now I'd been avoiding Kaval, or maybe she'd been avoiding me... or maybe we just didn't have that much to say to each other. As I drove, I wondered if I should try to talk to her, at least. To explain why I'd gone quiet, but it seemed like a very tall mountain to climb. Maybe it was fine to just leave things the way they were between us. Maybe whatever roles we were meant to play in each other's lives had come to an end.

※

I nursed the cup of coffee the shiny machine in the Sabsvari kitchen had spit out, watching Sohrab's face carefully as I pressed him for a hundred promises that he wouldn't ever tell a single soul what I was about to tell him.

Yes, my parents, and the Bay Area Muslim community, would probably find out about Bisma eventually. It wasn't the kind of thing that stayed secret for long, and she'd apparently been telling her arranged marriage prospects about the video. Still, it wasn't my story to tell anyone—well, except for Sohrab, obviously, because I needed his help.

My friend smiled at me in that wise man of the mountain way that he had and responded to my demand for secrecy with "If one promise from a man is worthless, then a hundred promises from him are worthless too."

There it was. Exactly the kind of brilliant insight I'd come to him for. Hopefully he hadn't used up all of his brain cells on that line, though, because he still had to solve my problem.

So, without mentioning her name, I told him about Bisma, about what had happened to her, and about how we'd been hanging out for months and that somehow, without realizing it, I'd found myself totally ensorcelled.

"Where is the sex tape?"

"Well...I mean, it's not a tape," I said. "It's like...a sex USB. Or a sex cloud."

"So there could be copies?"

"Yeah."

"That is suboptimal."

I shook my head. No one I know talks like that except Sohrab.

"It would be one thing for your family to deal with rumors. If it becomes something people can actually see..."

287

He trailed off and cocked his head, as if he'd heard something.

"What?" I asked.

"Nothing. It was probably just the house settling. Anyway, Danyal, I know it doesn't feel like it, but there are plenty of girls in the world. Your parents will find you someone who doesn't have these issues in her past. In fact, I think the odds are rather high you'll never have to deal with anything like this ever again. All you have to do is walk away."

"Sohrab, I really like this girl."

"Are you in love with her?"

"I..." I waved my arms in the air, as if they could express what I was saying better than words. "I don't know what it means when people say that. To be in love with someone, I mean. Isn't there supposed to be an epic storm? And in its rain, I should be dangling from a web and sharing a magical upside-down kiss with her and—"

"Like from the Spider-Man movie?"

I nodded. "Right. Everyone always says that when you're in love you just know it. I haven't gotten any sign, Sohrab. There's no shooting star that streaks from the heavens whenever I'm around her—"

"Like *Kuch Kuch Hota Hai*?"

"Yeah. If love isn't like that, then what is it like? How can I be sure? Where's my sign?"

Sohrab didn't answer the question. Instead, he said,

"Based on what you've told me, you should forget about this girl."

"What?"

"Never see her again. Just make a clean break. It'll be easier for you. It'll be better for your family. You should walk away from her, Danyal."

Never seeing Bisma Akram again...I couldn't even imagine it. It was an impossible thing. I'd come here, I realized, and I'd asked the wrong question. I didn't want to know whether I should be with Bisma. I wanted to know how to do it.

And now Sohrab was saying that I should just end everything with her?

Never see her smile again.

Never feel the almost accidental, almost innocent touch of her fingers against mine.

Never hear her laugh again. Never hear her talk again.

Live a life in which she was not present.

The thought of it made my chest hurt.

"I can't," I whispered. "I won't."

My friend nodded, as if that was what he'd expected me to say. He pointed a finger at me. "That's your sign."

It took me a second, then I got it. "Whoa. I see what you did there."

"I'm very clever. Now, is this a good time for us to talk about how your methods in pursuing this girl need to be halal and honorable, otherwise your soul will be in mortal peril?"

Oh. Right. There was another reason I hadn't asked Sohrab about Bisma earlier. He was a pain.

"As much fun as that sounds, it's kind of late. Let's do that some other time."

"All right," Sohrab said. "It can be something to look forward to."

CHAPTER TWENTY

How do you tell a girl you're in love with her?

More importantly, how do you tell a girl who has asked you not to make her any promises that you're in love with her?

You don't.

You just sit there, staring at her from across a library table while you're supposed to be working on a super important essay. At least, that was the strategy I'd decided upon. It wasn't great, but like Churchill said about democracy, it was the best I could come up with just then.

At least she was there. I'd been afraid that, after the way our dinner had ended, she wouldn't come to the library anymore. What would I do then? Wander around Berkeley searching for the microbiology lab? Microbiologists have labs, right? Yeah. That sounds right.

I couldn't go to her house. Not after the way I'd talked to her father. Plus, you know, that'd be pretty stalkery. If she hadn't come today, it would've meant that she didn't want to see me. I would've had to learn to respect that.

But she was here, so that meant—

"What's wrong?" Bisma asked, looking up from the textbook she was reading.

I love you and I don't know how to tell you because you don't want to hear it.

It was really unfair. Not of Bisma, of course, but of Allah. I mean, I'd spent so much time thinking about what kind of girl I'd like. I'd had to describe this fantasy woman to my parents, which should be the first thing to come up online when someone googles the word *awkward*. I'd seen the pictures of so many prospects, and I'd even met a bunch of them, and I'd gone through all of that to ultimately end up in a library with a girl who loved superheroes and books and wore glasses but never dresses or heels and wanted to study biology—except not in a fun, hands-on kind of way. She wasn't the kind of girl I'd imagined I wanted.

"Danyal?"

I'd been so wrong about what was important, though. All of that, except maybe for the part about the books, was surface-level stuff. I should have told my parents that I wanted someone who was quick to smile, who was patient when she had no reason to be, who made me feel good and took an interest in what I liked, and who cared about other people the way other people care about themselves.

292

I'd been looking for a beautiful face.

I should've been looking for a beautiful face pond.

"Hello? Danyal?"

I shook my head. "What?"

"What're you thinking?"

"Just that I love you. . . ."

Crap. Crap. Holy pot stickers. Damn it. Why am I such an idiot?

Breathe. Breathe. *Breathebreathebreathe.*

Fix it. But how?

Words. I needed words. *U* words.

Did I know any *U* words?

Umm.

Not a word. That's not a *word.*

Dude, this is taking too long, just pick something. Anything. The first *U* word you can think of. Say it. Say it *now.*

"Eulogies."

Bisma stared at me. "What?"

What the fuck is a eulogies? Why is that a word I know? Didn't matter. I was committed now.

"That's right. I love eulogies. Love it. Can't get enough of that eulogies. Eulogies is so great. So . . . uh . . . delicious, you know?"

Bisma pressed her lips together so hard they went white. She covered her mouth with her hand, and her small frame trembled with a mighty effort to keep her laughter in.

She failed.

One minute she was just sitting there, quietly doing

her reading, and the next her laughter was slaughtering the carefully preserved silence around us. When people tried to shush her, it only made her laugh harder for some reason.

We got kicked out of the library is what I'm saying.

Sitting on the hood of the van, when Bisma was able to talk again, she spoke to me as I typed into my phone. "If you're looking up *eulogies* right now, I'm going to die. I'm just letting you know. I'll be dead."

I stared at the screen. So. Not a *U* word, then.

I put my phone away. "That's not at all what I'm doing."

Bisma grinned and hopped down onto the concrete of the parking lot. She walked up to me, touched the side of my face, and said, "Well, for what it's worth, I think eulogies is pretty great too."

The next few weeks with Bisma weren't all fun and games. In fact, there was almost no fun at all. Renaissance Man was getting close, and Bisma was crazy intense about getting the essay to be as good as it could possibly be. I could tell she was tempted to rewrite entire sections for me, but she never did. She just gave notes. Lots and lots and lots of very, very long notes.

I was more of a one-draft person. If that. I'd never understood why people thought writing essays was hard. Writing essays was easy, as long as you were willing to pull an all-nighter and settle for a bad-to-okay grade. Revising was not my thing.

Honestly, if it had been anyone but Bisma trying to help me, I would've started to hate them a little, or at least gotten into a dozen fights with them. I listened to her, though, because she listened to me, and because I liked the sound of her voice. That was why we spoke over the phone a lot. I think she'd figured out I didn't like long texts. Too much like reading.

Weeks of back and forth, writing and rewriting and just plain whining, and then, one morning, Bisma called me. "I read the draft you sent me last night," she said. "It's good."

"But?"

"No. Danyal. I'm telling you. It is good."

"We're done?"

"Not yet."

We couldn't work on the presentation at the library because Bisma thought I had to rehearse it out loud—it was a performance, she said—so we went to Lake Elizabeth, a pretty big park in Fremont. It was kind of a great place for me to practice, actually, because while I was good at the talking bit—Bisma said I was compelling—I had a tendency to pace.

It's apparently not good to wander around aimlessly when you're giving a speech. You're supposed to move to underscore points or whatever, not just because you're restless.

Who sits around coming up with this crap is what I want to know.

Speaking of crap, Lake Elizabeth was basically a bathroom for geese. Their shit was everywhere, so my habit of walking while talking magically transformed into a desire to not move. I didn't want to step in anything.

"The spirit of Churchill," I told Bisma, even though she'd already heard this a bunch of times, "is the spirit of the tribe. Intense patriotism. Intense nationalism. Intense beliefs about racial and religious superiority—"

"Don't look at your notes so much," she said.

"I can't remember the exact words without—"

"Then use different words," she said.

"But we spent all this time writing these ones."

Bisma rolled her eyes.

I went on. "In that sense, it is a primitive spirit that humanity ought to seek to transcend, and not embrace. Even Churchill's contemporaries understood him to be a man who belonged in the past. Roosevelt called him a—"

"Stop." Bisma gestured for me to come closer.

Gingerly stepping over all kinds of stuff I didn't want to think about, I made my way over to her bench.

"Talk to me, Danyal."

"About what?"

"The presentation. You have to rehearse, but it can't

sound rehearsed. You have to engage your audience. The preparation is for you. It isn't for them."

I threw my arms up in the air. "That makes no sense."

"It will. Look, your notes, they're like a marinade."

I gave her a skeptical look. "Really?"

"Yes. When you marinade chicken, it's prep, right? The customer doesn't ever see that happen. The customer doesn't even see the marinade. They just taste all that work you did in the dish you give them. A dish that looks nothing like it did when you were making it. Does that make sense?"

"I think so, yeah."

"Good," she said. "Let's start from the beginning."

After what felt like a thousand practice sessions, Bisma decided it was time for a focus group. I met Sohrab at Zar's place and performed for them. It felt as weird as I'd told Bisma it would. She'd insisted, however, that it was important to get outside opinions and told me that it'd help get me used to the idea of having an audience.

Zar and Sohrab were a far cry from the four hundred or so people who'd watch the actual presentation in an auditorium, but I trusted that Bisma knew what she was talking about.

"... and that's all I've got," I told my friends, folding up my notes. When neither one of them said anything, I followed up with, "Guys?"

Intezar was the first to actually react. He grinned. "That was great, *yaar.*"

"Really?" I asked, looking to Sohrab for confirmation.

My somber friend nodded. "Absolutely. You're onto something important here. Western leaders have often been insulated from their own brutality, and Churchill is no different. Telling the truth about what they did, and continue to do, is vital. Otherwise, it's like Khataba, the village I told you about. You remember?"

Soldiers using knives to dig bullets out of bodies and lying about it? It was hard to forget. "I remember."

"We're fed stories that go unchallenged and they shape our view of the world. I mean, Harry Truman dropped atomic bombs on Hiroshima and Nagasaki, and he's practically sanctified by his biographers. FDR set up internment camps—"

"Is he doing his own presentation now?" Zar asked. "Because I only signed up for one."

Sohrab gave him an annoyed look. "I was just providing commentary."

"Thanks," I cut in before they could start arguing. "Both of you. Looks like I'll be fine. Right? Yeah. Definitely. It isn't a big deal."

Reassuring me that I'd do well, Sohrab took off, leaving me alone with Zar. "What did you think, really?"

He shrugged. "You know what Pirji said, right? He said you'd choke."

Right. Zar's holy man in Pakistan had predicted that I'd crash and burn in Renaissance Man, just like he'd predicted Zar would strike out with Natari. "You think it's going to be bad?"

"Nah. I think Pirji is about to lose a customer. You'll bring your fire, brownther. You'll burn the house down."

))/

A week later, it was the night before Renaissance Man. I wasn't nervous. I was just going to get up in front of hundreds of people and take a dump on the legacy of one of the greatest figures in modern history. Not a big deal.

At least spending the evening with Bisma had made time go by fast. Now that the library was closing, and we were going home, a long night awaited me.

"I got you something," Bisma said. She dropped her backpack down and knelt beside it. When she got up again, she was holding a bright yellow school tie with diagonal black stripes. As I took it, I noticed that there was a crest of some kind on it.

"What is this? Like a ferret?"

"It's a badger."

"Right. And its name is Hufflepuff?"

She grinned. "Don't worry about it. You should wear it tomorrow. It'll suit you."

It wouldn't really. I only had my blue suit, and while the yellow was fine, the black stripes could look a little out of place. Maybe if I wore black oxfords, it would work. I'd make it work. There was no way I wasn't going to wear a gift Bisma had gotten me.

"Thank you," I said. "And not just for this. For everything. It's like..."

I didn't know how to tell her what I wanted to tell her without sounding massively cheesy. It was like she'd made me taller or something. Like she'd seen where I could fit into the world and helped me get to that place.

Thankfully, once again, Bisma came to my rescue. "You're welcome," she said. "It was fun."

"Yeah. Definitely. So...uh, you'll be there for me tomorrow, right?"

"Are you kidding? I wouldn't miss it for the world."

CHAPTER TWENTY-ONE

"*You're going to* be late, *beta*."

I scowled at my reflection in the mirror. No matter how much I tried, I couldn't get the tie Bisma had given me on right. Sometimes it was too long, other times it was too short or just crooked. I'd been at it for a while.

My mother, who'd been lingering outside the door for some time, finally marched in and demanded I hand it over. "This wouldn't be a problem if you learned from your father instead of watching those stupid videos online."

That was possibly true, but I didn't want to admit it. So I just watched in silence as she rather expertly pulled a knot together for me. I couldn't imagine putting a tie on another person. I couldn't even put one on myself just then.

"I didn't know you could do that."

"The people you know best will surprise you some-times. Like you will surprise your father tonight, I think."

I stared at her. She couldn't possibly know that my pre-sentation about Churchill was going to be less than flattering. I hadn't told her.

"What do you mean?"

"Come on, Danyal," she said mildly, smiling as she adjusted my collar. "I've known you longer than you've been alive. How many secrets do you think you can keep from me?"

"When did you figure it out?"

Aisha Jilani laughed. "When your father told you to praise Churchill despite what you'd learned, I knew you wouldn't. You really do have a bad habit of being disobedi-ent when you think you're right."

I grinned. "I guess it's a good thing I don't think I'm right very often."

She gave my ear a playful tug and stepped back, look-ing me over, then nodded. "Also," she said, "you left your notes lying around in the living room."

"Oh. Yeah. That sounds like something I'd do. So, do you think Dad will be mad at me?"

"Maybe. It depends on how the night goes."

"No pressure, then."

"*Jaan*," she said, "poets say that there was a time under British rule when our people used to leave their homes feel-ing like they had their funeral shrouds wrapped around their heads. That was their metaphor for how they felt every day when they stood against the Empire. They felt like they were going to get killed and buried."

"What's your point?"

"That all you've had to do is put on a suit. So yes, there's no pressure. Whatever happens, you'll be fine." She placed a hand on my shoulder. "Break a leg. *Chalo.* Let's go."

"How is fracturing a bone a good idea right now?"

"It's just an expression. It means I hope you do well. Don't worry about it, okay? And please don't go around trying to hurt yourself on purpose...."

It was completely nuts backstage. Some contestants had teachers and family members huddled around them, while others stood in corners alone, trying to shove one last bit of information into their overflowing brains, or practicing the delivery of their lines.

I looked around for Tippett, just to see if he had any last-minute advice, but couldn't find him. Natari drifted over when she saw me.

"Hey," I greeted her. "Weren't we all supposed to vote on what order we're going to go in?"

Natari made a face. "We already did."

"Nice of you guys to wait for me."

"Sorry. It wouldn't have made a difference even if you'd been there. Alan's idea won by a lot. We're going by GPA, highest first."

I grimaced. It was like they were trying to make me feel bad. Now I was going to have to go last, which meant that I'd have to sit through everyone else's presentations and worry about all the things that could go wrong in mine.

"These guys really hate that I'm a part of this, huh?"

"For what it's worth," Natari said, "I voted to pick the order at random."

I smiled at her. "Thank you."

"Don't worry about it. Besides, I owed you one."

"What are you talking about?"

Natari grinned. "Intezar asked me out."

I stared at her. "Really? And you said..."

"Yes, obviously. He seems super sweet."

"He is. I'm glad. That's awesome."

"He told me you encouraged him, so yeah, I owed you one. By the way, he also said to show you this."

She held out her phone to show me a recent text from Zar. It was just a series of emojis. Prayer hands. Fingers crossed. Brown guy with turban, who I assumed was supposed to be Pirji. Stop sign. Fire. One hundred.

"What does that mean?" she asked.

"It's a little hard to tell with Zar," I joked, "but I think he's saying it's time to stop hoping and praying. It's time to go all in and be fire."

"Seems like good advice."

"Yeah. Anyway, I know you'll do great. Break a leg. That's an expression, by the way. I don't actually want you to get hurt."

Natari laughed. "Of course. Everyone knows that."

"Right," I said. "Totally. Everyone."

After Natari wandered away, I once again had no one to talk to, so I texted Bisma. **You here yet?**

I'm here, she wrote back instantly.

Any last words? I asked.

Bored with it all.

I shook my head and sent her an eye roll emoji. Those had been Churchill's last words. I put the phone away for a while, and just sat there, reminding myself that none of this was a big deal. I'd be fine. Nothing was going to go wrong.

When my phone buzzed, it was Bisma again.

Do you need me to be with you?

I started to tell her that yes, yes, definitely I did, but one of the teachers clapped their hands loudly and someone else shouted, "Places!"

"Guys," Alan Rhodes called. He was standing by the curtain, peering out at the crowd. "You have to see this."

The auditorium was packed. A sea of expectant faces was looking at the light-drenched stage, waiting for us. There were people standing in the back. I couldn't spot Bisma or my parents. I should've asked them where they were sitting.

There were three judges on the panel, and they were peering at score sheets, looking impatient to begin. I recognized Principal Weinberg, of course, but not the two men who were with her. I stepped away from the curtain, throat suddenly dry, heart pounding.

Natari touched my arm lightly. "You okay?"

"Fine," I said, taking a deep breath. "Just another Saturday night."

It began to get quiet as people started hurrying away to find their seats. Soon just the eight of us were left backstage, and no one seemed to feel like speaking. We stared at our hands or our feet, at the ceiling or the ground. We'd all be doing more than our share of talking soon.

I closed my eyes and tried to pray through the opening announcements, but I couldn't focus. By the time Alan's name was called and his presentation began, my chest was tight. I felt like my heart was stumbling over itself.

What was I doing here? This was just a bad joke gone wrong. I didn't belong with these brilliant, talented people. What had Tippett been thinking? This was going to be a disaster. My classmates would be telling their kids stories about how badly I'd bombed.

"My God," I whispered, only now realizing how completely I was going to be humiliated.

"You're sure you're fine?" Natari asked, leaning over to look closely at my face.

"What? Yeah. There's just no air in here, right? I feel like there's no air in here."

"Deep breaths," she suggested.

I concentrated on my breathing and tried to pay attention as Alan Rhodes wrapped up his speech and a polite round of applause broke out as he walked off the stage.

He'd been talking about some kind of math theorem or something. I'd understood exactly none of it.

"Thank you for that enlightening presentation, Mr. Rhodes. Another round of applause, ladies and gentlemen? Very good. Next, representing Ms. Nix's class in the field of geography, please welcome Natari Smith."

Natari gave my shoulder a squeeze, got to her feet, then confidently marched onto the stage.

She was incredible. I mean, I didn't manage to follow everything, partly because my stomach felt like Dwayne "The Rock" Johnson was squeezing it, but it was obvious that Natari was articulate, passionate, and persuasive. Geography was just her jumping-off point, as Tippett had predicted. Her real topic was climate change, and she was so interested in it that she made the audience interested in it too.

When she was done, there was loud clapping and hooting—the hooting almost exclusively from Zar, I was guessing—that didn't stop until after the next presenter was announced.

So, from what I've heard, as much as the end of the world will suck and stuff, the beginning of the afterlife is going to suck more. We're all going to get stuck in this place called *Barzakh*—purgatory—where we'll have to sweat while awaiting judgment. This will go on, apparently, until people start to feel that it'd be better to be in Hell than to be trapped where they were. They'll beg for the reckoning to begin.

This never made sense to me, until that night as I waited backstage, dreading my turn to speak, and at the same time, desperately wishing that whatever was going to happen happened quickly, so that life could go on.

It felt like I waited for hours.

Eventually, I was all alone. I was next.

I paced the length of the room and tried not to look at myself in the mirror. My hair was messed up because I hadn't been able to stop myself from running my hands through it over and over again. I was sweating, and I felt so hot that I'd had to mess with my mom's perfect knot and undo the top button of my collar. I mean, I was sure I still looked pretty good, because... well, you know, it was me, but I wasn't exactly going to project confidence out there.

"And our final presenter of the night..."

Oh shit. Okay. It was happening. It was fine. I clutched my notes to my chest. I just had to walk out there and not stumble on my own feet. That wasn't hard. I walked all the time. I'd been doing it for years. Practically since I was born, really, so—

"...representing Mr. Tippett and speaking for history, Danyal Jilani."

The crowd started clapping and I started to put one foot in front of the other. There were some cheers. Intezar called out, "That's my boy," and a few people laughed. I made it to the lectern. I did not fall.

It was boiling under the lights. I couldn't see much, but everyone could see me. My stomach clenched. I needed to throw up.

There were a few bottles of water on the lectern. I wanted to reach for one because I felt really thirsty, but my hands were shaking so badly that I was afraid I'd spill water all over my notes and then I'd be even more screwed than I was now.

I was familiar with panic. I panicked during pretty much every test I took. I knew that my fingers and toes would get cold, just as they were starting to now. I'd experienced the rising dread of coming failure so many times that I'd thought I could deal with it. I was wrong. The wave of fear rising inside me was different than anything I'd ever experienced before. It drowned out all my thoughts.

How long had I been standing here, anyway? Too long.

"Come on, Jilani," someone shouted from the crowd.

A few other voices joined in.

"Say something."

Then a familiar voice, loud and clear, rang out. I squinted and saw my father standing up. "You can do it!" he shouted. "Have some confidence."

Then my phone buzzed in my pocket.

And it buzzed again.

And again. And again.

Almost without thinking about it, I reached into my pocket and pulled it out.

Confused murmuring broke out in the crowd.

I'd gotten a bunch of texts. All of them were from Bisma.

I'm here with you.

Nothing that happens tonight will change the fact that I'm proud of you.

Or the fact that I'm in love with you.

I love you. I love you.

I love you.

CHAPTER TWENTY-TWO

"*Mr. Jilani?*" Principal Weinberg asked, her voice as sharp as vinegar.

I looked up from Bisma's messages. My heart, which had moments ago been plummeting, was now soaring, making me feel a little dazed as I looked down at the irritated judges.

She loved me. She loved me.

Nothing else mattered. The crowd. The contest. None of it.

It was just something I had to live through so that I could be with Bisma again.

"Mr. Jilani, what could possibly be so important that you're looking at your phone right now?"

"It's a girl," I said.

The audience started to laugh. I grinned at them.

Principal Weinberg sighed heavily into her microphone. "As thrilling as I'm sure your personal life is, Mr. Jilani, I think we'd all rather you get this over with."

I nodded. "Yeah. Sure. I'm ready to start."

I reached over and grabbed a bottle of water. My hand still trembled, but only slightly. I took a quick sip, then a deep breath, and began to speak.

"I hate Indians. They are a beastly people with a beastly religion."

A shocked silence fell over the hall.

Then the lights in the auditorium went dim. The projector came on, and a map of the world at night, all its major cities lit up like stars, went up behind me.

"Sir Winston Churchill said that. I'm guessing all of you know who he is. We learn about him in school. There are a bunch of movies about him. A lot of books too. I'm told there's a bust of him in the Oval Office, but I can't be sure. I've never been."

I looked down at the judges. Principal Weinberg was smiling up at me now, and the two men I didn't recognize seemed interested.

"Churchill was unique. Yes, he was a politician. It's what he's known for. He was more than that, though. In many ways, he was a Renaissance Man."

A few people cheered upon hearing the name of the contest dropped in.

"Churchill was a storyteller. Before he became prime minister, he was a reporter. After the Second World War, he was a historian. You know how they say that the winners get to write the history books? Churchill literally got to do that. He wrote a six-volume book about the war. His book framed the narrative of what happened in that war—a war that, more than any other, informs our world today."

I felt the urge to start pacing, but I closed my eyes for a moment, imagined I was surrounded by goose droppings, and stayed put.

"In his book, Churchill doesn't seem to want to talk much about the fact that he oversaw the deaths by starvation of three million people in Bengal."

I started by explaining that there had been no famines in that region since the British had left, and that recent scientific studies showed that the Bengal Famine of 1943 had not been caused by a lack of rainfall.

I took them through my next points quickly, outlining how Churchill's scorched-earth war policies, combined with decades of plundering of the province by the British, led to a famine that he then proceeded to ignore. Food was stockpiled elsewhere, because that was how Churchill chose to allocate the resources available to him.

"So, maybe you're asking yourself, why does it matter? Maybe Churchill was a hero. Maybe he was a monster too. I'm not sure if you guys know this, but he's been dead for a while now. Why are we talking about it?"

I took another sip of water.

"We're talking about it because the spirit of Churchill lives. Like I said, we still tell stories about him, we honor his memory. The stories we tell, who they're about, why we tell them, and how we tell them matters. The story of Churchill is the story of a man and of an age where people were not equal. For Churchill, white men were better than brown men, Christians were better than Hindus, Britishers were better than everyone."

My phone, resting on the lectern, buzzed again. A fresh wave of laughter ran through the crowd as the microphone picked up the sound.

Principal Weinberg sighed. "Would you like to share that note with the rest of the audience?"

I glanced at the text Bisma had sent.

You're doing so great.

"Sure. She thinks this is going really well."

More laughter.

Weird. I'd been so afraid, for so long, of everyone laughing at me, but now that it was happening, it didn't bother me at all.

"Anyway, my paper—and I—argue that our way of looking at the world today is the same as Churchill's way of looking at it. We're taught from an early age that America and Americans are special. That we're better than other countries. We aren't given any proof of this, of course—"

"America first!" someone shouted.

"Right. As you can see, we believe it anyway. The conviction that they were superior to everyone was central to the British colonizing mission, and it is the central belief of *our* colonizing mission. Churchill and the British

314

set out to bring enlightenment to other parts of the world, and we now go out to bring democracy to the world. The end result is the same: the exploitation and destruction of other people for financial gain. We are, sadly, still contemporaries of Churchill, who Franklin Roosevelt once called a mid-Victorian."

I took a deep breath. "In other words, myths of racial and national supremacy are still around. We must speak against them. There's no point in having a voice if you don't use it, and it isn't enough to use your voice to only speak your truth. If lies that oppress any people go unchallenged, if these lies are allowed to share space with the truth, they start to seem valid. They're not, though. So we've got to use our voices against narratives of inequality whenever they're repeated, even if we benefit from them. If we're silent in the face of injustice, then we're unjust too."

I turned my back to the audience, facing the map behind me.

"This is our world at night. This image is seen as a symbol of our development. We look at the pretty lights, and we pat ourselves on the back for all the progress we've made. But look at the dark places. Look at the places where there is no light. There are still people there, and they are just like us. We can tell ourselves we're better than them, but we're not. We live differently, mostly because of where we were born, but that doesn't give us the right to use and discard others. Our humanity is dependent upon our recognition of their humanity. Either we're all human, or none of us are. The darkness other people have to endure is the price for the light we enjoy. If history teaches us anything, it should teach us to not only look at the lights we kept on, but also the lights we put out."

I turned back to the audience.

"So the next time you use your cell phone, think about the places where they are made, where there have to be safety nets so workers won't kill themselves. Think about the kid in rags who stitched the clothes you're wearing. Think about who you are. Who we are. We may be the ones writing the present, but that doesn't mean we'll be the ones writing history. If we stay our course, history may not remember us kindly, and even if it does, I'm not sure it matters. History is not morality. I'm not sure when and why we started thinking it was."

Silence.

They weren't clapping. Weren't they supposed to be clapping?

Then the principal leaned forward into her own microphone and said, "Questions."

Right. I'd forgotten about those.

One of the other two judges, a wiry man with a thin, refined voice, said, "I do have a question, Mister..." He riffled through the pages before him, trying to find my name. Principal Weinberg leaned over and whispered in his ear. "Jilani."

"Okay," I said.

"The British modernized India. They built factories

and introduced the railway. Many feel that the Raj tremendously benefitted the subcontinent, and that the stewardship of the Empire was generally for the good of the people living there."

He stopped talking and looked up at me, as if expecting me to respond.

I shrugged. "Sure. I read about that."

"Well, I suppose my question to you is, what would you say to those people?"

Now for the first time, I had to look at my notes. There'd been no way to prepare for what the judges might ask, so this was one area where Bisma hadn't been able to help me.

I remembered there were numbers somewhere that would be useful. I just had to find them. In the meantime, I had to stall.

"Well...I guess I could tell them about the horrible ways in which Indians were treated by the British. I could tell them"—I found the page I was looking for and pulled it out—"that before being colonized, India made up twenty-three percent of the world economy, just like Europe did. By the end of the Raj, they made up just three percent. I'm not sure anyone can honestly argue that the British governed India for the benefit of Indians."

"Yes, Mr. Jilani," the judge drawled. "But with all due respect, I didn't ask what you *could* tell them. I asked what you *would* tell them."

"Oh. Well...that's easy. With all due respect, I'd probably just tell them to fuck off."

For a second, it was so quiet you could've heard a goose fart.

Then there was a roar of approval from one man, who stood up and screamed, *"Mera* cheetah!" and started clapping.

It was my dad.

Then my mom was standing, and then the lady next to her, and then the guy next to her. They rose like a human wave, until almost everyone was on their feet, and their applause went on and on until I finally walked off the stage.

Intezar rushed at me, pushing everyone else waiting to congratulate me out of the way, and wrapped me up in a bear hug. Sohrab followed close behind, apologizing to everyone for Zar as he went by them.

"That was awesome. You had me scared for a minute there."

I looked around for Bisma but couldn't find her.

"Thanks," I said. "I was pretty scared myself for a while."

Sohrab grinned. "Well, it was very impressive."

"Hell yeah, it was impressive," Zar said. "I can't believe you dropped the f-bomb onstage at Renaissance Man. You're going to be a legend, dude."

"Mr. Jilani."

All three of us cringed at the sound of Algie Tippett's familiar voice.

"Of course," Sohrab reminded us, "most legends are dead. Good luck."

I took a deep breath and turned to face our history teacher, who was walking toward me, a folder in his hand. "What did you think?"

"What did I think?" Tippett asked. "I think that was the stupidest thing I've ever seen a student do in my many years of teaching. Why would you curse at one of the judges, Danyal? Your presentation was decent. Your essay was surprisingly not entirely of low quality, despite the fact that I disagreed with your position. You could've won. Now, I think, it'll be very difficult. Ms. Smith was also very good."

I looked at the old man, who'd taught here for so many years, and who'd never had a student he nominated win the Renaissance Man.

"I guess I didn't want to mess up your losing streak, sir."

Tippett let out a sigh. "I was under the impression that I warned you against developing a wit." He thrust forward the folder he was holding. "Anyway, whatever happens, congratulations are still in order. You passed my class."

I took it from him and flipped it open. It was my essay, and on it, Tippett had written in green ink *A+*.

I just stood there and stared at the page.

Well...this was new.

I mean, I was looking forward to losing my virginity and all, but there was no way it would feel better than this.

By the time I looked up, Tippett was already walking away.

And standing before me was Kaval Sabsvari.

"So, after all that, you didn't use *any* of my notes," she said. There was a scowl on her face, and her arms were crossed in front of her. She sounded irritated, to put it mildly.

"Sorry. I decided to go in a different direction."

"Fuck. You. That whole speech was a giant middle finger for me, wasn't it? Just because I wanted you to be successful, just because I wanted you to do well, you thought what? That I was colonizing you? Using you for my financial benefit?"

"What? Kaval, I didn't say any of that. Come on. We're friends—"

"We're not friends, Danyal. We never were. I can't believe I wasted all that time on you. If all you wanted was a porn star, you should've just told me so, and I would've told you to go to hell."

I stared at her, stunned. How did she know? How could she possibly know?

"That's right. I overheard you talking to Sohrab at our house. That girlfriend of yours must've put on quite a show on that sex tape for you to just forget about me and— oh." Kaval suddenly turned pink and stepped back, and I realized she was looking at someone behind me. "Hi, Mr. Jilani. We were just..."

I turned around to look at my father, who had a plastic smile painted on his face.

"Sorry," he said, "I didn't mean to interrupt you young people."

"No, Dad. It's fine, I..."

That's when I finally saw Bisma. She was leaning against the back wall of the auditorium, arms folded, looking down at me with that heart-winning grin of hers radiating joy.

"I'll be right back," I said. "Excuse me."

As I ran up to Bisma, she started to say something—she was probably going to congratulate me—but the words never escaped her lips. I captured them.

It was a gentle, tentative, careful kiss. A light kiss.

A small thing and an immense thing at the same time.

Bisma pulled away a little and looked at me with eyes that set my heart on fire. "What are you doing?" she whispered.

"Making you a promise," I said.

Then I kissed her again.

And she kissed me back.

And I understood what an oasis is, when you're in the desert.

And what dawn is, when you're surrounded by darkness.

And what music is, when all you've known is silence.

And what hope is, when your heart is broken.

It was when the hooting and wolf whistles began that I remembered we weren't alone.

Bisma pulled away, blushing furiously.

Then her eyes went wide.

And she yelped.

And ducked.

I should've ducked too, I guess, but instead I turned around to see what had caused Bisma's reaction, and that was when one of my mom's slippers struck me square in the face.

I still hadn't fully realized what had happened when Aisha Jilani charged at me, armed with her remaining *chappal*, and started hitting me on the back with it. "You. Can't. Do. That. In. Public," Mom yelled, punctuating each word with a fresh strike. "*Besharam*. What. Is. Wrong. With. You?"

"Ow. Mom. Stop. Mom. Come on."

Bisma had turned traitor and was laughing at me.

Actually, everyone was laughing at me.

I felt my face go hot as my mother grabbed my ear and twisted it painfully.

"Ow. Someone call CPS."

Mentioning Child Protective Services earned me two more thwacks.

Bisma bent down and retrieved the slipper my mom had launched at me like a projectile—where had she learned to throw, anyway?—and handed it to my mother.

"Thank you, Bisma dear. That's very nice of you. I'm afraid you'll have to try to succeed where I failed and civilize this one."

"Might be a lost cause," Bisma said.

"I got stuck with him. You chose him, so you've got no excuse not to try," Aisha Jilani said, and then, still holding on to my ear, she began dragging me toward the exit.

Once we were alone by the van, my mom finally let me go. She swatted at my shirt to dust off the marks left by her footwear. "Sorry," she said. "Hope I didn't hit you too hard. There were so many other women from the community there. *Dekhana parta hai.* I had to hit you to show them that it isn't my fault that you turned out to be such a rascal."

"It kind of is your fault, though," I said.

"Yes, but they don't have to know that." She grinned at me. "So, first kiss, *haan*? How was it? Looked pretty good."

"Mom!"

"Oh, so now you're feeling some shame. Not when you're latching your face onto the Akram girl's in front of hundreds of people? Tell me, though. Didn't I do a good thing when I found her?"

"Yeah, Mom. You did."

She was all smiles until my father came to meet us, and she saw that he was not smiling.

CHAPTER TWENTY-THREE

"*I did a* horrible thing when I found this girl," Aisha Jilani said.

My parents were furious. Who would've thought they'd have zero chill about a sex tape? Right. Everybody. I hadn't planned to tell them, of course, but my father had overheard what Kaval had said, and there was no coming back from that.

"It isn't your fault. Your son knew everything—"

"*Acha.* Once again he is my son only, *haan*? Who just got up in front of all those people and called him his cheetah?"

Not. This. Again.

"Guys," I said. "It's not a big deal."

"Not a big deal," my mother said with a fake hysterical laugh. "Did you hear that, Ahmed? He thinks it isn't a big deal."

"If you didn't think it was a big deal," my father demanded, "then why did you hide it from us? You kept it buried like a cat buries its shit."

"I love this girl."

"No one cares about that," my mom says. "Every man loves his wife—"

My father gave an uncertain grunt, almost involuntarily I think, which got him a withering glare.

"No one is going to care about your love for her," she went on. "When people hear the words *sex tape*, that is all they're going to be thinking about. We can't give our name to a girl who has that kind of black mark on her character. What will everyone say?"

"What does it matter?"

My father held a hand to his head, like it was hurting really badly.

"Danyal, you know we love you, but you've got to grow up," my mother said. "We have to live in this world with other people. Their opinions matter, *beta*. We can't just cut off our noses in front of all society because you're infatuated with this girl."

"Okay," my father said. "I'm done talking about this now. The decision is made. Danyal, you are not to see this girl again—"

"It's going to be hard to marry her without seeing her again."

"This discussion," he growled, "is over. This is my house and my family, and my word is law."

"No."

My father's eyes went wider than I'd thought humanly possible.

"What did you say to me?"

"I'm nineteen years old. You can't just—"

"Go to your room," my father said, his voice as quiet as death. "Now."

So I went to my room. Not exactly a power move, but I knew my father. There was no reasoning with him just then. I'd try again tomorrow.

A text from Zar told me that I'd come in second at Renaissance Man. Natari had won. He sent a few pictures of them celebrating. There'd be time enough for me to congratulate them both. Just then I had to warn Bisma.

She . . . did not take it well.

Before I was even done telling her what my parents had said, she was crying. She just kept saying, "I told you, I told you this would happen, I told you," until Suri had to take the phone from her.

"This isn't fair, Danyal," Suri said.

"I know," I said. "I'm going to fix it."

"Promise?"

Making promises is a dangerous habit to get into. It's like a drug. You think you'll do it one time, and then, before you know it, your word is bound to impossible tasks.

"Yeah, Suri. I promise."

Bisma stopped showing up at the library. She stopped answering my texts and wouldn't take my calls. I sent her a long email, the longest thing I'd ever willingly written in my life, explaining what had happened, how I hadn't meant for her secret to get out, but she didn't reply.

I didn't know what to do.

I was alone. I couldn't talk to Zar because I didn't want to have to tell him Bisma's story, and for once Sohrab seemed to be out of helpful suggestions. He did tell me that Kaval felt really bad about what had happened, that she hadn't meant for my father to overhear anything about Bisma. Whatever. That did me no good.

My parents wouldn't talk to me about Bisma at all. They weren't talking to anyone else about her either, though, so at least her secret hadn't spread. It didn't matter much. Enough damage had been done.

A week went by. Zar, who had assumed I was bummed because I'd lost Renaissance Man to Natari, began to suspect something else was wrong and started asking questions. I tried to avoid him, saying I didn't feel like hanging out.

It was the truth. I didn't feel like doing anything, actually.

It was like all the colors had died.

When another week went by, Sohrab suggested, as

gently as he could, that maybe it was over. Maybe things do get screwed up so badly sometimes that there's nothing we can do to fix them.

That night I lay in bed and wondered if I should just ask Bisma if Sohrab was right. I'd been texting constantly, though she never replied. I picked up my phone and looked at our recent conversation. All the word bubbles were mine.

Please call me.

I'm sorry. Call me please.

Can we please talk?

Can we meet?

Just let me know you're okay.

She hadn't responded to any of those messages, but I still hoped to hear from her. What if I asked her if there was no chance, if it was really over like Sohrab said, and it ended up being the first time she did answer?

What would I do?

I took a deep breath.

I know I fucked up. I'm so sorry. Please let me fix it. Please.

I waited.

Okay. I'll leave you alone. I'm sorry I kept bothering you. It's just...I love you.

Nothing.

I wiped the tears that fell from my eyes, dropped the phone beside me, and turned off the light in my room. Sohrab had been right. I should've known. He was right about most things.

It was over.

I needed to sleep.

The tears would stop soon. Then I would sleep. It would be better in the morning.

Wouldn't it?

I was about to close my eyes, when the screen on my phone lit up.

$$\text{\textit{℆}}$$

The full moon was alone in the sky when I pulled into the library parking lot. No stars were out tonight.

I drove up to Bisma's Prius. She was already outside, standing next to her car, with Suri slouched over in the front seat, reluctantly playing chaperone for our midnight meeting.

As I got out, I couldn't help but notice that Bisma looked pale and tired and the skin around her eyes was swollen. Her hair was done up in a messy ponytail, and . . . well, she looked like she was recovering from the flu or something.

She smiled when she saw me, though, and I've never seen anything that beautiful.

Suri waved at me without getting out of the car.

I might have waved back. It was a little hard to think about anything but Bisma just then.

"You've been crying," she said softly.

"So have you."

Bisma shrugged. "I've been trying to get over a guy."

"Me too," I said. Then frowned. "I mean, you know, not . . . You know what I mean."

She stuffed her hands into the pockets of the hoodie she was wearing and was silent. Her text had just said she'd meet me at the library, so I didn't really know what she was thinking. She was here, though, at this late hour. That was something.

I stepped toward her. "I . . . don't want you to get over me."

"Good. Because I can't."

I didn't know what to say to that. Bisma spared me the search for words that wouldn't have been enough to express what was in my heart anyway. She rushed toward me and wrapped her arms around my neck. I held her, burying my face in her hair.

"I'm sorry," I told her.

"You can stop saying that now," she whispered.

"I love you."

"That you should keep saying. You know, we'd have been here sooner, if you'd said so earlier."

I leaned back and stared at her. Had I never said that to her? I hadn't. She'd texted it during my speech, when I'd been onstage. I hadn't exactly been in a position to write back. It wasn't until earlier tonight, in my last text, that I'd actually told her. "That's what you were waiting to hear? I mean, I kissed you."

330

"That's not the same thing."

"But...you knew, right? You knew I was in love with you."

"But did you know? Someone once told me you're not very bright."

"Oh. My. God. You two are so extra," Suri called from the car. I realized that she had her window down. "Is there a reason this couldn't wait until the morning? Did I really have to get dragged out of bed?"

No. It absolutely could not have waited. I was about to tell Suraiya that, when Bisma asked, "Did you mean what you said to Suri? That you can make this right?"

I nodded, hopefully sounding more certain than I was. "I think so. I've got a plan."

"Is it a good plan?" Bisma asked.

"Of course it's a good plan," I said. "Haven't you heard? I'm a Renaissance Man. Well...almost."

"And that's great," Suri called. "But we can talk about it later. I'm tired. Apa, can you kiss him already, so we can go home?"

She could.

She did.

"What are you doing to my kitchen?"

I gave my mother the very best smile I could pull together.

"Making food," I said.

"I can see that," she told me. "Why so much food prep first thing in the morning? Are you preparing for a party?"

"Yeah. I invited the Akrams over for dinner."

"You did *what*? Danyal, your father is going to end you."

"Mom. Help me make him understand. Please."

She shook her head. "I'm sorry." It sounded like she meant it. "I can't be with you on this, Danyal. What that girl did, it was a very big sin. And there is video evidence of it—"

"Only because someone violated her privacy and committed a crime. Why do you guys insist on punishing her?"

"She made a choice too. Now, I feel bad for her, and for you. I really do, but we all have to pay for our mistakes, *beta*."

"But how much? For how long?"

My mother shrugged. She'd never had a problem admitting when she didn't have all the answers. "I can help you with the food. If you want."

"Okay," I said. It was something. "That'd be great. Thank you."

$$\wr\wr$$

Like I told Bisma forever ago, food is a miracle.

It just is.

It has said so much over the centuries. It was probably how the first human beings expressed themselves, probably our very first gesture of friendship, of love and caring.

It was how we first spoke to animals.

It was why we first developed a relationship with the earth.

It is necessary and beautiful, basic and extra.

So that day, when I needed a miracle, I reached for the only one that was in my power.

I didn't make anything foreign. I wanted everyone to feel at home, to feel comfortable, so it had to be desi food.

Dum goat *biryani*, with Spanish saffron and long-grain basmati rice.

Seekh kabab laced with a hint of ghost pepper.

Chicken *tikka* seasoned with Iranian blue salt.

Naan, which I ordered from a restaurant, but brushed with my mother's homemade ghee.

Ras malai with crushed pistachios, and a *halwa* made from almonds.

When it was all done, I looked at Mom and asked, "Do you think it will be enough?"

"The trouble with using food as an apology and a prayer, *beta*," she said, "is that you still have to bring people to your table. You've done an amazing job here, but it is your words, I think, that you'll have to rely on."

Great.

I'd never really been good with those.

The handshake between my father and Mr. Akram was tense. I'd thought for a minute there, when Bisma's tall, distinguished father extended his arm, that my dad wouldn't take it. He'd looked at it like it was a thing to be mistrusted.

"You should have told us, Mr. Akram, about your daughter's situation."

"We told your boy. If you have a complaint, it isn't against us."

They both turned to look at me.

I waved at them a little.

Obviously, they didn't wave back.

Bisma looked hollowed out. Her eyes were still swollen from weeping, and she wouldn't look up at anyone. Not even me. I didn't want to think about the things that had probably been said to make her look like that. I'd seen how harsh her father could be, and convincing him to come here must've been ridiculously difficult.

As Suraiya walked past me, following our families into the formal living room, she whispered, "Tell me you got this."

"I got this," I said with absolutely zero confidence.

Suri's smile in response was equally weak.

We all sat in tense silence together, the only sound in the house the tinkling of glass against glass as Mom served pineapple juice. She gestured for me to start talking.

"So," I said, trying out a wide smile that no one returned. "I guess . . . I'm just going to say . . . things. I have this friend, Sohrab, and he spends way too much time at the mosque. I don't mean to sound like I think that's a bad thing, but it isn't for everyone and—"

"Is there a point to this?" Mr. Akram demanded.

"Let him speak." Bisma's voice was paper thin, and she managed nothing more than a whisper, but there was enough anger in it to cut and draw blood. I've always been surprised that paper can do that.

Her father fell silent, and I gave her a grateful look.

"Well," I went on, "Sohrab asked me to come to a lecture at the mosque once, and I learned about this thing called *qalb-e-saleem*. Have you heard of it?"

"A pure heart," Dad said. "What about it?"

"The Quran says that on the Day of Judgment people will only be saved if they've got one of those."

"How does that apply to anything—"

"It applies to everything, Mom. Don't you see? If Allah is going to look at your heart, don't you think he's going to look at my heart? And Bisma's heart?"

I caught Bisma's gaze.

"He'll look at them all. And when this God that we worship, the source of all love, of all justice, looks at her heart and finds it broken...what do you think He'll do? Ignore it? I think, maybe, He'll wonder who dared to break it and why. What will any of you do then?"

In the silence that answered my question, Bisma took a long, shuddering breath.

"I know I'm not...you know, wise or whatever, but the way I see it, by punishing people for what we judge to be sins, by hurting them, we all become sinners. The only thing we have to do with other people is to be careful with their hearts. That's all. Who is forgiven, who is punished, it's not our business."

No one would look me in the eye.

Well, except for Suri, who grinned and gave me a thumbs-up.

"Anyway," I said, "that's what I believe. No one has to agree with me. But that's why I don't care what anyone says about Bisma. Anyone who has anything to say about her should have a hundred things to say about themselves. I'm not going to let this amazing girl that I'm lucky enough to be in love with go because of the opinions of hypocrites."

I got up and walked over to where Bisma was sitting, next to Suraiya, and knelt down before her, like I'd done all those months ago when her father had been so cruel. "Hi," I said.

She sniffled and didn't say anything.

"You have the most beautiful face pond in all the world."

Bisma sort of sobbed and chuckled at the same time.

"Will you marry me?"

Her eyes started to drift away from mine, searching for her parents, and my parents.

"Listen," I said. "Look at me. I didn't ask them. I asked you. What do you want? Do you want to marry me?"

She nodded, fresh tears falling from her eyes. She

wiped at them, but kept nodding and said, so softly that I barely heard her, "I really do."

She held out her hand.

I took it.

We rose up together.

Suri pumped her fist in the air. "Fuck yes!"

"Language!" everyone cried at the same time, and Suraiya wilted back into her chair.

Ahmed Jilani got to his feet and walked over to me. He was a few inches taller than I was, and he stared me down. I swallowed. Bisma held my hand tighter. I met his gaze.

"Jaleel," he said finally, turning to Bisma's father, "when you came here today, you said that you'd told my boy about your daughter's circumstances. Now I have to tell you that there is no boy in this family for your daughter to marry. Don't you see? Today, my son is a man."

$$\mathcal{U}$$

And then we ate, which, by the way, is how all stories should end.

Nothing says happily ever after like a meal crafted with love.

I mean, of course, there was a lot of hugging and crying and asking for forgiveness before that, but in the end, we gathered around good food and were together, as one family.

Bisma and I didn't get any time alone, of course. That's

not how these things work. Still, we sat next to each other at the table, and if our eyes whispered promises to each other, or if I took her hand and kissed it when I thought our parents weren't looking . . . well, I don't think anyone has to know.

Acknowledgments

Having made it this far, I find that I have no words to adequately express my gratitude for the incredible people that made this novel possible. This too is a gift. If words are going to fail you, after the end of a story is not a bad place for it to happen.

I have to begin with my extraordinary agent, Melissa Edwards, who is always there to answer questions, provide guidance, open doors, vanquish obstacles, and can be counted on to see the potential of first drafts and respond: *THIS IS SO GOOD! Holy fudge. It's so good. This is a professional email.*

My editor, Deirdre Jones, is a marvel. She understood Danyal's story from the very beginning, somehow seeing it with clearer eyes than I did, and without her vision, wisdom, hard work, and patience, this book would not have come to life. I am incredibly fortunate that she, and Thorne Ryan, worked on this manuscript. You guys were right about the lemon bars.

I am aware that novels are written without the guidance of my mentors, Léonie Kelsall and Marty Mayberry, but how that happens I do not know. Thank you both for so generously using your time and energy to teach me the craft. If I weren't typing, this would be a serious heart-hands moment.

Thank you to my copyeditors, Annie McDonnell and Maya Frank-Levine, and my proofreaders, Christine Ma and Mary Auxier, for their thorough work. They are not to blame for any weird italicization choices in the text. Those are on me. Their work was impeccable, and I appreciate it. (Does that comma go there, guys? I'm pretty sure a comma goes there.)

My thanks to Megan Tingley, Alvina Ling, and the entire Little, Brown Books for Young Readers team. Thank you to the book's designer, Marcie Lawrence, and to Hallie Tibbetts and Anna Prendella. Thank you also to Sammy Moore, who brought Danyal and Bisma to life on the cover.

Thank you, Madelyn Burt of Stonesong and Addison Duffy of United Talent Agency. Thank you to the Pitch Wars Class of 2017, especially Elizabeth Chatsworth, Anne Raven, and Robin Winzenread Fritz, who went through the gauntlet with me.

Publishing is a long road, and an exhaustive list of people who've encouraged me, said kind words, or held out a helping hand is impossible to produce here. I'll just say that I remember all your kindnesses and will not forget them. Thank you.

Finally, thank you to Saad Ahmad, for *Mortal Kombat* and a friendship unbound by continents. Thank you to Lendyl D'Souza for our long Skype sessions and his constant enthusiastic support.

And to my wife, Amena, who makes writing feel possible and love stories seem real. "I love you. I love you. I love you."

And to my mother, Hajra Masood, who thought buying her kid novels would get him through the boredom of having chicken pox. She wasn't wrong, and that one magical gift completely altered the course of my life.

And to my father, Syed Manzar Masood, a man with a sound heart, who before he passed saw the dark clouds of bigotry and hatred gathering on the horizon of our world, and in that simple, matter-of-fact way of his, looked at me and said, "You should do something."

I did something, Papa. I just wish that you were here to read it. Miss you always.

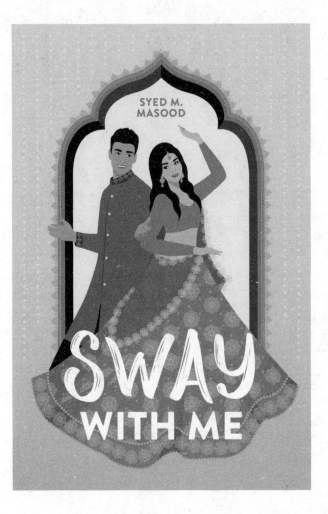

Chapter One

"Everything's going to be okay, Arsalan. You'll be fine."

That was a lie and, unfortunately, deceiving yourself when you already know the truth about something is almost impossible. As a result, I'd been standing in front of a full-length mirror in my bedroom for quite a while, struggling to convince my reflection that the quest upon which I was about to embark was no big deal. All I had to do was be cool.

But I knew that in my seventeen years on Earth, I had managed not a single moment of cool. Also, the task before me was actually daunting. Momentous. Herculean, even. Today, after school, I was going to talk to a girl about love.

"Are you quite done preening?"

I jumped at the sound of Nana's voice. My great-grandfather rarely came by my room. Stairs, like everything else in the world, irritated him. When I turned toward the door, I saw that he was hunched over his cane, still in his fraying velvet dressing gown, looking rather miserable. He was never agreeable until after I'd made him his morning tea.

"I wasn't preening...exactly," I protested. "I was making sure I was presentable."

Nana's critical gaze traveled from my freshly polished—though hopelessly scuffed—dress shoes, to my zealously ironed khaki pants, to my green blazer, and then to the laboriously perfected knot of my dull yellow tie. When his eyes fixed upon my hair—I'd made certain the side part I'd had since kindergarten was flawless—he asked, "Since when do you care about what you look like?"

That was a good question. Nana had a habit of asking those.

"And are you aware that you're running half an hour late?"

Nana also had a habit of asking a second question before I could answer his first. I wondered, sometimes, if I'd find him as endearing as I did if I hadn't spent almost all of my life with him.

I looked around and realized there was a lot more sunshine in my room than I was used to in the mornings. I'd lost track of time. That was unusual in the extreme. I had, in fact, never been late for school—not that this was all that much of an accomplishment. I'd only been going to Tennyson High for a few weeks. Nana had homeschooled me before that.

"I got distracted."

"Like Narcissus," he said.

I shook my head. That particular figure of Greek mythology had nothing in common with me. Narcissus had been so enchanted by his own beauty that he had spent his life staring at his own image. I knew perfectly well that I was not a pretty face. I'd just been trying to look a little better than I usually did, less like the definition of the word "dweeb."

"So," Nana asked, "I assume a young lady is responsible for your newfound vanity?"

"There is no—"

He raised his extraordinarily bushy eyebrows.

"Fine," I muttered, surrendering to his disbelief. Shoving my hands in my pockets, I admitted, "I was going to talk to a girl after school."

"Excellent," Nana cheered. "You will do marvelously with the fairer sex. After all, you have an exceptional vocabulary."

I rolled my eyes. "Right. As if that is relevant."

"Oh, but it is. Girls like nothing better than a strapping lad who sounds like he reads the thesaurus every night before bed."

I wasn't exactly a "strapping lad," and in my experience—limited as it was—Nana's theory about what impressed girls was more than a little incorrect. Either that or every single one of them at Tennyson was a brilliant actress in the making, pretending to be totally uninterested in my mastery of language.

I'd tried explaining this to Nana before, but he was nearly a hundred years old now and held the opinion that he had outgrown being wrong.

"You see, the size of your vocabulary tells a girl the size of your most precious organ."

I frowned, genuinely confused. "How?"

"It lets them know you've got a large brain, Arsalan."

Oh. Right. The brain. Also important.

"Syllables, my boy," he declared, "are irresistible."

"If you say so."

"Come, now. You look positively dejected. Muster some confidence."

"That's what I was trying to do when you walked in."

Nana waved a dismissive hand in the direction of my mirror. "You cannot rely on your looks. You have to show off your strength. What is the most impressive word you can think of?"

I shrugged. " 'Incomprehensibilities'?"

He made a face to show what he thought of that effort.

" 'Impedimenta'?"

"Adequate," he conceded.

" 'Sesquipedalianism.' "

Nana grinned. "There it is! Who would not be impressed with such brilliance, hmm? Tell me, do you not feel better about yourself?"

I had to admit that I did, actually, though maybe that was because Nana almost never gave out compliments.

Leaning heavily on his cane, Nana made his way over to place a hand on my shoulder. "Everything is going to be okay, Arsalan," he said, repeating what I'd been saying to my reflection. "You'll be fine."

At the end of the day, after classes were over, I made my way through the deserted corridors of Tennyson High and tried not to think about how deeply alone an empty school could seem. It was like walking into an abandoned mosque or a mall that had shut down. It felt wrong somehow.

It wasn't as if I didn't like being by myself. I was used to that. But there's something sad about stumbling upon solitude in places you don't expect to find it. It makes you miss strangers you've never met and friends you've never had.

Anyway, I didn't like it, so I walked as quickly as I could.

As the gym—not my natural habitat—neared, handmade signs told me I was drawing close to the dance audition where I knew I'd find Beenish Siraj. I'd waited until almost all the other students had gone home before seeking her out. This way, if I embarrassed myself, at least it wouldn't be in front of a large group of people.

My worries felt entirely justified. Beenish was terrifying. I didn't know her personally, but I'd heard tell. Apparently "Beans," despite being the younger sister of a teacher, had been suspended last year for punching some guy and breaking his nose. She was rumored to be prickly, stabby, and sharp. Definitely the kind of person I would usually avoid.

Why was I about to talk to her, then? Because Beenish was the daughter of Roshni Siraj, the premier matchmaking aunty of the Greater Sacramento Area. There was no one better at setting up arranged marriages in all of California.

Unfortunately, Roshni Aunty likely wouldn't help me if I reached out to her on my own. She had an exclusive client list. The men she did business with were always in possession of a good fortune and in need of a wife.

I was not a man, though I was scheduled to become one within a year.

Also, I didn't have a fortune. My total net worth was around twenty dollars.

Finally, I didn't really want to get married. I was too young for that. I needed a rishta aunty to work her magic on my behalf because I wanted an assurance—a guarantee— that no matter what happened, I wouldn't end up alone in the world.

I needed an engagement, and if I impressed Beenish maybe she'd convince her mother to find me a match.

"Clinomania," I whispered to remind myself of my conversation with Nana that morning. "Mellifluous. Surreptitious."

Never having been to a dance audition before, I'd imagined an event with music and lots of frantic activity. That wasn't the case. The gym was empty except for a single table at the exact center of it, where Beenish Siraj sat.

I took a deep, bracing breath, stepped toward her, and pasted on the biggest smile I could manage. I probably looked like the Cheshire Cat had escaped Wonderland.

"Greetings," I said—squeaked, actually—and bowed my head a little. "I would very much appreciate the opportunity to converse with you."

Not bad. The bow had been unnecessary, and I hadn't used any really big words yet, but it was a decent start.

Beenish, however, seemed distinctly unmoved by my performance.

For my part, I thought her rather remarkable. She had the darkest eyes I'd ever seen. They were pretty in an "is there even a soul inside this person" kind of way. I noticed also her black hair and her T-shirt, which said THE NIGHT in bold, capital letters.

"Maybe stop perving out and look at my face when you're talking to me?"

I blushed and yanked my gaze away from her shirt.

I'd *never*!

Okay, so perhaps "never" is overstating things a bit, but in this case I definitely hadn't been staring at...I hadn't been staring *there*.

"I was looking at what you're wearing. Honest."

"Sure."

"It's true," I insisted. "What does that mean, anyway, 'The Night'?"

"It means I'm dark and full of terrors."

There was a pause as she waited for me to react to what

she'd said. This happened a lot. People made pop culture references and then waited for me to get them. I usually didn't.

"Well, anyway, if it is not too much of an inconvenience, I was hoping to procure your assistance in a delicate and confidential enterprise. You see—"

"Why are you talking like that?" Beenish demanded.

"Like what?"

"Like you just stepped out of a Dickens novel."

I frowned. "I endeavor only to make a good impression."

That earned me a puzzled look. "Why would you want to impress me? I don't even know who the fuck you are."

I gasped. It wasn't so much her awful language that was shocking. It was the carelessness with which she'd used it, as if she said words like that all the time.

"Dude," she said with a grin. "You're a trip."

"I am, in fact, Arsalan Nizami," I corrected with as much dignity as I could manage in the circumstances.

"Uh-huh. And does Arsalan Nizami dance?"

"Not when people are watching. And also not when no one is watching."

She pointed to a sign saying this was a dance audition.

"That's not why I'm here," I explained. "I need your help finding a girl."

"You lose someone?"

"Yes. I mean...we've all lost someone. But I haven't lost any girls, no."

"Who'd you lose?" Beenish asked.

I blinked. That wasn't the kind of thing you asked people

you'd just met, was it? It was private. I'd come here to discuss completely impersonal things. Like marriage.

"I need your mother's help finding a girl," I clarified, hoping to get our conversation back on track.

"Oh. You're one of *those*. Look, Nerd Scout—"

"Nerd Scout?"

"Because of your outfit. What are you wearing?"

I adjusted the knot on my tie and tugged at the lapels of my sport coat. "It's my uniform."

"Tennyson doesn't have a uniform."

I shrugged. "The school doesn't. But I do."

Beenish didn't seem to know how to respond to that. "Whatever," she ultimately decided. "Look, my mother doesn't do that arranged marriage crap. My stepmother does."

"What difference does that make?"

That earned me a look that threatened to scald my soul. Apparently, it made a great deal of difference. "Sorry," I said, though I wasn't really sure what I'd done wrong.

"Why are you even bothering me?" Beenish asked. "Just have your parents call Roshni and set things up for you."

"This wasn't... This isn't an idea my parents came up with, exactly."

She looked at me as if I were completely incomprehensible. "You actually *want* to meet a rishta aunty to ask for an arranged marriage?"

I shrugged again. "I need help."

"Obviously. Listen, I'm sorry, all right? I don't get

involved in anything Roshni does. Ever. Now, as you can see"—she gestured expansively at the massive gym—"I'm super busy with this audition."

"No one is here," I pointed out.

"There's time," Beenish said. "People could still show up."

"Is this for cheerleading or something?"

"Do I seem like a cheerleader to you?"

I laughed at her dark tone. "Not even a little."

For some reason, that caused her eyes to narrow.

"What?"

"Get," she snapped, "out."

So I did.

In the school parking lot, I put my head down on the steering wheel of my great-grandfather's ancient Cadillac and closed my eyes. That had sucked. Not only was Beenish not going to help me, I already knew that some of the things she'd said with casual, thoughtless brutality would bother me for a long time.

I don't even know who the bleep *you are.*

Nerd Scout.

What are you wearing?

I'd remember it all for years.

I wondered if other people were like me, if small hurts haunted them the same way. Maybe I was the only one who obsessed over every faux pas I made and cringed at the memory of every minor slight I'd endured. I often felt bad for things that had happened forever ago and, at the same time, felt petty for obsessing over what were, after all, minor bruises. Surely the rest of humanity was better than I was. Surely.

I sat back up and glanced over at the passenger seat, where the beat-up briefcase I carried—Nana thought back-packs were juvenile—sat mocking me.

You are different, it said. *You're strange. Everyone laughs at you.*

I sighed and turned the ignition. The old car gasped, sputtered, sounded like it was preparing to perish, but then rumbled to life.

Before speaking to Beenish, I'd planned on going back to Nana's. Now the long silences my great-grandfather and I shared seemed like too heavy a burden to bear. My heart and mind were full. I needed to speak to someone who would listen to me without trying to offer advice, and with-out interruption.

There was only one person like that, and I always knew exactly where to find her.

"Hi, Mom," I said.

She didn't answer, but she never did.

Not anymore.

It was a nice autumn day. The sun was playing

hide-and-seek with a few scattered clouds. Birds I couldn't see chirped in trees that were still hanging on to their leaves. In a few months, the cemetery would no longer be full of their song.

"How are you?"

A cool breeze picked up slightly. I knew that it was not a response from my mother. And yet…

I lay down next to Mom. Up above, in the light blue of the sky, I thought I could just make out the moon, which was always there, but often veiled by the brightness of the sun.

"I finally spoke to that Beenish girl I told you about. It didn't go great."

I really shouldn't have to do this, I thought. *You should be here.* But there was no reason to be unkind. As a general rule, I tried not to complain about my life when I visited my mother. Whatever my troubles, she had it worse, being dead and all.

"Anyway, what about you? Anything interesting happening?"

I closed my eyes and listened to the silence around me.

Two years ago, I'd have been freaked out by the thought of being in a graveyard as the sun began to fall from the sky. Now I knew it was a peaceful place where I could be around the only person who'd ever really known me.

Of course, she wasn't actually present. This was just where her body was. Her spirit was elsewhere. I wondered what that felt like. Maybe it felt like a dream.

I don't remember the room. I want to say it was cold and clinical, but I've forgotten a lot of details about that day, even though it ended up being the most important one of my life.

I remember holding my mom's hand as she lay on the hospital bed. I remember how little it seemed to weigh. There were deep, ugly, purple bruises on her face, but they didn't look so bad. Not bad enough to die from.

It's internal bleeding, doctors told me. *You can't see it.*

Where's your father?

I didn't know.

Do you know if your mother has insurance? Are you eighteen yet? There are these forms that... We'll give you a moment.

A moment. A moment to hold her hand.

Allah said he made human beings from clay.

You forget that, until they break.

Then she opened her eyes and I dared to hope.

She managed a smile. It was small, but it was the world.

"Hey," she said, very, very softly, her parched lips struggling to part.

"Hi, Mom."

"How much time do I have?"

"What are you talking about? There's nothing wrong with you."

"You know you shouldn't lie, Arsalan."

I remember crying and crying and crying and not being able to stop.

I remember her stroking my hair as best she could.

"Everything's going to be okay, Arsalan," she whispered. "You'll be fine."

"I don't know how to live without you, Mommy."

She was in tears too now. Her hand dropped away; her breathing came faster. "You will. Search for love and you'll see. Life is beautiful."

Her eyes closed and she couldn't open them.

They sedated me and darkness fell upon me too.

I woke up.

She never did.

SYED M. MASOOD

grew up in Karachi, Pakistan, and now lives with his wife and children in Sacramento, California, where he is a practicing attorney. He wrote a few couplets in Urdu when he was a teenager, and his family still tells everyone he is an Urdu poet. He is not. Syed is the author of *More Than Just a Pretty Face*, *Sway with Me*, and *The Bad Muslim Discount*, and he invites you to visit him online at syed-masood.com.